page-turning journey with two very different women who must somehow find their way together. This is more than a novel about friendship; it is also a story *for* friendship: you will find yourself sharing it with everyone you love. Dive in; the storytelling is delicious!"

—Patti Callahan Henry, *New York Times* bestselling author of *Becoming Mrs. Lewis*

"Harvey creates genuine, capable, flawed protagonists and fun secondary characters, and readers will appreciate the thoughtful depiction of women supporting one another in an easy, breezy story. Fans of Mary Kay Andrews and Mary Alice Monroe should add this to their beach read lists."

—*Booklist*

Praise for *The Southern Side of Paradise*

"Kristy Woodson Harvey has done it again! Perfectly tying together the stories of Ansley, Caroline, Sloane, and Emerson (and their men!), *The Southern Side of Paradise* is full of humor, charm, and family. Fans of the Peachtree Bluff series will not be disappointed!"

—Lauren K. Denton, *USA Today* bestselling author of *Hurricane Season*

"As the eldest of three sisters, I know you're not supposed to pick favorites—but *The Southern Side of Paradise* is Kristy Woodson Harvey's very best. The heartwarming finale to the Peachtree Bluff series, this novel had me laughing, crying, and wanting to hop on a plane and head south. I loved every page."

—Camille Pagán, bestselling author of *I'm Fine and Neither Are You*

"Woodson Harvey has been called a major voice in Southern fiction, and her latest novel—the third in the Peachtree Bluff series—delivers a healthy dose of her signature wit, charm, and heart."

—*Woman's World*

Praise for *The Secret to Southern Charm*

"*The Secret to Southern Charm* is a compelling, beautifully drawn tale of love, hope, and small-town secrets. The richly detailed backdrop of a charming coastal town and the struggles and joys of four generations of women solidifies Kristy Woodson Harvey's spot as a rising star of Southern fiction."

—Mary Alice Monroe, *New York Times*
bestselling author of *Beach House for Rent*

"The characters will leap off the page and into your heart, and you'll find yourself rooting for them so fervently, you'll forget they're not actually real. Kristy Woodson Harvey has delivered another masterpiece. . . . Let's just say that this one had better have a sequel too, because I'm not ready to leave these charming ladies behind."

—Kristin Harmel, international bestselling author
of *The Room on Rue Amélie*

"Harvey's growing fan base will find another great beach read in this second novel in her Peachtree Bluff trilogy. . . . Harvey is an up-and-coming Southern writer with staying power."

—*Booklist*

Praise for *Slightly South of Simple*

"Kristy Woodson Harvey really knows how to tell a Southern tale. Every single time her stories unwind gently, like a soft wind in Georgia, then that wind catches you off guard and throws you into her characters' tumultuous lives. I loved it."

—Cathy Lamb, *New York Times* bestselling author

"My prediction is that writers come and writers go, but Kristy Woodson Harvey is here to stay. The warmth, wit, and wisdom of this novel pave her way into the exclusive sisterhood of Southern writers."

—*HuffPost*

"With a charming, coastal Southern setting, *Slightly South of Simple* is a heartfelt story about the universal themes of love, loss, forgiveness, and family. I'm thrilled to hear that this book is part of a series and look forward to getting to know this cast of strong Southern women even better."

—*Deep South Magazine*

KRISTY WOODSON HARVEY

Under the Southern Sky

A NOVEL

G

Gallery Books

New York   London   Toronto   Sydney   New Delhi

G

Gallery Books
An Imprint of Simon & Schuster, Inc.
1230 Avenue of the Americas
New York, NY 10020

First Gallery Books trade paperback edition April 2021

GALLERY BOOKS and colophon are registered trademarks of Simon & Schuster, Inc.

For information about special discounts for bulk purchases, please contact Simon & Schuster Special Sales at 1-866-506-1949 or business@simonandschuster.com.

The Simon & Schuster Speakers Bureau can bring authors to your live event. For more information or to book an event, contact the Simon & Schuster Speakers Bureau at 1-866-248-3049 or visit our website at www.simonspeakers.com.

Interior design by Davina Mock-Maniscalco

Manufactured in the United States of America

10 9 8 7 6 5 4 3 2 1

Library of Congress Cataloging-in-Publication Data

Names: Woodson Harvey, Kristy, author.
Title: Under the southern sky / Kristy Woodson Harvey.
Identifiers: LCCN 2020024600 (print) | LCCN 2020024601 (ebook) |
    ISBN 9781982117726 (trade paperback) | ISBN 9781982117733 (ebook)
Subjects: LCSH: Domestic fiction. | GSAFD: Love stories.
Classification: LCC PS3623.O6785 U53 2021 (print) | LCC PS3623.O6785
    (ebook) | DDC 813/.6—dc23
LC record available at https://lccn.loc.gov/2020024600
LC ebook record available at https://lccn.loc.gov/2020024601

ISBN 978-1-9821-1772-6
ISBN 978-1-9821-1773-3 (ebook)

To my friend Beth Heins,
who sparked the idea for this story . . .

My "little sister" Brooke Smith,
who made me sit down and write it . . .

And all the families,
created through extraordinary circumstances,
whose journeys inspired this book in ways little and big.

Amelia

MODERN LOVE

I FOUND OUT MY MARRIAGE was over the day my "Modern Love" piece appeared in the *New York Times*. The Modern Love piece about my thoroughly modern love with my husband, Thad, about our decision not to have children, about how we were choosing travel and wanderlust instead, living life on our own terms.

Little did I know that he was *really* living life on his own terms. While I was going to work every morning and he was "writing his first novel" in the dated downtown Palm Beach apartment that his octogenarian grandmother rented to us for next to nothing, he was actually playing house with a CrossFit obsessed god named Chase. In fact, when I ran home from work to show Thad my piece at nine that morning, it wasn't Thad I found on the wood-framed yellow couch in our living room. It was Chase. I knew him because he was a hairdresser.

My hairdresser. But I had never seen him quite like this: his neon green boxer briefs accenting his spray-tanned abs—both of which clashed horribly with the sofa, I might add—sitting nonchalantly under the portrait of Thad's grandmother. She smirked inside her gilded frame, hair in a bouffant, choker pearls tight around her neck, earlobes dripping with rhinestones. It didn't take long for me to put the pieces together.

I dropped the newspaper, the pages falling through the air in slow motion.

I wondered if Chase had bathed in the pink tub in the tiny master bath, if he had watched soap drip off his toes against the green tiles with hand-painted daisies, chipped and faded with age. I wondered if he had drunk vodka out of our crystal glasses, the ones I was certain were of a vintage that potentially contained lead and that, every now and then, I was positive were poisoning me.

As the last page drifted to the floor, I realized I had just written my love story for the entire world to read. And now it was over.

A baffled, wet-haired Thad emerged from the pink-and-green bathroom, a floral-print towel wrapped around his waist, and explained that I never came back home once I left for work, as though I were somehow in the wrong for discovering his affair. *Lie to me. I promise I'll believe you*, I thought. But he didn't. Instead, he tossed out the idea of the three of us—Thad, Chase, and me—living together. Ironically, our love was not that modern.

When people would console me later about the divorce, they would say, "Well, at least you split up before you had children." I didn't include in the column that I'd abandoned the idea of motherhood when I found out I was infertile at age fourteen. And I definitely left out the part about how the egregious number of baby showers I had attended over the past several years had made me curious about what it was like to feel flutter kicks in your belly. It had made me wonder what it might be like to take part in a rite of passage that was as normal to my friends as getting our first training bras or learning to drive a stick shift.

Their words made me realize how alone I felt, how I had made a decision to never let anyone into my life who would love me unconditionally, or, maybe more important, that I would love unconditionally. People always think being loved will change them. But that's not true. It's really, truly loving—with the kind of love you couldn't take away even if you wanted to—that turns you inside out.

Cold panic washed over me. I felt myself back against the wall and slide down it until I was on the floor, the last page of newspaper crumpled in my hand. That paper was the only thing keeping me tethered to earth. As it always did when I felt like I was losing control, my recurring nightmare flashed through my mind. In it, Daddy is washing his old Cadillac in the gravel driveway of Dogwood, the sprawling waterfront home that has been in my family since before the Revolution. My father is a small farmer, and, well, the family money has all but run out. They could sell the valuable property, make a nice life for themselves somewhere else. But then, my mother argued, where would that leave Aunt Tilley?

Daddy's nearly vintage Cadillac is dripping wet, and he is wearing one of those infomercial shammy gloves, rubbing soap circles on the car's body.

The house starts off in good shape, like it is in real life, largely because Daddy, my brother, Robby, and I can fix absolutely anything. I could paint trim better than any professional by the time I was twelve years old. Robby can fix a refrigerator, rewire a car, splice cable, anything you need. Even still, as a child I always had the feeling that the grand home filled with heirlooms—the mahogany dinner table where Washington once carved his initials, the gilded china, the monogrammed sterling silver—was falling in around us. The fading opulence seemed incongruous with the too-small dresses I was squeezing into for the third year in a row.

As Daddy washes his car in the driveway, Aunt Tilley walks out on the porch in one of her Victorian getups, complete with corset and parasol, which she took to wearing after she lost her mind, before I was even born.

Only, when I look up, it isn't Aunt Tilley who is residing in the east wing now. It's me. Old, alone, and crazy as a bat, with my beloved family home falling down around me. And Trina, my sister-in-law, is calling, "Amelia, darling." That's when I wake up, sweaty and cold.

Some people dream about losing their teeth. I dream about losing Dogwood.

I never told Thad about the nightmare. Now I was glad I

hadn't. Because, it seemed, I was destined to become the spinster aunt in the attic, the subject of many a good Southern cautionary tale. Just like my poor, dear aunt Tilley. She was a little unhinged, but she was still my favorite.

No! I scolded myself. I was not Aunt Tilley. I was Amelia Saxton, investigative reporter, award-winning journalist, seeker of truth and lover of righteousness. I tried to convince myself, as I walked out the door, completely unable to hear what Thad was saying as he ran after me, that this was better. This facilitated my life plan: Rise to the top of my game as a journalist. Check. Become executive editor. Check. Become managing editor. Check. Next stop: editor in chief. My husband, Thad, was an anchor around my neck. Of course, true love had also been a part of my life plan. That was when the tears began. He had been the one my heart searched for. He had been the one that changed everything. The thought split me in two: *How will I live without him?*

But I was a girl who had grown up huddling by the cast-iron radiator in my too-big room when we didn't have enough money for the heat bill. I was a teenager who had replastered living room ceilings after a storm caused them to cave in. I was a woman who had discovered pay inequities in local manufacturing and exposed that the largest business owner in town was preventing women from exercising their legal right to pump breast milk at work. I was a warrior. I always had been. The dissolution of my marriage was nothing more than a bump in the road.

No use crying over what could have been, I reassured myself as I wiped my eyes, stood up straighter, cleared my throat, and dug around for my concealer. Modern Love, take two, equaled solitude. It equaled throwing myself into work. My writing had always been my only real safe place. By getting lost in someone else's story, I could blissfully forget my own, at least for a little while.

And the interview I had scheduled that morning would lead to a story that I felt in the marrow of my bones would be groundbreaking. It had taken me months to get this interview in the first place, and I knew I could never reschedule, despite the fact that my entire life had just gone up in flames. Even as sure as I felt, though, I couldn't have predicted how important that one interview would turn out to be.

But life is like that. Sometimes the nothing moments are everything.

Greer

JULY 21, 2016

I KNOW THIS IS THE last time I will be able to write, can feel the strength slipping from my fingers and the clarity slipping from my mind. There is so much to say when you are running out of time. It all feels so important, and yet also absurdly trivial. I am just one person. My struggles have so little bearing on the rest of the larger, wider world. At the beginning, I rushed, worried, finding people to take over my newspaper column and my Instagram account. I hurried to pass off all my responsibilities at the nonprofit, to train new people so Daddy wouldn't have so much to do at the company. Now it all seems so pointless. What does it matter?

Even still, I hope I made a difference in my short time. I think about a woman who came to hear me speak this last time, who looked sad and troubled, who looked like life had won. She told me that my words had helped her through her divorce, had given her the strength to go forward and find a new career she loved, had eased her fear of starting over. I think about the woman we built a house for, the one who had lost everything in a fire, the way her tears felt against my cheek when we stood in the front yard staring at it, when she was too emotional to even step inside. I think about the children who drew their mothers cards to congratulate them when they finished our job skills training program and we helped them find employment.

I wouldn't go so far as to call it a legacy. But I'm surprised to find that I don't care about that anymore. A legacy means nothing. It's a life that matters. And I know, without a doubt, that we helped to give those women lives they could own, that they could celebrate. It fills my heart, even now.

I can't imagine that, even in heaven—if there is such a place—I won't feel the pain of losing Parker, of being away from my beloved husband. I worry about leaving him behind, about what he will do. I worry that I have ruined his life, even though he says that I have made it. I feel deep anguish and guilt about the pain I have caused him, about the tasks that he has had to perform these past few months. It terrifies me to know that the worst is yet to come, the lifting and feeding and bathing will give way to much worse. And now I can only pray that it's fast.

I can't imagine that, even so far away, I won't pine for the babies we never got to have, those embryos I had to leave behind, put back into that cold and impersonal freezer. A mother should never have to say goodbye to her children—even the ones that might never be.

I know that being with my own mother there in the great beyond will be a comfort. It soothes me as I begin a slow walk down a narrow corridor that I hope is leading somewhere even more glorious than I can imagine. It helps me push away the fear that there is nothing waiting for me on the other side, only darkness.

When I was growing up, when I would get in bed at night, my mind would often race with scary scenarios or bad dreams. My mother would tell me to think happy thoughts, to fill my head with chocolate drops and peppermints, ballet slippers and tutus. Now I fill my mind with my first wedding dance with Parker, the way the lights twinkled around us, the way he held me so close, how I knew I would always be safe in his arms. Even now, I may be leaving, but I am still safe in his arms.

I don't know if Parker will ever read my journals, but I suspect he will. I would. So, Parker, if you are reading this, please know that leaving you is the worst thing I have ever faced. Worse than losing my mother, worse than dying myself.

I think you might find in these pages some parts of myself that I am ashamed of, some parts that, if I'm honest, I'd rather you never knew. For those parts, I am sorry, my love. I truly am. But please know that nothing in these pages changes the absolute certainty in my heart that you were my only one.

I am writing you a letter, and I will leave it with your mom, who, as you know, I loved almost as if she were my own.

She will give it to you when the time is right. She will know. Mothers always do.

Amelia

DREAM JOB

AS I OPENED THE DOOR to Palm Beach Conceptions only an hour after the most emotional scene of my life, I realized I should have been sitting at one of my friends' houses, sobbing into a pint of Häagen-Dazs and a glass of rosé. But, damn it, I had been working on getting this interview for more than three months. Crying wouldn't help. Writing, I knew, would.

I waved to two of the women in the waiting room, who called, "Hi, Amelia." I'm sure they were wondering why I was here, if Thad and I were trying to have a baby. Even the gossipiest socialites in town couldn't already know about my new, Thadless life, could they?

The thought gave me heartburn. What if *everyone* knew? What if I was the only person in all of Palm Beach who had been out of the loop on the truth about Thad? I couldn't stay here now. I couldn't bear to stick around knowing that I was the scandal of the week.

Maybe I could go back home to North Carolina. I had a decent amount of contacts now. I could freelance. But I wasn't sure if I could make enough money freelancing to live. And try as they might, my parents weren't in a position to help me. Plus, there wouldn't be any alimony. I'd been the one paying our bills, while Thad "focused on his novel"—which I now knew was code for focusing on Chase.

I couldn't very well throw Thad out of his own grandmother's apartment. Even if I could, I'm pretty sure no one wants to sleep in the chintz-filled bedroom where her husband has been having sex with someone else.

All at once, this terrified, vulnerable feeling came over me. But at least I still had my job.

I didn't have a single friend who still had the same job as when they graduated from college, so I guess that made me a little bit different. But getting hired at *Clematis* magazine had been my dream. Growing up, the daughter of two very refined Southerners, *Clematis* had been as much a part of my life as church on Sunday and my grandmother's pearls around my neck. *Clematis* was aspirational, a symbol of the person that I might become one day, someone well traveled and well-read. Someone who could speak authoritatively on art and new museum exhibits and the importance of music in society. Someone like my mother.

I had taken early on to investigative pieces. Getting to the bottom of a secret, discovering a sordid underbelly, was my real forte. But I also loved to tell people's stories. Real stories about life and love, hardship and heartache. About the way that people get back up when they fall down. In fact, my very first piece at *Clematis* had been about a disgraced young heiress whose father had been caught up in the Enron scandal. In a matter of days, she lost everything, the cushy, beautiful life she'd always known pulled out from under her. Years later, only in her midtwenties, she had begged and borrowed from every friend she had left to launch a makeup line that had sold for millions to Sephora, landing her back on top once again. Storytelling showed me that it's not our failures that matter; it's what we do after that counts.

There was no doubt about it: I was in the midst of the biggest, baddest failure of my life. I guess, in retrospect, there had been signs, a few rumors. Being from North Carolina, I should have known that where there's smoke, there's fire. But Thad laughed the rumors away.

I knew when I walked out of the apartment that this wouldn't be a normal divorce. If Thad had left me for another woman, people would rally around me, curse him for how he had betrayed me. But now that he was leaving me for a man?

Well, of course my girlfriends would hate him. They didn't have a choice. But strangers, and acquaintances, and *society*? They would all cut him slack. He was finally living his truth. There would be pity for me, of course. And maybe even whispers that our marriage had been for appearances.

I exchanged pleasantries with the women I knew, forcing a smile, getting close enough to smell their Jo Malone perfume and see the diamonds sparkling in their ears, hoping that they couldn't see how I was dying inside.

As I sat down in one of the chic leather chairs, I couldn't help but realize how different this was from the waiting rooms of my youth with their standard-issue medical office chairs with the upholstery that itched the backs of my legs. This waiting room smelled of soothing essential oils, not antiseptic.

As I picked up the latest issue of *Clematis*—as though I couldn't have practically recited its contents—all I could think about was that I should have stayed in Raleigh. If I had continued on at the little newspaper outside of town I interned at for two summers in college, if I had taken the job they offered me, my entire life could have been different.

I'd loved working for that little newspaper; I had loved getting to do absolutely everything, from writing to editing, proofreading to graphic design. I had even learned to take a decent photo or two. Those summers made me the journalist I am today. I wasn't a one-trick pony. I knew every element of putting out a publication.

But when I saw the salary package they could offer, I realized that even I, a single girl in a small town, couldn't live on it. And, to be honest, I felt a little bit ashamed. I had been number one in my journalism school class, the editor of my college magazine. By all accounts, I was destined for journalistic greatness. I couldn't work at a small-town newspaper for the rest of my life.

Even still, I actually didn't expect to get the job at *Clematis*. It was a smaller, core group of journalists. And if it didn't work out, I was stuck in Palm Beach—which, admittedly, isn't a bad place to be stuck—with no New York City publication on my résumé. If I'm honest with myself, I was scared. When I was in college, I said I stayed in Raleigh so that I could be close to the beach, drive home on the weekends to soak up the summer rays. And I guess that was true, in some ways. But when you got right down to it, I was terrified of being in a big city, scared to leave home, intimidated by the great, wide world beyond the South.

Plus, *Clematis* was my dream job. And even though it was less money and a less prestigious position in the eyes of the world than a New York magazine, I believed with all my heart that if I took it, it would pay off. At a midsized publication like *Clematis*, I could have the opportunity to write both investigative stories and profile pieces.

I had been so nervous moving to Palm Beach, renting the smallest apartment on the least noteworthy street with a girl from Craigslist who I had never met. (My parents would have killed me if they'd known.) I didn't have any friends. In some ways, it was a much bigger risk than going to New York with a handful of college friends. But there were vestiges of my Southern upbringing everywhere. The trappings of city life, but the manners and protocols of a small town.

And then I met Thad. He was handsome and kind and made me feel like I was at home in this new world.

I had gotten my dreams early. So I guess I was getting my comeuppance early, too. I was only thirty-five, and I was going to be joking about my starter husband.

I knew I was in real danger of crying when a very pleasant nurse with Texas-sized hair opened the door to the waiting room and said, "Mrs. Williams, Dr. Wright will see you now."

Mrs. Williams. I wasn't going to be Mrs. Williams anymore. I was going to go back, as quickly as possible, to being Miss Saxton.

On autopilot, I followed the nurse as she opened the door to Dr. Wright's office, which was so sparse it was clear he didn't do a lot of actual work in here. I put my game face back on like my daddy taught me on long days at the softball field. "Are you the one who has to call the patients?" I asked.

"We all take turns," she said. I could tell she wasn't sure if she was supposed to talk to me. I supposed a reporter in a doctor's office usually didn't mean much good. But I wasn't there to get her in trouble. I was there to sniff out a trail; I was writing about what happens to frozen embryos once they are no longer needed.

I wanted to talk to parents of these fertilized eggs. Did they destroy them? Adopt them out? Donate them to science? Did they have more children because they couldn't stand the idea of doing any of the above?

"So you only call them when it's time to make a decision?"

She shrugged. And then she made a tiny, simple gesture that would end up thrusting my life so far off its axis that my divorce would seem like a blip on the radar. She pointed to a thin stack of paper on Dr. Wright's desk. "Yeah, once they've been in there for three years with no activity, we start calling the parents. They pay a bundle to keep them frozen, and our freezer space is always at a premium, so we try to keep on top of them." She paused. "But that list is the ones we can't get in touch with. After a few years of being unable to reach a contact, of not being paid for storage, we consider them abandoned."

I nodded. "Then what?"

She shrugged. "That's the hard part. We don't want to destroy them or donate them for research without the parents' consent, but eventually, we're going to have to make some hard decisions." She paused. "Dr. Wright is a little behind, but he should be here shortly."

I smiled cheerily, wanting more than anything for her to get the hell out of the room so I could snoop. "Please tell him to take his time," I said. "And please reassure him I'll be brief."

As soon as the door closed, I practically pounced on the first page of that list. I didn't know what I was looking for, but one of the hurdles I was facing was finding parents to interview for this article. I needed real-life patients to tell me why they'd decided to destroy their embryos, adopt them out, etc., and the listing I had placed on HARO, a website where journalists and sources connect, wasn't doing much good. In this case, no one wanted to help a reporter out.

Maybe I would know someone on this list and could lead them into a discussion without their knowing I had broken all kinds of laws and without their doctor breaking HIPAA, which I was one hundred percent sure Dr. Wright wouldn't do. This was the kind of office with a secret entrance for its high-profile patients.

I scanned the *A*s, flipping quickly through the alphabet. When I got to the *T*s, my eyes focused, and I gasped audibly. I heard a hand on the doorknob and practically flung myself into my seat, trying to look calm, even though my heart was racing out of my chest.

I breezed through my cursory list of questions. I just needed Dr. Wright as a quoted source on questions I knew the answers to, so it wasn't that hard. I actually skipped a few because I needed to be alone with this moral dilemma.

I had seen a name on that list that I recognized. I wasn't supposed to know that those embryos had been abandoned. *It isn't any of my business*, I repeated to myself. But what if he didn't know that his embryos were even here? What if a decision was made about them that he wouldn't want?

As I walked out the door, I said nonchalantly to the nurse, "Thanks. And good luck."

Without even looking up from her paperwork, she said, "Thanks, hon."

I stopped on the street and took a deep breath, realizing that I was walking in the direction of a home that wasn't mine anymore. I'd just check into the Breakers and luxuriate for a few breaths before I decided what to do. I stuck my thumb on my banking app. Nope. Maybe I'd check into the Colony instead. One of my friends, the marketing manager there, had promised me a too-good-to-be-true media rate if I ever wanted it.

I closed my eyes for just a moment, trying to make the swirling in my head—which had become so fast and furious I almost felt like I could see it—stop. All I could see was their names: Thaysden, Greer and Parker.

Hadn't I already inserted myself way too far into their lives once before? I decided I had, as I began walking in the direction of my car, planning to go straight to the Colony. But walking away—from my life, my marriage, and even someone else's problems—wasn't something I was capable of.

I tried to tell myself again that I couldn't, I wouldn't. But I had no choice, really. I could never live with myself if I didn't tell him.

"Hey, Siri," I said, "call Parker Thaysden."

Parker

INSTANTANEOUS NOTHING

PEOPLE TALK A LOT ABOUT widows, but you don't hear that much about widowers. I couldn't think of a single famous one. That morning, I tried to because Greer's *Us Weekly*, the one that had autorenewed for the three years since she died, was sitting on top of the stack of mail. Same with her *Southern Coast*, a magazine her father teased her mercilessly for loving, since it was not owned by her family company, McCann Media.

Maybe it's because men bounce back faster and move on with their lives. People kept telling me, "At least you don't have kids. You can make a clean break."

They didn't get it. I wanted to be a father, and I would have given anything for a kid with Greer's blond hair and fearlessness. My wife was born bold. She didn't take any prisoners and took down anything that got in her way. Anything except for ovarian cancer, which proved to be her kryptonite.

I lifted my head from my cereal bowl and glanced over at the neat stack of large black Moleskine journals on the white quartz counter. Greer was a creature of habit, introspective. She was the kind of person life coaches would call "self-aware." Those journals were part of her daily routine. Sometimes she wrote a lot. Sometimes a little. Every entry, from the mundane to the extraordinary, was a part of the woman who had been so steadfast and confident that I'd believed she was invincible. I never would have imagined that I would be sitting here alone at the table she'd picked out—like she had everything in this house—over a bowl of soggy cereal, in the small Palm Beach home we had purchased six years earlier. The view of the Intracoastal didn't seem nearly as awe-inspiring now that she was gone.

As I raised the spoon to my mouth I could almost hear Greer saying, *Cereal has no nutritional value.* She would have been in the kitchen throwing all varieties of plant matter into the Vitamix, going over the day's schedule, and making something that looked disgusting but somehow tasted amazing. Although she would have been doing that at six, not nearly eleven. Now I stayed at the office almost all night sometimes. I was in charge of Mergers and Acquisitions for McCann Media, which meant my days revolved around finding new publications to purchase and transitioning their teams into the world of McCann once I did. That often meant corporate restructuring, which wasn't always savory. But someone had to do it.

After Greer died, I couldn't sleep, so I had rearranged my

schedule, grabbing a few hours of rest in the early morning before heading back to the office. If he didn't approve, the boss—
my father-in-law—never said so. Everyone was still treating
me like I'd crumble if they looked at me wrong. I would.

This morning I crumbled at the thought of Greer in a fitted black work dress and shoes that cost more than my first
car. She was petite and pretty, but that girl was powerful. She
would have taken the time to sit on my lap, to kiss me, to
make plans for the night. She ran her own Florida-based arm
of her family's national media conglomerate, the nonprofit
she had created, and the world. But she always took the time
to make sure people knew how much she loved them.

And me? She loved me a whole damn lot. But not a tenth
as much as I loved her. I stood up straighter when she walked
in the door. I loved to look at her across the room at a party
and know that she would be leaving with me, to see her throw
her head back in laughter and know that I could make her
laugh like that. She had been mine to protect. And I had let
her down.

Everyone told me I had to move on, that this pain and
emptiness would ruin me if I didn't get back out there. I was
young. I could still have everything I wanted out of life. That
was what they said. But she was what I wanted out of life.

It had gotten to the point that my mother—my own
Southern, pearl-wearing, churchgoing, never-said-a-dirty-
word-in-her-life mother—had said that maybe I should consider a one-night stand. That is a conversation one does not
ever want to have with one's mother.

My friends had suggested I move. This neighborhood was full of wealthy, retired snowbirds. It was too stuffy for me. But Greer had wanted to be near her family when we had children. This was her world. How could I leave it? Leaving would mean taking the clothes out of her closet, throwing the rows of shoes from their racks into boxes, removing the purses from their storage containers and giving them away. I couldn't do it.

I looked over at the journals, debating which one I would pack to take with me on my trip home to Cape Carolina the next day. I let myself read one entry every day, chosen at random. It was my way of holding on to her. Every day, I fought the urge to sit down and read them all, all at once. I held myself back so that I could stretch out the joy of those fresh words. When I had read through them, I planned to start all over again, read them in order. But then they wouldn't be new. Then they would be a memory.

And then I would have to admit that she wasn't coming back.

My phone rang in the bathroom, finally tearing me away from my soggy cereal. I got up, barely even noticing the pink-and-green lattice wallpaper that Greer had said was "very Palm Beach," glancing at my hair, which seemed darker since it was wet, in the shiny white mirror, running my hand across the three-day stubble that I needed to shave before work. I was deeply tanned, even though it was December. Winters were mild in Palm Beach, and solitary days on the boat were what kept me breathing—the sea, the sky, the wind. Every day the water outside my door held something new. I kept think-ing that maybe it would bring me something new, too, erase the fact that Greer was gone. As of yet, no luck.

A familiar but confusing number lit up my black iPhone screen. "Amelia Saxton." Her Facebook profile picture popped up too. Her exuberant face on the screen, the way her wavy dark blond hair fell over her shoulders and her blue eyes shone, so full of life even on camera, almost made me smile back at her happiness. *Almost.* I briefly considered sending it to voice mail, but I didn't. Instead, I answered, thrusting my-self onto the sword of whatever inconvenience was on the line.

Just seeing Amelia's name brought back the memory of the day Greer told me she wanted to end her life—before the cancer could. It took my breath away.

When Greer told me, my first reaction was to tell her no. But no one tells Greer McCann no. Not even her husband. When she said it, this eerie calm came over me, as though I were outside myself, receiving news that didn't pertain to me. I had just faced that Greer was sick. I had never considered that my wife would die. She was too real to actually die. When she brought the subject up in our usual restaurant with my usual steak and merlot, I had nearly forgotten, seeing the way the light reflected off her pretty face, that she was even sick.

We had just been talking about how we would decorate a nursery when she got well, for Pete's sake.

I swallowed a sip of wine, my stomach turning over. This was the only woman I had ever loved. I had changed so much of who I was and what I wanted because being with her was so much better than anything else. She made me happy in a new way, one I had never experienced before. My first thought, looking across the table, was, *They're going to have to kill me, too.*

I would have given anything to trade places.

After that, I couldn't stop touching Greer. I followed her everywhere, gauging her moves and her actions, trying to decide if she was getting worse, trying to keep her here with me. I didn't necessarily agree with her idea to announce her plans via *Clematis*. But, again, Greer and "no" never mixed well. She wanted to frame the story to bring attention to her charity. I didn't care what she did as long as I got to hover over her and breathe life into her while she did it.

She wouldn't let me stay in the room with Amelia—the reporter who also happened to be my childhood friend. But I stood at the door. I could make out only snippets of the conversation. When I showed Amelia out of the house, I could tell she was shell-shocked. I'd known her since I was born. She was so quiet. "I'm sorry" was all she managed as she engulfed me in a familiar hug.

I nodded. "Me too."

That was it, but maybe it was all we needed.

Back in the house, I found Greer in the shower, and I climbed in behind her.

I kissed her, quite intent on making love to her right then and there. In that simple gesture, something as familiar to me by then as brushing my hair, I finally broke down. Sobs escaped me, and, naked as the day I was born, I wept on the black-and-white marble floor of our walk-in shower.

"Babe," Greer said calmly, "what is the matter?"

I pulled her down onto the floor with me, holding her in my arms. "I can't know it's the last time," I said, pressing my face into her neck. She didn't smell like death yet. She still smelled like her, like Shiseido shampoo and rose body oil.

She ran her fingers down my back, laying her head on my shoulder, the water dripping around us. "What do you mean?"

"I can't have it planned, G. I can't know when you're going to go. I can't know that it's the last time I'm going to make love to you, or kiss you, or feel you in my arms." I paused, catching my breath. "I know all that is coming, but it has to be a progression. I can't know ahead of time."

My dying wife was the one consoling me. I thought I was tough, but she was stronger. I expected her to argue with me. Instead, she whispered, "Okay."

I looked up at her. "Really?"

She nodded sadly. "I wanted to get it over with for you. I didn't want you to have to watch me go downhill. But if that's what you need, if that will help your healing process, then that's what we'll do."

"It's like a really bleak 'Gift of the Magi,'" I said, kissing her.

"I always thought that story was pretty bleak anyway," she joked, trying to make me smile.

She got up, washing the soap out of her hair like we hadn't just had one of the most emotional scenes of our lives. She pulled me up and said, "Parker Thaysden, you are the best decision I ever made, and I will love you for all eternity. Even when I'm not here."

I kissed her again. "No man has ever loved a woman the way I love you."

She smiled. "I agree wholeheartedly."

The shower is where most people go to think. But for me, now, the shower is memory central. There isn't a single morning I step in that I don't think about that night. I feel guilty about it, but I stand firm in my decision. We had more time than we were told we would. I cherish every moment of it, even the bad parts.

With all of that weighing so heavily on my mind, I knew I couldn't talk about Greer. Not even to Amelia, who I'd known all my life. Not to anyone. But then again, my urgently ringing phone reminded me, Amelia could potentially have some pressing news from Cape Carolina. Or maybe she wanted to do an article about the foundation, which would bring attention to the great work we were doing. Greer would want that.

The phone had already rung four times when I slid to answer and hit the speaker button. "Hello."

"Parker," Amelia said cheerily. Too cheerily. So cheerily that something was clearly up.

"What's going on, Amelia?" I asked.

"Oh, same old," she said. She was lying. Amelia and Greer were totally, completely different people, but they had similar sparks that made it impossible for them to sit still. Amelia was always moving forward, just like Greer. I admired that about her, especially since, as my inability to talk about my dead wife in the past tense for three solid years indicated, moving forward was not my strong suit.

I didn't say anything. That was the tactic I always used when I wanted someone to get to the point.

It worked. "Listen, Parker," she said. "I need to meet up with you. It's important."

Suspicious. The casseroles had started flooding in the day after Greer died. If I hadn't been so devastated, it would have been a huge ego boost. For a moment, I wondered if Amelia might be coming on to me. But then I remembered that she was married to Thad, a fact that I tended to conveniently forget. My family had teased me for years about my crush on Amelia.

"You're-on-a-tight-deadline-and-need-a-quote important? Or a-secret-uncle-has-died-and-left-me-twenty-million-dollars important?" I smirked.

"Um." She paused. "It's decidedly more important than either of those things."

"Can't you just tell me now? My interest is piqued."

She was quiet. I could tell she was deciding. "Yeah, no. I don't think so. It's a face-to-face kind of thing."

"Well, damn," I said.

"I'm leaving for Cape Carolina in the morning," she said apologetically. "Maybe next week?"

"Oh my God," I said. "It's my mom. Or my dad. It is, isn't it?"

She laughed. "No, Parker. You're killing me. Everything is fine. Let's just get coffee when I get back to Palm Beach." I could hear noise on the other end of the phone, and as I was saying, "Well, you might be seeing me sooner than you think," she was talking over me, saying, "I'll text you to set it up. I have to run!"

I am a harper. Once I want to know something, I can't think about anything else. Fortunately, I was heading to Cape Carolina tomorrow, too. So I wouldn't have that long to wait.

When we hung up, I rubbed shaving cream on my cheeks and chin and saw that I was smiling. Human interaction wasn't my favorite thing these days, but that phone call had been less painful than most. It had to be that Cape Carolina connection.

When my face was smooth, I tapped my American Airlines app and checked in for my nine a.m. flight. I hadn't been home in months, but now had seemed like a good time. I had all those points piled up, waiting. But who wants to take a vacation alone? I didn't. All being on the beach would do was remind me that Greer wasn't lying beside me. When I was at her office, I could be surrounded by her: her employees, her things, her energy. That's why I had gone there almost every day since her death. Even more than our house, that office had become home.

Tomorrow, I would be in Cape Carolina, where I was defined by my baseball stats, not my marriage to a deceased heiress. Where I was the guy who made orangeades at the soda fountain after school, not the one running his dead wife's company.

I walked into my bedroom. Even after three years, it still smelled like Greer. I pulled the green lattice comforter, which matched the wallpaper, up over the sheets so the bed was sort of made. I threw three shirts, three pairs of khakis, and three pairs of boxers in my roller bag.

As I walked out the door, heading to work, turning to put my key into the lock, it occurred to me, for the first time, that what Amelia had to say might be good news.

Greer

FEBRUARY 16, 2015

IT'S WEIRD HOW SOMETHING YOU'VE never considered can suddenly become all you can think about. Like the minute they came in and told me that I had ovarian cancer, all I thought about was my babies. The babies I didn't have. The babies that, after three years of marriage, Parker and I had just started talking about. In some ways, I still feel too young to be a mother. None of my friends have kids yet. But the biological reality at thirty-one is that, whether our New York to Palm Beach lifestyles and our workaholism allow for it or not, eventually our biological clocks are going to start ticking loudly.

So, as Parker was asking the doctor how early she thought it was and about treatment options and heredity, all I asked was, "Can you save my eggs?"

Parker was near hysterics. "Your *eggs*? Are you serious right now, Greer? Who gives a shit about your eggs? All I care about is you."

I just looked back at the doctor, who said, "I don't see any obvious signs of cancer on your right ovary. I would suggest removing it to be safe, but we can retrieve your eggs from it."

I told her I'd like to freeze embryos because I hear they have a better success rate than that of eggs frozen unfertilized.

Parker looked truly astounded. But I didn't know how he didn't know that. Articles about it were everywhere.

He kind of freaked out and said something like, "How about we discuss the major surgery you're having tomorrow? Would that be okay with you?"

Parker is usually very calm. But that man loves me. He loves me hard. And I know his panic was from considering a world without me in it. To be honest, I can't even consider a world without me in it, so I am, instead, considering what I will do after I am declared cancer-free.

What I will do is IVF.

I know what I am up against. I watched my mother go up against it, too. I watched her lose a swift but painful battle with what proved to be the only adversary that had ever beaten Karen McCann. I don't want to think about it. I don't want to focus on calling my dad or my sister or on my surgery or my chemo or what they might find inside me.

So instead, I will focus on making my poor, shell-shocked husband deposit his sperm on the way to my surgery. Because I will beat this. I will win. And when I do, we will be so happy to have these beautiful embryos waiting to become babies, ready for us to hold them in our arms.

Amelia

GLORY DAYS

I DIDN'T CONSIDER MYSELF THE kind of girl who runs home to her mother, but as soon as I left that doctor's office, I wasn't able to control my urge to buy a plane ticket home. Maybe I needed something familiar to anchor me back to earth, or maybe I wanted to get the unpleasantness of telling my family over with.

After a sleepless night in a hotel that was quite luxurious but left me feeling even lonelier, I boarded a plane home that early morning, sunglasses over my eyes, which were swollen and blurry from crying and lack of sleep. As I shoved my carry-on into the overhead compartment, a simple *ding* on my phone—a reminder of Martin's birthday party— sent me back into sobs, prompting the woman in front of me to look at me with a mixture of pity and disgust. Thad and I loved Martin's birthday parties. And Martin was *my* friend. I got to keep him in the divorce.

I wanted to tell Martin so, but I couldn't risk anyone knowing what was going on until I told my parents. They were going to be outraged and devastated; the last thing I needed was for them to hear the news from someone else first.

I sat down in my window seat in the very last row of the plane, the only seat available so last-minute. I pulled out my phone and texted Nanette, my editor. So sorry, N. I can't make it in today. Major emergency. Flying home to Cape Carolina. I will fill you in on all when I get back.

Typing bubbles appeared immediately, followed by Nanette's response: Oh no, babe. You okay? Can I help? Anything you need. Take as much time as you want. I'm here for you.

I knew she was. I also knew she was panicking because we were supposed to be putting the December issue of *Clematis* to bed today, and while Nanette had the technical skills and know-how to do it herself, she depended on me, her managing editor, the deputy to her sheriff, for far more than I thought she even realized.

I tapped my thumb on the group text my oldest friends, Sarah, Jennifer, and Madison, kept going at all times. We had grown up together, and the three of them had returned to Cape Carolina. I was the only outlier who had moved away for good. I wanted to tell them. I *needed* to tell them—at least that I was coming home, if not the reason why. But I couldn't quite bring myself to do it yet.

As I leaned my head against the plane window, watching Palm Beach become smaller and smaller and then fade to white, I couldn't think about next steps. All I could think about was how to tell my mother. My mother loved me more than anything, but she also had ideas about how my life was going to turn out. I thought she would be disappointed in me. My divorce was a mark on her sterling reputation.

But then I had a thought that neither consoled me nor made me feel worse: Thad had never really been mine. I had been a part of a life he was trying to live, a pawn in a game that he had tried to play and lost. A tiny part of me pitied him, felt sad he had spent years living a life that must have felt like it was the wrong size and color. But I think what worried me most of all was that I really, truly hadn't known.

In fact, I used to feel sorry for my friends. Their marriages were so *boring*. Thad and I went dancing, we took art classes, we traveled on a whim, we laughed all the time. I couldn't reconcile how the man who told me how beautiful I was, who looked at me with pure admiration, was the one who had betrayed me.

Thad had called and texted me no fewer than twenty-five times. I didn't want to read his texts, but I couldn't help it. The last one was a gut punch. Amelia, I'm so sorry. I never wanted to hurt you.

It was a relief. I hadn't been that stupid. Thad and I did have real love. It was just the lust part that was missing. I'll admit that we hadn't had a hot and steamy sex life. Maybe it wasn't as good as our conversations over coffee about the art opening we'd gone to the night before or our long, rambling walks through Palm Beach's elite neighborhoods, where Thad would have me in stitches over his renditions of the secret lives behind those bougainvillea walls.

I reasoned that a girl can't have everything. While my friends complained about their husbands not wanting to take them out or go on vacations or watch Bravo, my small concern seemed paltry. Thad and I had fun. We had love. The lust would be gone eventually anyway, I justified. I was married to my best friend.

I fell asleep, my face pressed against the plastic window, jolting awake when the plane touched down. Shocked that I'd slept through the entire flight, I powered my phone up, and, momentarily forgetting what had transpired, I, out of habit, said sleepily, "Hey, Siri, text Thad. *Landed.*"

My phone rang, and I immediately realized my mistake. This was going to take some getting used to. "Thad," I said quietly. "I don't want to talk to you."

"Oh, Amelia," he said. "I'm so sorry. I was going to tell you. I swear I was."

"But it never seemed like the right time to destroy my entire life?" I responded angrily.

"Let's talk about this," he said.

"I can't. I have to go ruin my parents' lives now, too."

"Amelia," he said sadly. "I do love you. I swear I do. I wanted to be different for you. I tried."

"Do not make me feel sorry for you, Thad," I said softly, knowing he was telling the truth. "I can't go there yet."

"Okay," he whispered. "Please just promise you'll call me. Please, Amelia." Then he added, "I miss you already."

I wanted to say something sarcastic like, *Well, I'm sure Chase will soothe your hurt feelings*, but I could tell he meant it. For a brief moment, I thought maybe we could move forward in a different way. But no. I didn't want to live a lie. I felt like all the blood was draining out of my body into my feet. I was light-headed from a sorrow so deep tears felt too ordinary, too trite.

"I'll let you know when I get back," I said noncommittally. "But I'm not sure I can be around you right now."

"I understand," he said softly. "But please call me if you need me. Please let me know if I can help." He paused. "I really am sorry," he added one more time. "I didn't want to lose you, and that was selfish."

"Goodbye, Thad," I said, his name foreign in my mouth. It wasn't a *Bye for now!* or a *See you next week!* It was goodbye. For good.

After leaning on my carry-on in the cramped aisle of the plane for an interminably long time, I walked down the steps and onto the tarmac, wrapping my sweater tighter around me. The two-gate airport was small, clean, bright, and lovely in every way. Home.

Remembering I still had Thad's credit card, I charged a rental Mercedes convertible that he couldn't afford and, with Taylor Swift blaring over the Bluetooth, put the top down and cranked the heat. As I pulled out of the parking lot, I felt free. With the wind in my hair and water all around me, maybe I would be okay.

•   •   •

My parents' house in Cape Carolina could only be described as rambling. And thank goodness. Because thirty-eight years earlier, my aunt Tilley had—as Southerners describe it—gotten "the vapors." She still had them. People said my mama and daddy should put her in a home.

My father was all for it. But my mother said she wasn't going to abandon her sister. So the east wing was converted into an apartment for Aunt Tilley, with a bedroom, bathroom, living room, dining room, and a kitchenette with a refrigerator and microwave—nothing that Aunt Tilley could use to burn the house down. Or so my parents thought. The fire department had to come that one time Aunt Tilley put a frozen macaroni and cheese into the microwave for sixty minutes instead of six minutes. But Chris at the appliance store rewired it so that it would only turn on for one minute at a time, an idea of my brother Robby's that he hadn't been able to figure out how to implement.

Chris had been two grades above me in high school, and he could rewire anything, including Principal Trusken's car. How he got it onto the roof of the school remains an urban legend. He and his friends all had to go to summer school and didn't graduate on time because of it, but if they could, they would do it again. Glory days are fleeting. One must make the absolute most of them.

The classic white colonial might have seemed out of place compared to the beach houses that had taken up residence all around it, with their cedar shakes and hardy board siding. But this grand estate at the long end of a narrow peninsula—alone except for the Thaysdens' house beside it—was the oldest home on the beach. Saxtons had lived in this house for hundreds of years. We had moved into it when I was seven, after my grandparents retired to Florida. I knew every back staircase and hidden nook, every ghost, every creak of the stairwell. And I loved it all. As I drove down the long, live-oak-lined street, I smiled at how the ancient trees made a canopy over me. Not for the first time, I thought that I would love to live here one day. It seemed a little bit crazy, since I wouldn't have children to brighten the shadowy corners or fill the antique beds.

But Robby and his wife, Trina, already had three adorable but very rowdy boys. They, no doubt, would be the next Saxtons to inhabit Dogwood. I always teased them that when they moved in, I would take over Aunt Tilley's apartment. Every Southerner needed a batty relative living in the attic—or, in this case, the east wing. Trina would squeal and go on and on about how much fun we would have while Robby looked horrified. I shuddered, thinking of it now. It had been all fun and games until my recurring nightmare about turning into Aunt Tilley had started.

I had a hard time deciding whether to go see Daddy at the farm first or to head straight home. I figured that, either way, my parents' worlds were about to be shattered by the news that their golden girl had disappointed them.

I decided to go home first. As much as they drove me

crazy, I really couldn't get enough of Mom and Aunt Tilley, especially when they were together, a little codependent disaster area full of hairspray.

I pulled into the grassy lot—well, mostly dead grass, since it was winter—that served as Dogwood's overflow parking, opened the door, and was finally embraced by the smell of the salt air that had begun wafting in through the lowered convertible top the moment I reached the beach. As I stepped out of the car, it actually brought tears to my eyes. When I lived here, I got used to it, couldn't smell it. After a day or two, I would lose it again. But, for now, it was the scent of coming home.

Despite the near-Christmas chill in the air, Mom and Tilley were sitting side by side in rocking chairs on the front porch when I pulled up in my rental car, Mom in a pair of sensible but stylish black pants and a yellow double-breasted jacket and Aunt Tilley in a white lace corset dress with matching parasol. She really seemed normal a lot of the time. This was not one of those times.

They both stood and began squealing for me to hurry up, waving their arms and gesturing to me, but they wouldn't step off the porch, as though contained by an invisible fence. The porch floor was, as always, painted black for winter, to attract heat and keep it warmer. In the summer, it would return to the palest gray. The ceiling remained blue all year long to keep the evil spirits away. (And the mosquitoes.) But my separation from Thad was one evil spirit even the bluest of blue couldn't scare off. Long and healthy marriages were a hallmark of the Saxton family, and I was ruining that streak.

"My baby!" Mom said, as Tilley lilted, "Liabelle!"

Even their joy couldn't keep me from noticing the two broken spindles on the front porch and that the house, which would look stately to anyone else, seemed to sag a little. If I'd had time to think about it, it would have scared me. But I didn't have time to be afraid because I had barely gotten over the threshold, the expansive water view beyond the porch nearly blinding, before "You are much too thin" and "Darlin', you look exhausted" began. Tilley was dragging me inside, toward the kitchen. Stepping over the threshold felt so good. I loved the worn Persian rugs and the English antiques that had been inside this house for generations. I loved that I could see the soothing water from almost every room. Tilley was cutting me a slice of fresh pecan pie on the familiar blue-and-white tile counter when the doorbell rang and Mom went out to answer it.

I had just swallowed the first sweet, delicious bite when I heard Mom say, "Why, Parker Thaysden! To what do we owe the pleasure?" On her lips, the words sounded like "Parkah" and "pleashah."

Aunt Tilley gasped and pointed her fork at me. "You are seeing Parker Thaysden, aren't you? Admit it!"

"Aunt Tilley, I'm married to"—I cleared my throat—"to Thad."

She was saying, "You can take the girl out of Cape Caro-lina—" but stopped herself when Mom and Parker walked into the kitchen, Mom saying, "Liabelle, you have a visitor."

"A gentleman caller!" Tilley trilled.

I rolled my eyes and whispered, "He is not a gentleman caller."

"Well, he's a gentleman, and he's not calling on us old ladies," Tilley said, kissing Parker on both cheeks.

Parker looked terribly amused, while I was hoping the floor would open up and swallow me. I grabbed his wrist and said, "I am so sorry, Parker. Let's go out on the porch."

"But I want some of Aunt Tilley's pie," he whined.

"Oh, I'll bring you some, sugah," she said.

"What the hell are you doing here?" I whisper-shouted as we made our way to the door.

I had grown up with Parker, thinking of him as that an-noying younger boy who wouldn't leave me alone at church. I mean, he had always been cute, obviously. But I wasn't a member of his fan club, one of the hordes of girls that swooned over him.

No one had been more shocked when one of my idols had chosen to marry *him*. I wanted to call Greer up and say, *Parker Thaysden? Do you realize that this kid used to hang worms out of his nostrils?*

But I had gained a new respect for Parker when Greer had died. He had loved her in the way that every woman dreams of being loved. He honored her every day during and since, some might say too much. But I thought people were too cynical. They had forgotten that true love never dies. I guessed I would never know what that was like.

"Amelia, you can't tell a man that you have something really important to talk to him about and then leave him hanging like that," he said as Aunt Tilley wordlessly delivered a piece of pie to him and slipped away as best one could in a five-foot hoopskirt.

I rolled my eyes. "This is a little bit insane."

He shrugged. "I tried to tell you yesterday that I was on my way here, but you hung up too quickly."

"Ohhhh . . ." Well, that made more sense.

We both sat down, and he looked at me expectantly. I hadn't planned what I would say yet, how I would deliver this earthshaking news. I had other earthshaking news I'd been preoccupied with delivering.

"Hey," he whispered between bites. "I'm really sorry about Thad."

"Parker!" I hissed, looking around.

"I know, I know. I figured you came home to tell them. But it's a small town. Word gets around."

I rolled my eyes. "It's been, like, a day."

He shrugged. "Chase does my copy editor's hair." He added, behind his hand, conspiratorially, "And if it makes you feel better, word around the salon is that he had no idea that Thad was married, and he is *pissed*. They are done. Chase isn't anyone's side piece." He looked at me very seriously.

While he worked hard to hold a straight face, I had my first good laugh since yesterday morning. That maybe Thad

wasn't going to get his happily ever after made me feel the tiniest bit better.

"Thank you," I said. "That helps. Even though there is no
way in the world he didn't know Thad and I were married."

"Okay," Parker said impatiently. "We've done you. What
about me?"

I took both his hands in mine and looked him in the eyes.
Something like panic crossed his face, and I dropped them.
"Oh my God. This isn't like a confession of love or something.
You wish."

He smirked. "Okay, well, I mean, I don't know. It wouldn't
be the first one I've gotten in the past few years. I'm not totally unlovable."

I shook my head, but he was right. He wasn't. Sometimes
when you've known someone his whole life, you forget that
his blue eyes are incredibly soulful and his tousled hair is both
boyish and manly at the same time. "I found out something
that I shouldn't know, and I shouldn't tell you, but I feel like I
have to." I paused. "There's an off chance that you don't want
to know or that you already know, and that I'm sticking my
nose in where it isn't—"

"For God's sake, Amelia, spit it out," Parker said.

"Wanted," I whispered. I bit my lip. I wanted to stall, to re-
wind and figure out how to deliver this news tactfully, with
grace. But he was right in front of me, so that seemed more
than a little out of the question now. For half a beat, I wondered if, when the dust settled, Parker would let me interview

him for my story. But I scolded myself. This was more important than any story.

"Look, I was reporting on what people do when they
don't use their embryos, and I sort of accidentally saw that
your embryos are on the abandoned list. And maybe you're
ignoring them and quit paying for storage on purpose, and
that's fine . . ."

I rambled while he looked at me blankly.

"You know," I added, "the embryos that you and Greer
froze—"

"I know which embryos," he practically spat.

"I'm sorry," I whispered.

He pulled out his phone, which I thought was an odd reaction. I thought maybe I should leave. But then he said, "Yes.
This is Parker Thaysden, and I want to check on my embryos.
I wasn't sure if there was an invoice I missed or something."
He paused. "They are not *abandoned*," he said, venom in his
voice. "Uh-huh. Well, yeah. It would be hard for Mrs. Thaysden to return your calls from that number, since she has been
dead for three years." He rolled his eyes.

He pulled out his wallet, removed his credit card, read
off the numbers, and then hung up the phone. He looked at
me, but I could tell he wasn't seeing me. "What now?" he
asked.

It was not the response I was imagining. "What do you
mean, what now? I have absolutely no idea."

"I can't destroy them," he said. "They're all I have left of her."

"You could adopt them out," I suggested warily.

He shot me a look. "Are you serious? They're Greer's. I can't give them to a stranger."

I shook my head. "Well," I said quietly, "there are a lot of people who donate theirs to science. I bet they could be used for something really targeted, maybe even ovarian cancer research, something that would honor Greer's memory."

Parker nodded. He leaned forward and rubbed his temples. "Maybe so," he said.

"I shouldn't have told you, should I?" I whispered.

Parker opened his eyes, but he didn't answer. "Aunt Tilley," he called in the direction of the screen door. "I'm gonna need the rest of that pie!"

I smiled at him cautiously, one hundred percent sure that he was cracking up, but then cracking up myself when I saw that Aunt Tilley was actually delivering the entire pie pan— minus the two pieces we had already eaten—with a fork.

"I'm not sure pie is going to take care of the problem," I said, smirking.

"You don't know that," Parker said, his mouth full.

"My pie can solve absolutely anything," Aunt Tilley said.

Maybe she was right. Because by the time he had finished that pie (The whole thing. I'm serious.), I got the sneaking suspicion that, even though he hadn't deemed it appropriate to share with me yet, Parker Thaysden knew exactly what he was going to do.

Parker

A LITTLE LIGHT

SITTING IN THE FRONT SEAT of my rental car, still in Amelia's yard, I took three deep breaths. Sometimes it hit me hard, at moments like this, that I was alone. Really, truly alone.

What I was thinking about now was absolutely ridiculous. No, not ridiculous. Mad. Unhinged. They should put me in a twin bed across the room from Tilley so they could keep an eye on me.

I remembered being in church as a kid, and the minister told us that when we were struggling with something, we should pray really hard and then open the Bible to a random page. God would speak to us through that page and tell us what to do. Well, I figured that God had enough on his hands without having to prove himself to me through some game with the Bible.

But once Greer died, I figured she didn't have as much

going on as God, so maybe I could ask her to shed a little light through her journals. I had only brought one with me from Palm Beach. It was lying in the passenger seat like a therapy dog. And when I got back in the car after Amelia dropped the bomb on me, I said out loud, "G, if you can hear me thinking, then you're probably thinking I'm crazy. I know I am. But if you could help me decide what to do, that really would help me out."

I opened the notebook randomly. That's when I realized that, even though I thought I had known everything about Greer, no one ever really knows *all* of anyone.

Greer

MAY 16, 2016

I ASKED TO SEE THEM today. I was supposed to go to the oncologist's office, but at this point, I didn't see a reason to: I was dying; it was as simple and as complicated as that. So, instead, I drove to the fertility clinic.

I walked through the double doors, past the front desk with its sliding glass windows, with several nurses protesting, down a hall with modern art and low lighting, and directly into Dr. Wright's office. If he was surprised to see me, behind his imposing desk, a pair of giant computer monitors flanking his head, he didn't let on.

I asked to see them, and he was like, "See what?"

My babies, obviously.

How was it that only a few short months ago making these embryos felt hopeful? It felt easy, like cancer would be a blip on my radar and, in no time, I would be back in action.

Dr. Wright didn't argue with me. And, in retrospect, I'm sure that walking me into his lab must have wrecked his schedule, that the rest of the day was filled with angry women. I wondered briefly what Parker would have thought of this, of me there, standing over a microscope, my tears blurring the eyepiece as I asked Dr. Wright to switch the slides. They were just a few cells, my babies. But each one already looked different. One was a ladybug with its wings out. Another a beautiful flower about to bloom. A four-leaf clover. A teddy bear. They were actual, real-life embryos, a part of Parker and a part of me. One would have grown up to like her hair in braided pigtails, the other in sparkly clips. One would have wanted a basketball party when he turned five, another a firefighter party. One would hate peas, one would love carrots, one would be a gifted pianist, another not able to carry a tune. They were unique and they were special and they were beautiful. They were gifts. But they would never be.

I knew I was dying. I had made peace with that. But what I couldn't reconcile is that they would die with me. I could imagine rocking them to sleep as babies, holding their chubby hands as they stepped into the ocean for the first time as toddlers, fighting over math homework and curfews, Parker teaching them to drive, even sitting in the front pew at their weddings. I wouldn't get to do any of that, but what was so much worse, neither would they.

Pain and sadness drenched every part of me, making it difficult to breathe. I wouldn't make a scene; I'd never do something like that. But this ache was so raw and so pure that I felt like I couldn't move. I couldn't walk away from them. When I did, my brief and painful attempt at motherhood, the one maternal thing I would ever do in my life, would be gone.

Dr. Wright put his hand on my shoulder and asked if I wanted him to call Parker. I sniffed and shook my head. I didn't want Parker to know about this. He shouldn't. He couldn't. He was going to have so much to deal with. I couldn't ask him to share this pain and this loss, too. I hoped that he would never think about it again, although it hurt something deep and low and dark in my heart to think of my babies here in this freezer. My ladybug, flower, four-leaf clover, and teddy bear. My legacy. My family. All the life that nearly was.

It seems crazy now, but I almost took them with me. I almost put my babies in my pocket and carried them out of there. What did it matter? They were just going back into some cold, anonymous freezer. They would never know the warmth of my body. They would never grow inside of me, come out of me, be held in my arms. They would never know the two parents who loved them more than life. They would be yet another decision that poor Parker had to make once I was gone. What to do with the embryos. I had put a lot of clauses in my will to make things easier for him, but that was one I had left alone. A mother shouldn't have to make such decisions.

And so back to the freezer they went. My ladybug, flower,

clover, and bear. And I know that Parker will make the best decision he possibly can, that he will weigh all the information and do what he thinks is best, like he always does.

God, I love that man. I love our babies. I love the life we have together. And what I wouldn't give for just a little more time.

Parker

⁓⌘⁓

GOOD GRACES

I COULDN'T MOVE, COULDN'T BREATHE. I just sat there, shaking a little, in the front seat of my rental car, in the grass lot outside the Saxtons' house, Greer's journal on my lap, tears pouring down my face like they hadn't since her funeral. For a few minutes, Greer had been here in this car. Her soothing voice had been in my ear, telling me a secret. I didn't know those cells had become such a part of her.

My chest was in physical pain, like my heart was being torn in two. It was a feeling I was used to, one I'd had often when I was watching my beautiful wife endure treatments, when I held her hand while she was in the kind of pain people dread.

This wasn't the first time I had let a journal help me decide. I was clutching it tightly, like I was clinging to her. Greer would have known what to do. Greer would have been sure.

Most of the time, like that Bible test, I could interpret Greer's words however I wanted to. But this entry was pretty cut-and-dried. She was damn attached to those embryos. I couldn't see just handing them over for scientific research or throwing them out with the hypodermic needles.

Was being in Cape Carolina exacerbating this feeling somehow? Here, there was no doubt, I had always known I would grow up to be a husband and a father. Once I got back to Palm Beach, would everything feel different?

I was certain that my mother had already heard somehow that I was back and was wondering and worrying why I hadn't made it home yet. Hell, she'd probably seen the rental car in the Saxtons' driveway next door and intuited it was me in that Southern mother way of hers.

I almost didn't want to go home now, but what was my option? I could check into the Holiday Inn on the highway, get back on a plane—maybe to Tahiti?—or sneak into one of the four empty bedrooms at Amelia's house. That house had gone downhill since the last time I'd seen it. It wasn't terrible, but it needed a few things fixed, paint in some places. No doubt about it: Dogwood was a lot of house, probably bordered on being a burden. I decided to grab the guys and do some maintenance around there the next day. Mr. Saxton had his hands full with the farm. Looking around at the paltry grass, I respected him even more. It took a Herculean effort to create viable growing conditions here, especially to run the size of operation that he did. Dad was always saying Mr. Saxton should sell. But I understood needing to hold on to the past.

I almost didn't bother taking the car down Amelia's driveway and into mine. It would have been shorter to walk through the side gate. But I drove anyway. And just as I thought, my mom was sitting on the front porch.

"Well, there you are, darlin'," she said as I walked up the steps, as though I had wandered down to the store for some milk. She handed me a glass as I leaned down to kiss her cheek.

I took a big gulp of what I thought was sweet tea; it was sweet tea and bourbon. I coughed.

"I don't know what you're doing here unannounced," she said, "but I figured whatever it was, you probably needed a drink."

My mother had never treated me like a little boy. From the time I could walk, I was a man. I was supposed to open doors for her and help with yard work and, when I got old enough, drink bourbon.

I sat down beside her, looking out over the driveway. Our Georgian-style house wasn't mammoth like the Saxtons. But it was where the Christmas tree sat and where all my friends spent the night and where I played basketball in the driveway. And, while some people moved to the big city and scorned their small-town upbringings, I was the opposite. I appreciated mine even more.

From the brief time I'd spent in New York, I felt like I knew a little of the city that never sleeps. And I was grateful that I'd been raised in a town that slept all the time—especially after the full lunch we had every day.

"You want to go to the church softball game this afternoon?" Mom asked.

I smiled at her. "Do I have a choice?"

She didn't answer, just turned back toward the driveway and kept rocking. This was another way my mother had taught me to be a man. She didn't tell me what to do, and she let me tell her what was on my mind when I was ready. It was an unspoken rule in our world that whatever Mama said was what we did. And when Mama didn't say, we did what she wanted us to anyway. Because there was nothing that could tear me up quite like being out of that woman's good graces.

It had trained me well to be married to the one and only Greer McCann.

I held up my glass. "I'm gonna need another one of these."

I walked in the house, its dark paneling and floors made bright by the sunlight reflecting off the water and through the windows. I took a deep breath. Cinnamon buns. My favorite. I would never tell my mother, but, even though her cinnamon buns were good, nothing was as delicious as Aunt Tilley's pie. I set down my glass to refill it just in time. My brother, Mason, was running through the hall, tackling me to the floor before I could even say hello. Widower CEO Parker Thaysden thought this was ridiculous tomfoolery. Little brother Parker Thaysden got Mason in a headlock. I vaguely heard the front door slam and my mother sigh and say, "Boys, please go outside if you're going to do that. I don't want any blood on the new rug. It's impossible to clean."

We were laughing too hard to hear her. Three minutes

later, Mason had me pinned to the floor. I could have fought harder, but the kid needed a win.

My brother still lived in one of Mom and Dad's houses on the property and "worked" for Dad, which basically meant that he played video games all day until it was time to start drinking. It annoyed me. I mean, yeah, I was definitely the A student in the family, but he was plenty smart. He could have gone into sales with Dad. He could have moved away and become a sports agent—a job he was offered numerous times after the accident. He could have coached a high school team, taught a few classes, too. My brother had a lot to offer the world, a lot more than just his once-great pitching arm. I wished he could see that. But he couldn't. Greer and I used to joke that when Mom and Dad died we would get custody of Mason. But it really wasn't that funny because it was true.

Mason had been Cape Carolina's star pitcher. In a town where baseball is as important as oxygen, that is the top honor a boy can hope for. I spent my childhood on the sidelines, my activities and practices always taking a back seat to his. I had a love-hate relationship with Mason's stardom: When it got in my way, it was a pain. But when it got me something I wanted, it was awesome. When people would talk about the kid from Cape Carolina who was the next Babe Ruth, I'd casually say, "Oh yeah. That's my brother." And then, suddenly, all eyes were on me. I was famous by extension.

Even as a kid, I knew I had a lot of things Mason didn't— I was smart. I had goals and ambitions. I had a big imagination. I was a good writer.

Mason could pitch; that was it. Even when I was really young, I realized that Mason was cool and a good athlete, but that was all he had. As a kid, though, that's all that matters. I wanted to be him so badly I could taste it.

Sometimes, when I'm questioning the type of man I really am, I think I almost wanted that night to happen. But of course I didn't. I'd never have wished this life for him.

Sometimes I envied his lack of responsibility. But I knew he carried pain. He had lost the love of his life, too. Only, the love of his life was baseball. In some ways, his complete devolvement was a lesson. When Greer died, I knew I couldn't end up like Mason. I'd seen that there was a fine line between grieving and living in your old bedroom. Her death was the worst thing that could have happened to me, but I didn't want my mom doing my laundry for the rest of my life.

"Good to have you home, ass face," Mason said as he helped me up.

Ah, my brother.

＊　＊　＊

An hour later, I was on the lawn of St. Timothy's. I had spent every Sunday morning of the first eighteen years of my life inside this early 1800s church filled with stained glass and dark wood pews. The quiet was otherworldly inside that church. Even when it was empty, you could walk inside and know you weren't alone. My mother had made me serve as an acolyte every Sunday from the time I was big enough to carry the cross until the week I left for college. Sometimes, when the days were really hard, I could close my eyes and picture myself sitting in a chair beside the altar, wearing my vestment, and everything inside me would get still.

I saw my dad walking across the lawn and greeted him with a bear hug. Everybody said my dad could have spit me out. We were both just over six feet tall, with the same dimples and the same skinny legs. I got Mom's blond hair, not his dark, but now that he'd gone gray, the difference wasn't so pronounced.

"Son," he said, clapping his hand on my shoulder. "Glad to have you home."

Dad still owned his family's farmland, but had scarcely seen a tractor since he was eighteen years old. He'd thought he'd break his dad's heart by telling him that he wasn't going to go into farming. He was going to go into insurance. He had been shocked when his parents were relieved.

Of all the jobs in the world, farming might be the toughest. In a life where little can be controlled, farming is a job where *nothing*—not the rain or the sun or the yield or the pests—can be controlled. Hurricane season is a horror, and tornado season is almost as bad. Ironically—or maybe not—my dad had gone into a business where he helped people safeguard against tragedy. After a life of living and dying by the corn season, he knew exactly what was at stake.

Looking around the front lawn at the old brick church, I saw my history. My family had lived in this town forever; these people scattered around eating lemon squares were my people. They would all hug me and ask me how I was, and for a minute, between the people who loved me and the two bourbons, I would feel like maybe I was okay.

I heard squeals coming from the adjacent softball field and laughed to see my brother pitching, underhanded, to a group of kids. He was laughing, too, which made me happy. For years and years he couldn't even drive by this softball field, much less step onto it and throw a pitch. My brother was healing.

A hand clamped my shoulder and I turned to hug my friend Bart Steele, who I'd known since we were in diapers. "Watson, Spence, and I are fishing. Leaving the dock at five. You in?" The thing about having known someone since you were babies is you don't have to make small talk.

I nodded. I'd been fishing offshore with those three guys, my best buddies, with our dads since we were three, and by ourselves since we were fifteen—which, in retrospect, was too young. If you can't drive a car, you probably shouldn't be able to take a Sportfish thirty miles out into the ocean. "Want me to bring fried chicken or sandwiches?" This was our ritual. Melon, sandwiches, fried chicken, and someone's mom's brownies. Well, now, someone's wife's brownies.

He winked at me. "Just beer."

I made eye contact with Amelia, who was sipping lemonade and laughing with Mary Lou Jackson. She smiled apologetically, and I walked toward her. Kind of like when neighbors bond over a natural disaster or a shitty landlord, we had been thrust together. She was the only breathing person who knew my current situation.

I wasn't ready to broach the topic with my parents. My dad, who I was positive had never changed a diaper, would think I had lost my mind. My mother, who had raised me to be the kind of man my dad was, would think I wasn't capable. I couldn't take that energy right now. Not when this idea was so fresh and new. It wasn't real yet, and it never had to be real. I could just think about it and feel happy.

Mary Lou slyly walked away as I made my way toward Amelia. "Am I crazy?" I asked.

She shook her head. "Damn," she said. "So you *are* thinking about it! I knew it."

I felt a prickle of happiness like that really great feeling you get from a big idea, like starting a new business or building a new house. You haven't considered yet how much work it might be, how hard it might be, how much your life is going to change. You just feel the good parts. That's where I was.

"They're half of her, Lia," I said. "I have four little babies waiting for me that are half-Greer."

She sighed. "Parker, you're being dramatic."

I looked at her skeptically.

"Parker, look," she continued. "One of the things everyone loves about you is that you're a romantic. You see the starry-eyed version of the truth. But come on. You're young. You'll remarry. You'll have babies with a new love. If you do this, it'll prevent that. You'll never want to move on."

"I *don't* want to move on," I said, feeling indignant.

She took a sip of her lemonade and shrugged. "I can't be

responsible for this. I mean, you're going to do what? Hire a surrogate? Quit your job and stay home with kids?"

I hadn't thought of that yet. Stupid logistics licked the red off my candy. I couldn't really see being a stay-at-home dad. But Greer wouldn't have been a stay-at-home mom, either, so that didn't matter.

"And what if you have girls? What are you going to do when they get their period?"

I laughed. "I'm sorry. What?"

"Well, it's just an example. There are all these mom things that happen in life that you aren't going to be able to give your kids."

I crossed my arms. "Plenty of people grow up without mothers and turn out fine."

She bit her lip. I could feel her softening. "I think it's sweet," she said. "I really do. But, Park, it's not reality. This isn't some romantic comedy where the clueless dad and a pair of charming, well-trained Labradors endure the hilarious misadventures of spit-up and dirty diapers. It isn't that easy. Being a parent is really hard, and it's real work. You have to be realistic about this."

I nodded. I knew she was absolutely, one hundred percent right.

I would get a pair of Labs, too.

Greer

MAY 22, 2011

I KNOW I DON'T HAVE *time to date* is sort of the refrain of my journal. But it isn't an excuse, like my mother says it is. It honestly isn't. It's just that my life is so full right now.

But today was different. Today changed everything. I'm in Manhattan for the week to help Daddy, and I was rushing from a meeting in SoHo all the way back to Michael's for lunch with a publisher who was interested in my writing a memoir. Me! I mean, I'm twenty-seven years old. What do I know?

I figured they wanted a McCann family exposé, which is laughable. If I'm not going to grant an interview—which I never have—I'm obviously not going to write a book about all my deep, dark family secrets. But that's not the point.

The point is that I was running late, my driver was stuck in traffic, and I grabbed a cab. I paid the driver, dashed out, and a full half hour later I realized I'd left my phone in the back seat.

My stomach sank. With thousands of cabs all around this city, how would I even attempt to find it? I was trying to focus on what the young, fresh-faced, and slightly nervous editor was saying about spreading my message of female empowerment and greater good to the world—I liked that a lot, by the way; I might have been wrong about the family exposé thing—and all I could think about was my missing phone. I was going to have to spend my afternoon going to the Verizon store, waiting in line forever, shutting my old phone off, getting a new one.

But I needed to be at a family foundation meeting that afternoon. I had some pet projects that I wanted to be funded this quarter, and they wouldn't get done if I wasn't there.

Even though I'm usually levelheaded, I could feel myself begin to panic, mostly because my phone was the keeper of everything. What if all my numbers weren't backed up on the Cloud? What if I lost pictures and messages? What if someone found my phone, hacked into it, and stole my identity? I was about to say, *I'm so sorry. I'm going to have to run*, when I felt a tap on my shoulder.

I turned around and there was a man standing over me, the light from the plate-glass window streaming behind him, making his handsome face radiant and otherworldly. He was tall but not too tall, with sandy blond hair that was tousled but not sloppy. Blue eyes twinkling, he smiled at me with the straightest, whitest row of teeth.

I stood up, though I'm not sure why, and he said, "I think this might belong to you," in the most swoon-worthy Southern drawl I'd ever heard.

I was so relieved I threw my arms around his neck and said something super cheesy and embarrassing like, "Chivalry is not dead! Knights in shining armor do exist."

He smiled, showing off this adorable cleft in his chin and saying that his mother raised him right.

"She did," I whispered, forgetting that I was in a restaurant, that I was supposed to be talking about a book. "Wait, how did you find me?" I asked. This was great but also probably some sort of major security breach I couldn't let happen again.

"Your dad called, I answered, and he told me where you were." He grinned again. "Nice guy."

"Let me buy you a drink to thank you," I said impulsively, suddenly feeling something I never felt: shy.

He shook his head. "How about I buy you dinner to thank you?"

"Thank me? For what?"

"For leaving your phone in that cab so I'd have to come find you."

His name is Parker Thaysden. He is from North Carolina, which my mother will absolutely despise. He went to Princeton, and he's brilliant, but he doesn't know it. He's in marketing, which my father will love. Now I'm looking at my watch every five minutes waiting for him to call. I can't even think straight. And I'm dreading getting on that plane back to Palm Beach tomorrow because Parker isn't in Palm Beach. I'm already figuring out how I can work in New York more and he can take long weekends in Florida. And, just like that, maybe I have time to date after all.

Amelia

RIPTIDE

AFTER THAT SOFTBALL GAME, I couldn't have eaten dinner if my life depended on it. And not because I ate too many lemon squares.

I made certain my sister-in-law, Trina, was sitting beside me at family dinner, where I had to break the news about Thad and Chase. I loved Trina. She was pretty and sweet and the most involved mother I knew. Bless her precious, manicured, highlighted heart, no matter what storm was brewing in our family, she was as steady as the tide.

I hoped she wouldn't be worried for me, that she would just give me that sweet smile of hers and say something optimistic. Because this was going to be ugly. I felt so sick I hadn't even touched the pimento cheese and crackers Mom put out before dinner, which was really saying something because her pimento cheese was the best in the world. I swallowed a sip of chardonnay from a crystal goblet, which I also worried contained lead, for courage. If I didn't get this over with, I was going to be too sick for dessert, too. And that would really be bad.

"Mom, Dad, Aunt Tilley, I have something to say."

"Oh my Lord, you are finally pregnant!" Aunt Tilley exclaimed.

Trina gasped excitedly beside me, but a quick shake of my head told her that this wasn't good news. She made a pouty face and took my hand. I instantly felt better. This was why I loved Trina.

"Tilley, you know she can't get pregnant," Daddy had scolded.

"I know you don't want to imagine all that, but just because her daddy doesn't think she can doesn't mean a girl can't get pregnant."

"Oh, good Lord, Tilley," Daddy replied.

I had taken a deep breath and said, "It's okay, Daddy."

Mom interjected, "Why didn't Thad come with you, anyway? Darlin', that article you wrote about him . . ." She clutched her napkin to her chest, and I noticed a small hole in it. Certainly a hole in a hundred-year-old napkin was to be expected, but it bothered me that Mom hadn't noticed it. "It was just the most beautiful thing I've ever read."

"And the *New York Times*," Tilley said proudly. "Girly, you have made it."

"Well, that's sort of what I need to talk to you about."

Trina hit Robby with her napkin. "Why don't you write

things like that about me? Does Amelia love Thad more than you love me?"

She stuck her lower lip out, and Tilley said, "She doesn't love Robby more than I do."

Mom rolled her eyes. Tilley's boyfriend, who had died in a freak farming accident, had been named Robert. "Why in the world would you name your child Robby, Mother? It's too confusing for her," I'd scolded years ago.

"He's my son, I named him after my father, and I can call him whatever the hell I want," she'd retorted.

I had never heard my mother say "hell," so, suffice it to say, I never brought it up again.

As I was readying myself to get this ship back on course, though, my nephews came tearing into the dining room, one of them hollering, "I did not take the last chicken leg!"

"Did too!"

"Did not!"

As Momma was saying, "Now, boys," and Trina was saying, "William James, did you hide chicken legs in your pockets again so your brother couldn't have any?" I decided I couldn't take it a minute longer.

I cleared my throat and shouted, "I'm getting a divorce!"

The room was suddenly silent. Even the little boys knew this was more important than chicken. They ran back into the kitchen, the door between the two rooms swinging behind them.

"A divorce?" my mother said in a high, raised, outraged voice. I loved her, but she had this propensity to act so damn scandalized by every little thing. I mean, people got divorced. Constantly. Half the time. She acted like this was the first time she had ever heard the word. "A *divorce*?"

It was out now, and I couldn't take it back. I almost took joy in saying, "Yes, Mom. Turns out Thad is a little more interested in men."

Her jaw dropped, and Daddy slammed his napkin down on the table. "No one disrespects my little girl," he said. "I am outraged by this."

Aunt Tilley was uncharacteristically silent. Then she almost whispered, "So what now, darlin'?"

Robby mouthed *Sorry* to me across the table, as well he should have. He had been giving me so much crap earlier about registering to vote in Florida. But I'd lived there for thirteen years. It was a little impractical to fly home to vote. But he planned on running for mayor, and now mine was one less vote he would get. I wanted to point out that it didn't much matter. He was a Saxton. He would win the election.

My dad was stepping down as mayor of Cape Carolina. His sister, the first female mayor, held the position for sixteen years. And their daddy was mayor before that, their granddaddy before that, and so on and so forth. If your last name wasn't Saxton, you didn't have much of a prayer in the mayoral race. We joked that people thought great-great-granddaddy Saxton was still mayor. In a world where politics were often dirty and self-interested, I was proud to have a family who stood steadfastly on the side of inclusion and doing what was right.

Daddy's friends and political colleagues had asked him to

run for higher office when he decided to step down. But he wouldn't hear of it. His life, his obligation, and most of all, his true love—bless his heart—my mom, were in Cape Carolina. He didn't want to be anywhere else. Even still, Mom and Daddy had driven the almost twelve hours to see me every other month since I'd moved to Palm Beach. They were proud of me. Well, they *had* been proud of me before this. But pride isn't as pressing as plain, old-fashioned wanting your daughter home, where you can keep an eye on her.

"'What now?'" I responded to Aunt Tilley, "is the big question, isn't it?"

I set my napkin on the table, tears springing to my eyes, the weight of my situation hitting me. Now that I didn't have to worry about telling my family, I had to worry about what came next. I had no husband. No house. But I did have a home. And as inhospitable as it was feeling at this current moment, it was here.

Mom and Tilley shared a look. I felt badly for Daddy. I honestly did. It was like he had married two of them. And they were two peas in a pod, two forces to be reckoned with.

Mom put her head in her hands, and Tilley patted her back and *tsk*ed supportively. "At least she isn't pregnant," Trina trilled.

I gestured at her. "Exactly. Silver lining."

Everyone was talking all at once again, and I felt like I needed to escape.

Over the din, I could make out Mom saying, "There has never been a divorce in the Saxton family," as I slipped out from the table. I couldn't do anything about that now. I walked out the back door and down the dock, avoiding the planks that were sitting a little too high and needed repair. Even in my sorrow, I made a mental note to fix them and the pickets on the front porch the next day. I sat down, legs crossed, and took a deep breath. Out here, all you could see was water, with little islands of marsh grass interspersed. It was the place I had always felt the most alive, the freest. There is peace in the calm and quiet of the sound. And peace was what I needed more than anything right now. Tears rolled down my cheeks.

I imagined that, in some ways, having seen Chase with Thad would make my divorce easier. When I thought about the good times with Thad, I realized they had all been a lie. Our life and our love had been a total sham.

Why couldn't life be like journalism? The story could take you anywhere, but the formula was tried and true. If you did the research, if you conducted the interviews, if you put in the work, the story would come. Why hadn't my marriage followed that same pattern?

I wiped my eyes, and when I looked over to my left, I could see someone else sitting on the end of the Thaysdens' dock next door, not twenty feet away.

"Is it done?" Parker asked.

The way the moon reflected on the water was so beautiful here. "Oh yeah. It's done. I'm done. Everything's done."

"You are not done," Parker said. "You're just getting started."

I nodded, even though, in that moment, I didn't believe it. Not even a little.

"Hey, Park?"

"Yeah."

"So are you."

He nodded.

He didn't say anything else, and neither did I. We just sat there, the silence washing over us. How had we gotten so far off course? I wished that, just for a minute, we could go back to being those same kids on these same docks, fishing with cane poles and swimming every chance we got. I knew I had to move forward. And Parker did, too. But sometimes in order to do that, you have to go back first. And I think that's what scared us most of all.

· · ·

The first time I saw Parker, he was eighteen years old. Well, the first time I actually laid eyes on him, I was three and he was three days old, and my mom and I had taken a chicken potpie to his mom, as if crust and a little gravy could cure her split-open insides. Even then, I was leery of childbirth. Maybe my body knew already it was something that would never happen for me.

His mom had this frilly bassinet set up in their living room, and I peeked in to look at him. I wasn't sure what all the fuss was about. My baby dolls were so pretty. He just looked kind of red to me.

Our parents were best friends, which meant Parker and I

necessarily saw each other. Labor Day picnics, Christmas Eve get-togethers, lemonade on the lawn at church, that type of forced family fun, so I saw him all the time. But the first time I *really* saw him was the summer before my junior year of college.

As the friend who lived at the beach, I was pretty popular in the summer. And I always had my friends down for at least a week or two. The summer we all turned twenty-one, Dogwood resembled a sorority house. The girls were always impressed that I could drive the boat over to the beach myself, so I took every opportunity to wow them.

One day, we all walked out onto the sand, feeling cool and invincible in a way that only twenty-one-year-olds can, and saw Parker throwing a Frisbee with some of his friends. He waved at me. Well, less a wave and more that two-fingered salute thing guys did to acknowledge you without really acknowledging you. He was heading off to Princeton at the end of the summer, which didn't surprise me much. He had always been smart—and obnoxious.

One of my friends was like, "Who's the hottie?"

I had rolled my eyes and said, "Ew. That's Parker Thaysden, and he just graduated high school."

"So he's legal?" another friend chimed in, and we all laughed in the way of people who have another year of zero responsibilities, a rocking bikini body, and fewer than zero cares in the world.

We all made our way to the ocean. It seemed calmer than usual as we swam out past the breakers. I remember diving over one of them, loving the way it felt for my entire person to be submerged in the salty sea, certainly one of God's finest creations. As the water reached my chest, I had the unsettling feeling that maybe we were out too far, that we should come back in, and just as I turned to tell my friends, I felt something I had never felt in my twenty-one years of communing with this particular spot of ocean on this exact stretch of sand: a riptide. I tried to swim in, but no matter how hard I fought, the sea kept pulling me out.

I had heard my entire life that you never fight the riptide, you don't swim against it. You swim to the side to get out of it.

That advice was completely useless in the moment as the raging sea kept pulling me under for longer and longer stretches. I would emerge, gasping, long enough to uselessly attempt to cough out the saltwater filling my mouth and nose. My friends were waving their arms at the shore, I saw as I attempted to keep my eyes open despite their intense burning. But who could help me now? There were no lifeguards on this part of the beach. I started to panic, the worst thing you can do when caught in a riptide. I was going to die, I realized, as it pulled me under again, this time for longer. With a sudden surge of adrenaline, I tried again to swim to my right to get out of this thing. I could just make out someone running toward me.

A minute later, when I felt an arm loop around my waist, I wasn't sure if it was real or my imagination. But when I looked into the face that had come to rescue me, it was the same one I had known since he was three days old. It was Parker. "Put your arms around my neck and kick if you can," he shouted breathlessly.

As we got to the shallows, I wrapped my legs around his waist and he carried me piggyback to shore like we were back at one of those picnics, doing a partner race.

As we reached the sand, he dropped me, and I lay on my back, panting. He was crouched over me, his face near mine, hands on either side of me. And he was saying, "You're okay, Amelia. I'm not going to let anything happen to you."

As my friends ran up beside us, and Parker still looked down at me, I saw him for the first time. I mean, I really saw him. His words, the bulk and shape of his upper body, and the way we were both panting made me envision, just for a second, that this moment was something entirely different, something much less pure.

All at once, he wasn't just the annoying kid who used to hide out in the branches of the trees in our yard and jump down to scare me, or the one Mom made me drive to school when he was a freshman, who clearly only listened to music that his friends thought was cool. He was a man. Or, at least, he was on the verge of becoming one. He had saved me. He had protected me. We were connected by more than just the gate between our yards and the cigarettes that we'd occasionally shared at high school parties.

I bought Parker and his friends beer all summer. It was a paltry gift in exchange for my life, but it was what I had to give, despite my friends' insistence that beer was not what Parker wanted from me. I mostly ignored it.

But every time I had seen Parker since, I hugged him a little longer, I mentally thanked him a little more. Because he had truly saved my life. Later, a part of me believed he could save Greer, too, just through sheer force of will. I had hoped he could, had wanted him to. But no such luck.

Fourteen years later, back in Cape Carolina, I looked at him across the marsh, sitting on his dock. Even in the dark, I could see the dimple in his chin that came out when he grinned, the way that, even though he could laugh again now, really laugh, something around his edges seemed to sag a little, sad and defeated and lost.

Talking about those babies made him so happy. Anyone in his right mind would know having those babies was the craziest idea of all time. Some men might be capable of picking a surrogate and being a single dad to their dead wife's babies. I mean, I didn't know any of those men, but they did probably exist.

I thought back to the last time I had seen Greer alive, how even that close to death, Parker had made her laugh, how he had kept the trauma he was facing zipped up inside himself and dedicated everything to her, given her his all. Hell, maybe he could do it. Maybe he was that man. Maybe I had stumbled into that clinic and seen that record and made that phone call because Parker was supposed to be a single dad.

I had been thinking for years that I wanted to do something important with my life. I had been thinking for years that I wanted to repay Parker for saving me.

All those years ago, Parker Thaysden had given me life. As his eyes caught mine across the water, I had the odd, tingling sensation that maybe the right thing to do was to give it right back to him.

Elizabeth

~~~~~~

SABOTAGE

"I KNEW HE WAS WRONG for her," Tilley hissed as I handed her dish after dish to dry. I scrubbed them a tad too hard, the dish gloves Olivia had given me for Christmas—the whimsical ones with the long red fingernails and the huge fake diamond painted on—filling with water when I dipped them too far into the bubbles.

"Well, we all knew it, Tilley. But I never thought he'd do *this* to her."

Deep down we'd both known this was exactly how this would end. But we were ladies, so we hadn't said so.

Even in my anger at Thad, my hurt for my daughter, and my physical discomfort at having wet, soapy water sloshing around inside my gloves, I paused to be grateful. My sister was here tonight. She was herself. She was in this world, with me, where she belonged. I couldn't count the number of people who said I should put her somewhere where "they could take care of her." How could they even say such a thing? Who could take care of her better than I could?

I prayed every day—every single day—that she'd pass on one day before I did. I couldn't bear the thought of her being without me. Who would take care of her then? I didn't want Amelia and Robby to feel burdened. And, really, after everything she had meant to me, everything she had done for me, it was the least I could do. I prayed for other things, too, but that one was the most persistent.

"Well, I blame Mason," Tilley said, interrupting my thoughts.

I rolled my eyes, pulling the plug inside the sink and taking my gloves off, hanging them inside out over the drying rack. I leaned on the counter's chipped blue-and-white tiles. *Make up your corner of the world neat and tidy and it will be enough.* I said this to myself every day. Keeping Dogwood together was like squeezing sand as hard as you could inside your palm and wondering why it slipped through your fingers. But I would worry about that tomorrow.

Mason and Amelia had dated very briefly right before his accident. But their coming together had felt like kismet. Olivia and I had dreamed of it our entire lives. Anyone could see they were perfect for each other: the son and daughter of two best friends, the star pitcher and the valedictorian. And then, after it all fell apart for him, he just disappeared. He didn't call her, didn't write. I understood retreating. But without a word to my daughter? He had told her they were going to be together, had guaranteed her a future. No one knew better than I did that high school romances faded. But there are right ways to do things. And Olivia just let her son abandon Amelia. It was the biggest fight we'd ever had.

She said I didn't understand, that she had a different relationship with her children than I did with mine. I should certainly hope so. I would *never* have let my children behave that way, and especially not at eighteen years old. I took a deep breath to keep myself from getting worked up, picked up another drying towel, and started in on the goblets. People with dishwashers didn't have these conversations. They were missing out.

"She *has* sabotaged every relationship she has had since Mason," I mused.

Tilley nodded. "You're telling me."

"But surely she didn't know about Thad."

"But we *told* her," Tilley said, crossing her arms, all pretense of drying the dishes now over.

I rolled my eyes. "That girl just never listens."

"Mother! Don't say that!" Tilley snapped. "I'm standing right here!"

And, just like that, she was gone. My sister, who had been so lucid and clear a heartbeat ago was gone again. Thirty-seven years and it still broke my heart every time. Thirty-seven years of doctors telling me they couldn't find a cure—or, even, a diagnosis. Thirty-seven years of answers like, *Well, it seems akin to delusional disorder, but not quite consistent with that.* And *IT appears to be triggered by stress.* The ones who made me the maddest were the doctors who said she was faking. Who would fake such a thing?

"Not you, darling," I soothed. "You're the best girl I know."

She smiled just a little. "Really?"

I took her hand and said, "Let's get you to bed. It has been a big night."

She nodded. "And tomorrow I have a date with Robert."

Robert. Even though Tilley's boyfriend had died almost four decades ago, it was easier to agree with her, I had learned from experience. The whole town had, really. My heart swelled with pride and gratitude that Cape Carolina, like our family, had fallen into step with Tilley. If she showed up as herself, fine. If she appeared as Queen Victoria, great. If she discussed gardening tips, they were thrilled. If she wanted to wax poetic about her fictional wedding plans with her deceased boyfriend, they nodded and smiled.

"That's right, dear. And you will look positively beautiful."

As I helped her into her nightgown, made sure she brushed her teeth, and tucked her in, Tilley said, "I do believe I'm a little tired."

I had to admit that, in that moment, I felt a little tired, too. Tired from decades of this emotional roller coaster, tired from worrying about where my daughter's life would take her now, tired from the spoils and secrets of more than six decades.

I walked silently down the stairs, skipping the squeaky spots that I had become accustomed to stepping around roughly fifty-five years ago. I opened the back door and stepped out on the deck, overlooking the night sky, the silent sound with its still marsh grass, and took a deep breath. This home, this land, this water, and this sky had held me for an entire lifetime. It had guided me through the most difficult moments and the most joyous.

I caught a glimpse of my sad, defeated daughter sitting at the end of our dock, her hair blowing in the breeze. From the time she was a toddler Amelia had simply looked like a little girl who belonged on this beach, whose natural beauty, golden skin and sun-kissed hair melded seamlessly with the scenery around her. I almost went down to her. But then I saw another child I knew nearly as well sitting at the end of his dock right next door. And I realized that it wasn't only this place that had taken care of us so well; it was the people, too. The ones that were here and the ones that had passed on, who had left this house in body but who, I couldn't help but feel, were always here with us just the same. All I hoped now was that this place would provide the same healing for Amelia that it always had for me—and that I could hold on to it long enough for her to find her fresh start.

Greer

— ❧ —

AUGUST 21, 2015

I DIDN'T TELL PARKER I had an appointment today. I didn't tell him because I already assumed what the verdict would be. I didn't want to believe it, but this shit is living in my body. How could I not know? When the doctor came in with a grave expression and said, "Greer, I don't know how to tell you this, but the treatment appears not to be working," I just said, "I know."

You could tell she wasn't used to that. She was used to tears and panicking, but those aren't things I really do well. I do stiff upper lip well. So that's what I did. That's what I'm doing.

She droned on about clinical trials and alternative therapies, but I already knew I wasn't going to do any of them. I'm not going to put Parker or my father or my sister or myself through that. I am going to just go ahead and go, on my own terms. I watched my mother's agonizing death, and I'm not going to let that happen to me. There are peaceful ways to die, places and people who help you do it. That's what I want, so that's what I'm going to have.

Thinking about telling Parker breaks me apart inside. I'll wait a little longer, let him have hope as long as he can. I only wish that I could still hope, too.

Amelia

HELL IN A HANDBASKET

JUST THREE DAYS AT HOME had cured me. Okay. So maybe it hadn't cured me. But it had given me three days to ignore Thad's texts and calls and to avoid the fact that my life was in shambles. It had also given me three days to paint and hammer and caulk around Dogwood like old times. It had given me three days to drink way too much with my forever friends Jennifer, Madison, and Sarah and to ascertain that I could crash with my Palm Beach friend Sheree and her husband, Philip, until I got back on my feet—after they promised, of course, that they would not praise Thad for following his truth in front of me.

I had thought about leaving town, staying in North Carolina or maybe even finding a job in New York. But Palm Beach had been my fantasy. I had dreamed a big dream, and I had gotten it. And I only had one rung left to climb on the ladder.

Nanette would go to New York like she had always said, and I would be editor in chief. I would be the boss, the one with the big corner office. I would have made it. I could see it that morning on the drive from the airport straight to the office.

I could see it, that is, until I walked into the building. I was prepared for a bit of chaos since I had missed Monday. I rarely took a day off, and I generally never unplugged for even an hour. But yesterday I had needed it. I had needed to reassess who I was and what I was doing. I had needed some clarity and calm to decide if I could really help Parker in his quest to expand his family.

I had decided, thank goodness, that it was a ridiculous notion. I mean, sure, yeah, I had been a little bit curious lately about what it would be like to carry a baby, to bring life into the world. And, yes, it would be a nice thing to do. Maybe. Or maybe the whole idea was totally misguided and I was just contributing to the chaos. Either way, back in Palm Beach I had realized that it was utterly absurd. Parker could choose to ruin his life, but he wasn't going to take me down with him—not that he was trying to, of course.

While I felt relieved, my decision also shone a light on the fact that this job was all I had.

As I walked into the *Clematis* building that morning, I could actually feel the way the energy had changed before I even got to my office. Usually when I arrived, people were sitting in their cubicles, writing, on the phone. There was an electric hum. Today, people were walking around, out of their desks, seemingly frantic.

I was confused. Finally, I stopped Philip, grabbing his sport-coat-clad arm. Philip was one of the coolest people I knew. The product of an Irish mother and an Italian father who had met, in true American dream style, on the day they'd become citizens, he had his father's athleticism, his mother's eyes, and a sense of what would make a layout come to life that I'd never seen before. That was evident from the day I first interviewed him. He had played pro soccer for two years before realizing that graphic design was his true love. "What is going on?" I whispered.

He engulfed me in a hug. His familiar scent soothed me. "Sheree and I are so sorry."

Philip and Sheree were one of the most perfect couples I had ever known in real life and two of my very best friends. They were both fun and free and rode the line between responsible and irresponsible absolutely perfectly. They threw the best parties in town—meaning the most fun. In Palm Beach you had to clarify because, to a lot of people, the "best" meant the stuffiest and most overdone. Philip had invited Thad and me over for dinner his first week at *Clematis* and Sheree and I had spent five hours drinking wine and divulging our entire life histories to each other. It hasn't happened to me often in my adult life, but sometimes you meet someone, and you just know you're going to be friends forever. That's what had happened with us. Philip and Sheree had even come to Cape Carolina for the Summer Splash and Fish—the town's biggest celebration of the season—a few years ago.

I waved his words away. I couldn't confide in my friend

without falling apart. "There's nothing we can do about that now. What's going on here?"

"Where have you been?"

I raised my eyebrow. "In North Carolina."

"Well, I know where you were physically. But where have you been in the world? *Clematis* was sold to McCann Media."

My eyes widened in shock. *Clematis* had been independently owned forever—that was one of the best things about it. I loved the family feel, how I actually knew the powers that be, how we had the space to make our own decisions because we weren't owned by the big guys. Everything was changing. Everything had changed. The one stable thing I had left was suddenly unstable.

"Why didn't you tell me?"

He looked mystified. "Well . . . you're my boss. I assumed you knew."

I took a deep breath and stood up straighter. And I realized that, across the way, one of my writers was crying. "Heather, what is going on?"

But I didn't need her to answer. When your friend is putting the contents of her desk in a box that previously held printer paper, the dots are fairly easy to connect.

When Philip said, "Nanette needs to see you in her office," it honestly didn't even occur to me to be nervous. I mean, I was the managing editor, for heaven's sake. She was the ideas; I was the execution. She was the big picture; I was the details. We had been a seamless team for three years, working so well together that it was hard to know where I ended and she began.

I tipped a fake hat to Philip, walked into Nanette's corner office with the killer view, and closed the door behind me. *My office one day* . . . now was not the time. She was visibly shaken. But this was Nanette. She was shaken; I was steady. "Look," I said. "Whatever McCann throws at us, we've got this, sister. We are an unstoppable team, and we will keep *Clematis* a preeminent magazine no matter who owns us."

I sat down in the white slipper chair across from her desk and noticed she and the chair were precisely the same color. Wow. Nanette was easily ruffled, but I had never seen her like this. "Amelia, you are my best friend," she began. I thought that was a little sad. I mean, I loved Nanette. But she was my work wife. We never socialized outside of the office. I had sacrificed a lot for this job, but not as much as Nanette had.

I smiled wanly at her. "It's all going to be—"

"Please stop," she said. That was when I started to feel sick. "I'm the new managing editor," she whispered.

For a half second, I had the ridiculous thought that I was going to be the new editor in chief. But when I saw the tears in her eyes, I realized I was most certainly not getting promoted. I sucked in my breath. "And me?"

She shook her head. "You're getting three months' severance."

I was gobsmacked. I leaned back in the chair, feeling as if I'd been punched in the stomach. I had devoted thirteen years of my life to this company. Yes, I knew that magazines were merging staffs and recycling content, that media jobs were fewer and farther between, that for everything the Internet had given us, it had also taken away something really big. And you couldn't help but see the irony: McCann Media.

Nanette handed me a letter. "I wrote you the most glowing, most amazing recommendation I have ever written. I will do anything for you, and any publication would be lucky to have you, Amelia. You know that. You are the girl wonder. You took this company by storm. You'll do it again."

I was on the verge of tears. And furious. And I knew exactly who to take my anger out on.

.   .   .

As I thundered out of the magazine, I knew I was overreacting. But I'm not a fully rational human—no one is, really. Every now and then I'd get a nasty comment online and feel like quitting my job, throwing everything I'd worked for out the window. Or a friend wouldn't text me back for a couple days, and I'd decide she hated me for some perceived slight. My mom would say something snide about my heels being too high or my face looking a little round, and I would fume that I wasn't going home for Christmas.

I never let it show at work, though. I was the consummate professional; I kept everyone in line. I picked up everyone's slack. I didn't want to be the one to say it, but Nanette wasn't half as good as I was at actually putting out a magazine. She was the Google think tank. I was the assembly line.

My layoff, all the layoffs, were probably not Parker's fault. Probably. I looked at my watch. Eight ten. The high-and-mighty boss of McCann Media wouldn't be in yet at 8:10. This was what happened when companies got too big and quit caring about the peons that made it all possible. Greer would never have stood for this.

"Parker!" I screamed, as I banged on the back door, realizing that maybe, just maybe, a small part of my freak-out had to do with the fact that I had run out of the hormones I took every day to make my body not think it was in menopause. He emerged at the door, bleary-eyed, in his boxers.

"Oh, it's you," he said sleepily.

"So you'd just open the door to any stranger off the street in your underwear?" I crossed my arms, trying to not think about how hot he was practically naked and barely awake.

He yawned and gestured for me to come in, saying nothing.

As I followed him inside, I said, "Well, this is rich. By now, I've usually already been at the magazine for an hour preparing for the day, making lists, putting finishing edits on articles. You haven't even gotten out of bed yet, and *I'm* the one who's fired?"

He rubbed his eyes. "Coffee."

"I get laid off from the company I have dedicated my entire adult life to, the company that *you* run, and all you can say is 'Coffee'?" I was doing something uncomfortably close to shouting. Proper Southern ladies do not shout.

He put his hand up, and I didn't want to notice his abs, but really, you couldn't help it. On the flip side, this was the same kid who had hidden a lizard in my backpack my first day of fourth grade. I shuddered. What was wrong with me?

His Nespresso spit as I looked around. Everything was the

same. Not one single knickknack or design book had moved an inch since I was in this house four years ago, though now the book covers had faded. Four years ago, I had just gotten engaged, and I had just found out Greer was dying. Four years ago, I'd found out that my dumb kid neighbor was capable of loving a woman beyond anything I could imagine. I softened toward him.

I took in my surroundings. Greer's house. Greer's husband. I was thrust violently back into the past. Four years ago, I'd felt a little foolish admitting how entirely obsessed I was with Greer Thaysden. But, really, who wasn't? She'd been *the* account to follow on Instagram, had hosted one of the most successful podcasts on iTunes when podcasts were in their infancy. I had read her first book, like, five times, was on the waiting list for a goal-setting notebook she had collaborated with Moleskine on. Let's just say, she was one of my idols. The one thing that I couldn't wrap my head around was why beautiful, perfect, together Greer had married boy-next-door, little-brother-annoying Parker Thaysden. Thank goodness, though. Without that lapse in judgment, I never would have met my heroine.

Word was starting to get out that Greer, Palm Beach royalty and all-around maven, had been diagnosed with ovarian cancer—just like her mother had been. Every publication wanted to do a story on her. She declined absolutely everyone, as she always had. Everyone, that is, until me.

I hadn't been able to attend Parker and Greer's wedding—a fact that Parker's mother and my mother might not ever let me live down—because I had been at a bachelorette party in Mykonos. The very pricey plane ticket was non-refundable. I wasn't canceling it, no matter who was getting married.

But my path had certainly crossed with Greer's more than a few times in Palm Beach and at home in Cape Carolina. We hadn't been friends, per se, but I blamed myself for that. Sure, we ran in slightly different circles, but I felt now that we could have been close if it weren't for my being so intimidated by her. In my defense, Greer was a woman on the rise, on every Thirty Under Thirty list and, most notably, one of *Town & Country*'s Modern Swans that year, which was quite a coveted position to say the least. She was a woman with taste and fame, brains and power, and a good heart at the center of it all. The Goodness Greer column she had started, which not only talked about what she was wearing, reading, and watching, and where she was traveling, but also maintained this incredible thread of positivity and empowerment, had been so successful that she'd used its tidy proceeds to start one of the city's most influential new nonprofits.

She was single-handedly responsible for solving the problem of many of West Palm Beach's homeless mothers and children. She wasn't just a total badass. She was my heroine. Since I was a little girl, all I had wanted to do was write and help people. I hoped the articles I published would do both. And getting this interview would be a huge step toward that goal.

I cried when I found out Greer was sick. I barely knew

this woman, and here I was weeping to Thad. But I *did* know her, which was hard to explain. I had read her columns about her mother's death, bought shoes that she'd recommended, made family recipes she'd shared. She didn't know me from Adam's house cat, but, as foolish as I knew it made me sound, I positively worshipped the woman.

I consoled myself with the thought that Greer Thaysden didn't let anything stop her. She would beat cancer and be back to saving the world before I got this story to press.

In some ways, it seemed voyeuristic, but I knew with all my heart that I would protect Greer, that I would tell the story that needed to be told, the one that would portray her in all her glory. In Palm Beach and New York, *Clematis*'s biggest readerships, a sick Swan was big news. Somebody was going to break it. As Parker's mom, Olivia—who had been the one to talk Greer into giving me the story—had said, "Might as well be someone with a little tact and Southern charm."

Even still, I was nervous as I rang the doorbell that morning. One wrong word said, and I could irreparably offend a woman I idolized—and put myself out of a job.

Greer greeted me at the door in a hot pink sheath dress. She was so petite, even in sky-high nude pumps, that my five feet seven inches felt practically Amazonian. Her hair was freshly blown out, her nails smooth and rounded, her skin dewy, soft, and unlined. And she smelled like a pleasant breeze on a perfect spring day, like honeysuckle and gardenia but mixed with salt air. She didn't look sick. The sight of her cracked me open with happiness. She was going to be okay. I knew it.

She hugged me, smiled warmly, and said, "How are your parents? Any Cape Carolina news?"

I thought it would be a little impolite to say that Greer *was* the Cape Carolina news, so I just said, "Oh, you know, same old, same old. Nothing ever changes in that town."

We both laughed and she said, "I think that's what makes it so special, right?" She paused. "Thank you for doing this, Amelia. I'm glad it's you. Oh, and I'd really prefer no tape recorders," she said, signaling that the small talk was over.

I nodded. "They're so invasive." I never used them. Nothing made a subject clam up quite like putting a black box in front of their face. Plus, listening to a bunch of tape wasn't authentic to me. The feedback-riddled, staticky sound didn't quite capture the heart of the story. The story was a living, breathing thing that would begin formulating in my mind the second I met the subject.

Greer Thaysden moves through her Palm Beach home with all the elegance of the swan she is.

"Could I get you a cup of tea or coffee or anything?"

I shook my head.

She is kind and warm, with a graciousness that exudes from every pore.

"The story you're getting today may not be the one you imagined," she said as she sat down on the white leather couch in the open, airy room and gestured for me to do the same at the other end. I would have preferred to be across from her in a chair; sitting beside her felt so intimate. I knew already that what was coming next wasn't something I was going to want to hear. I glanced out the window at the totally unobstructed view of the Intracoastal beyond.

"I am dying, Amelia," she said. "I know you think you're here to publish a story about my valiant battle with ovarian cancer, but this is going to be a different story."

The tears in my eyes embarrassed me.

"I invited you here today because I am planning to move to a right-to-die state so that I can take my own life. My cancer is not responding to treatments, and I will not have my family or my husband remember me as a rotting vegetable."

I felt my entire body go numb. "You can't do that!" I exclaimed, shocking myself.

She crossed her arms. "Are you one of those journalists who thinks every piece is an opinion piece? Because, if so, this isn't really going to work."

She actually smiled when she said it, as though we were discussing the possibility of her running for governor, not some Dr. Kevorkian wannabe sticking a needle in her arm as her family watched the breath leave her body. I closed my notebook and put my pen down beside me. I wasn't going to take notes on this. This was a story I was going to rewrite.

"No, I just mean, with all the medical advances being made, you don't know what could happen. Maybe alternative treatments would work for you. Look at Kris Carr."

She looked shocked. Clearly, this wasn't the interview she'd been expecting, either. I wondered if anyone in her life ever argued with Greer McCann Thaysden. Judging from the expression on her face, I'd say not. Her shock was turning to amusement. "I find it strange that you seem to be taking this harder than some of my best friends."

I turned away from her, so she wouldn't see the blush creeping up my cheeks. If I wasn't uncomfortable enough already, with her in her perfectly fitted dress and me in the skirt and top that I had thought were so fashionable when I had put them on that morning but now realized were far too trendy, this was adding insult to injury. I think this was why Greer and I had never become close. When I was around her, I always felt less than, through no fault of hers. And then . . . maybe it was in my head, but I also couldn't help but feel like any time Parker and I were simply chatting at a party, she suddenly appeared. Or when we shared a laugh or an inside joke, it grated on her nerves. Then again, I would always remind myself, Greer Thaysden couldn't possibly feel threatened by anyone.

I wasn't sure why I felt so passionately about this stranger's very personal choice. But she had ignited something inside me. "We need you, Greer. Women like me need women like you to look up to. We need you to show us how we can follow our dreams and still do good in the world. We need you to show us how to fight the good fight. So fight it, won't you?"

She bit her lip, and I knew I was making her uncomfortable, but I couldn't stop myself. My heart suddenly ripped in two for Parker, and I felt so protective of him, so cognizant of his pain, that I added, "What about poor Parker, Greer?

Surely this is killing him. If you can't fight for yourself, if you can't fight for the women who need you, please, please, Greer, fight for Parker."

She didn't say anything for a second and then nodded her head toward my pad. "So, your story?"

I stood up. "If I run a story about your right to die, then you might feel like you can't change your mind. So I'm going to give you a week to think about this."

Greer followed me to the door. She looked me squarely in the eye and said, "Fine. But you should know: I never change my mind."

I hoped and prayed that she would, almost as hard as I hoped and prayed Nanette wouldn't fire me when I told her that I hadn't gotten the story after all. This was a fireable offense. If Greer did change her mind, and I did the interview in a week, it would give me only one day to file it and meet my deadline, assuming I stayed up all night. I almost called her back to apologize. But then I realized that this was her life we were talking about here. If I were choosing her life over my story, I would do that any day, even if it meant losing my dream job and flying back to North Carolina a failure, my tail between my legs.

I usually kept these things confidential until they went to press, but I had to tell *someone*. Mom had scolded me, had made me imagine what it had been like for Greer to watch her own mother suffer with this same disease. I guessed I had overstepped, and I felt like a fool. I felt like a fool, that is, right up until four days later, when I got a call from Greer. She didn't say hello or exchange pleasantries. She said, "Come back tomorrow. Let's write a different story."

"Greer," I said, a smile in my voice, "writing a different story is what life is all about."

Easy for me to say. Up until that point, my life had gone perfectly according to plan.

Parker handed me a cup of espresso and motioned toward the couch, bringing me back to the here and now, where I had just gotten fired from my job. He came back three minutes later wearing a T-shirt—so threadbare it was full of pinholes— and a pair of gym shorts.

"I didn't fire you, Amelia. I would never do that."

I was calmer now. Maybe it was the lilac scent from the flowers on the coffee table or the pair of white couches flanking the fireplace with the mirrored coffee table and the abstract art. "I know," I said quietly.

"Greer would not have wanted someone with your talent and drive fired."

I took a sip of my espresso. "Smart woman."

"Hang on a second, and let me make a call," Parker said.

"No!" I protested from a place of pride inside myself that I didn't know I still had. "I can't get my job back because Parker Thaysden made a call."

He studied me. "But isn't that why you came here? So I could fix this for you?"

I wrapped my hands around the coffee mug, feeling the warmth seep into my hands and fingers. Why had I come here? Had I wanted to see Parker? I took a sip of coffee, allowing myself a pause before I answered. Maybe, I realized, I had relied for far too long on other people to fix things for me. "I think this is something I have to fix for myself, unfortunately," I said. "I just don't really know what that looks like yet."

Parker smiled at me. "You've always been so brave, Lia. Maybe this as an opportunity, a time to write a new story."

Greer hadn't been around to see the new story I wrote for her play out. She hadn't gotten to spend a lifetime with the man who loved her more than the moon and the stars. She hadn't gotten to have her babies and watch them grow. I had been one of the ones who had let her believe in a miracle. A miracle that hadn't come. And now I was sitting here complaining about a job? She had lost her life. Her bright, beautiful life. Compared to that, a job was meaningless.

"I'm sorry, Parker," I said. "I feel really dumb. I'm going to go now."

"Please don't," he whispered.

"What?" I asked, surprised.

"Please don't go. I couldn't sleep last night, and I need some company this morning."

I understood that. "Are you still thinking about . . . well, you know."

He nodded. "I can't move on," he said. "Greer was just it for me."

I nodded knowingly, looking down into my mug. "Yup. Thad was pretty much it for me, too."

We both laughed. Same sentence, totally different meanings.

He smiled at me. "I just can't imagine that Thad was actually it for you, Lia. That as much as you have to offer, as kind and beautiful and brilliant as you are, you won't eventually give in to one of the men flinging themselves at you."

I laughed again. "Flinging themselves at me, huh?" It sliced through me how untrue that was. My friends always complained about the dating scene, but it never affected me because I had Thad. A study I'd read said that women find men most attractive that are their own ages, but the women most attractive to men were always twenty-two. I would never be twenty-two again. And thank God, really. But, at thirty-five, in Palm Beach, I had a solid chance of becoming a fourth trophy wife. That was about the extent of my options.

"Don't worry about your job," Parker said. "I'll give you any job you want at McCann. I'm sure it wasn't personal, just corporate restructuring."

I smiled sadly.

He followed me to the door, where my eye stopped on the bookcase beside it. It was filled with Greer's second book, *Other People's Problems*.

"Is it hard? Having her everywhere? Being able to open a book and hear her voice?"

He thought for a second. "I think it makes it easier. But longer. Does that make sense?"

I nodded.

"It still amazes me how she did her best work when she was so close to death," he said.

"Her best?"

"I think so. I thought her second book was better than her first."

I had read them so many times it was hard for me to tell. I was too close to see them objectively. "Okay. Well, bye, Park."

"Wait," he said. He went to the kitchen and returned with a folder. "Can you help me pick?"

"Pick what?"

"A surrogate. I haven't told anyone else yet, and it's a big responsibility."

I took the folder from him. "For the record, I think this is a really bad idea."

He grinned at me. "I know. But you don't want kids. You don't get it." He paused and took the folder back, removing two sheets of paper. Then he put them back inside. "Actually," he said, "you should read these, too. They're from Greer's journal."

It felt nosy, to say the least. A sneak peek into her heart and mind when she wasn't even here. But I took it, shaking my head. "This is weird, Parker. We didn't even know each other that well." Even as I said it, I knew I was kind of lying. In fact, I would venture to say that, in the end, I'd known Greer better than most people. But Parker didn't know why.

He shrugged. "Sometimes that makes it easier."

Easier . . . I had a flash of brilliance. "I will help you pick a surrogate if you'll help me get the rest of my things from Thad's place."

He nodded. "Sure thing. Do you need some furniture moved or something?"

Greer

SEPTEMBER 18, 2011

I NEVER IMAGINED I COULD be so excited about meeting a man's parents. That's usually the part that annoys me, the part that means that we're getting too close. It's the part I try to avoid. But it has been almost four months now, and Parker was going home to North Carolina, and he wanted me to come with him.

I have to say, as much as I love him and as brilliant and wonderful as I think he is, I was definitely prepared to have to pretend to like Cape Carolina. I thought it would be Podunk, but I was totally wrong. I mean, it's small. But it is one of the most beautiful places I have ever been. Parker and I stayed in the guesthouse, out on the end of a wide peninsula. There are views of this pristine blue water with marsh grass interspersed. And Mrs. Thaysden has impeccable taste.

Parker and I jumped off the dock and swam and kayaked.

We lay on the teak chaise lounges at night and looked at the stars and talked for hours. I told him I loved him, which I have never done first. But I do love him. And I love his town, and its amazing coffee shop and two of the best restaurants I've ever been to and a handful of perfectly curated stores. It's totally noncommercial and super quaint, like Palm Beach was about a million years ago.

And his *parents* are a total dream. His mother is this tiny woman who wears pearls all the time. She was soft-spoken and cooked this amazing meal for us. I have a feeling that Parker had a super-traditional childhood with a mom who stayed home and a dad who worked and his grandparents, like, two miles up the road.

It worried me because that's not what he would be getting with me. When I told him that, he laughed. And he said the most perfect thing: "Greer, I love you for you, who you are now and the woman you will become. The last time I checked, you fall in love with a person, not a lifestyle."

He's right, of course. But I have seen more people than you can imagine fall in love with a lifestyle and not a person. And, at a certain age, I understand how that can happen, how the search for the love of your life can become the search for a person you could be happy with.

Is it crazy that I'm almost positive Parker Thaysden is both?

Amelia

LEGACY

PARKER DIDN'T SAY ONE WORD as he drove me to my old apartment, and I loved him for that. I was deep in thought about what I wanted to say, what Thad might say. And I felt this dark sadness wash through my very veins. Last week, I had been professing my love for the entire world to read. I had been that sure of my happily ever after. And now here I was: alone. Well, except for Parker.

Thad couldn't help it if he liked men. But he didn't have to marry me. He didn't have to sweep me up into a fantasy of being starving(ish) writers together and living this romantic footloose and fancy-free, child-free life together.

"Liabelle, where are you staying?" Parker asked when we were almost to the apartment building that I had called home for so many years. "Do you want to stay with me?"

For a moment, it seemed like a tempting offer, but I

waved it away. "Remember Philip who works for *Clematis*?" I couldn't control the jealous pang that shot through me that he was still there and I was gone.

Parker nodded. "Oh, sure. I know Philip. Cool guy. Sheree is great too. I've seen them out and about."

As we pulled into the parking lot, Parker put the car in park, looked over at me, and said, "Are you sure about this?"

I nodded resolutely.

Thad was standing in the doorway. He grabbed my hand, and I pulled it away. "Don't!" I hissed, realizing how visceral my anger was.

"This way," I said to Parker, as Thad trailed behind saying, "Amelia, I made a huge mistake. It was just an experiment."

"Experiments are for college, Thad. Not your midthirties," I said calmly as I emptied my drawers into my duffel bag. Parker emerged from my closet with a huge armful of clothes, and I couldn't help myself. "Oh my God. Every man in my life is coming out of the closet these days."

Parker laughed, not even nervously, as he left the room.

"But that's just it," Thad said. "It isn't about that. It's all about love. And I love you, Amelia. I really do."

I stopped then and looked at him. "Thad, you have known me for six years. Does this seem like something that I am going to be okay with? Do you think the Amelia Saxton that you know is going to say, 'Oh, Thad, I forgive your long and torrid love affair with the only man who has ever given me proper highlights?'" I slammed the drawer I was holding down on the bed.

Thad walked up to me and said soothingly, "People make mistakes. I made a mistake. Please give me another chance at our life."

I wondered briefly if I was being hasty. I put my finger up and ran down the steps to the car, where Parker was deeply entrenched in a pile of hanging clothes.

"If I caught him with another woman, would I give him another chance?" I asked.

"Oh, um," Parker said, "I'm not really—"

"I mean, am I being biased and judgmental in some way here?"

"Well, I—"

"No," I decided, picturing a woman in her underwear on my couch. "No. I would be done either way. Hell, I'd be *more* done, if that's possible."

"So this is really more of a rhetorical line of questioning?" Parker said, pulling his head out of the car.

"Sorry," I said. "I just want to make sure that I'm doing the right thing. Can you imagine that he wants me back? Of all the absurd things."

"Well, sure, I can imagine that. You're pretty irreplaceable."

I smiled. That was nice.

Then I marched back upstairs and was startled to find that, in the time I had been gone, Kitty, Thad's grandmother—wearing her choker pearls and pearl earrings instead of rhinestones— had appeared and was now sitting on the couch underneath her portrait, which was a little creepy.

She patted the space beside her. "Hi, Kitty," I said.

"Hi, darling." She leaned over, offering a cheek for a kiss. She smiled at me disapprovingly. "You're making a mistake. That's a good boy in there."

I wasn't just losing Thad. I was losing his family. His grandmother, his parents, his brother and sister, his aunts and uncles, nieces and nephews.

"Amelia, dear," she continued, "I know that girls these days have certain ideas about their lives . . ." She trailed off, pursing her shockingly red lips. "But men have always had their little . . ." She waved her hand with a flourish. "Dalliances. But that's all they are. Dalliances. You're the wife."

I rolled my eyes. Was she serious? "Kitty, I'm not going to spend my life as the woman who looks the other way."

She gave me that vivacious smile of hers that I loved so much. "But, darling, you're not looking the other way. No, no. This is freedom. While he's doing what he wants to, you're doing what you want to. No harm, no foul." As she was painting the picture with her hands, it all started coming together for me. All the glamorous pictures of the sophisticated pool parties and Kitty and Bob arm in arm at galas and fundraisers, drinking champagne and dancing and laughing. It was an arrangement; it was not forsaking all others until death do us part. My heart sank. Kitty and Bob weren't true love. Thad and I weren't, either. Maybe the mere idea of that kind of love was as fake as the rhinestones Kitty wore in that portrait.

Kitty interrupted my thoughts. "Do you understand, darling?"

I searched for someone to share a look of disbelief with, but the room was empty. Was she serious? All the pieces of the puzzle were coming together now. Kitty was funding Thad's carefree "aspiring novelist" lifestyle—well, Kitty and I were. And if he didn't do what she wanted, that was going to be over. Maybe Kitty didn't want a divorced grandson. Maybe she didn't want a gay grandson. Whatever her reasons, she wanted her grandson to stay married and had somehow persuaded him that he should try to do so. It was absurd, but not surprising. Kitty had Thad wrapped around her little finger, and if she was upset he could barely function.

Thad emerged from the bedroom, looking sheepish. I glared at him and said, "So *this* is why you want me back?"

I became even surer of my theory when Kitty chimed in, "I'm willing to make this worth your while."

I locked eyes with Kitty and said, "If you think I can be bought, you don't know me at all."

Thad said, "No one is saying you can be bought, Amelia."

Parker emerged from the bedroom, too, out of breath, his arms full and a duffel bag hanging off each shoulder. "I think that's the last of it," he said, huffing.

"It sure as hell is," I said, following him out and slamming the door.

Embarrassingly, I burst into tears as I got into his front seat. Parker, sweaty, out of breath, and so cute it defied explanation, put his arm around my shoulder. "Anyone who cheats on you isn't worth the price of the paper they're printed on, Liabelle." It didn't make sense, but I found it oddly comforting.

He removed his arm, started the ignition, and said, "You know what we're going to do?"

I shrugged sullenly.

"We're going to go pay a visit to my friend Hannah."

I raised my eyebrows.

"She is the most vicious divorce attorney you'll ever meet."

I sniffed and nodded.

Parker added: "Then we're going to go get Sheree and Philip, and I'm going to take you all to dinner to celebrate that Amelia Saxton is free, and the world is hers for the taking."

My life, in less than a week, had gone to hell in a handbasket. But I had to admit that, when he put it that way, it didn't sound half-bad.

• • •

Parker Thaysden can dance. I don't know why I was so surprised by that. Sure, I figured he'd learned to waltz at cotillion. But I didn't know he had, like, moves.

When we got back to Philip and Sheree's place and were about to call it a night, I was only half-surprised to find twenty-plus cars in the driveway and all the furniture in the front two rooms moved out.

"It's the Amelia Saxton Freedom Festival!" Philip shouted.

I laughed at the *Old School* reference, and, before I could worry about a party of this magnitude on a work night, realized I didn't have a single place to be. "Philip, will you two ever grow up?"

He nodded emphatically. "Most certainly not, if we can help it."

I kissed him on the cheek. "You are amazing. Thank you for letting me crash."

I felt Sheree's arm appear from behind me. Her curly hair was long and free down below her shoulders, and her pale skin was flushed from dancing. "Friends don't let friends stay at cheap motels while they are having major life crises."

I smiled, and she whispered, "I think Parker likes you."

"Sheree, you're a little tipsy."

"Even still . . ." She trailed off as Parker came up, grabbed my hand, and pulled me out into the empty living room-turned-dance floor.

"I love this song!" he shouted to me.

I smiled at his enthusiasm as he spun me around and Fergie shouted through the speakers, "Tonight's gonna be a good night. Tonight's gonna be a good, good night!" I could never have imagined when I woke up this morning that I would have agreed with her.

"Thank you for tonight," I said in his ear as he pulled me to him. "I feel much better."

"Was it the champagne, the sushi, or the fact that Hannah thinks you can weasel cash out of Kitty if you sign an NDA?"

I laughed. "Thirty-three percent, thirty-three percent, thirty-three percent."

Parker laughed, too, with a laugh I hadn't seen since we

were kids, throwing his head back, dimples showing. He was just too adorable for words. I was glad to see him a little bit happy after so much sadness.

A couple hours later, I walked him to his car. "Thank you again for everything, Parker. There aren't a lot of men who would give a woman who woke them up and chewed them out such an amazing day. I couldn't have faced all the hard stuff without you."

"Cape Carolina peeps have to stick together," he said, raising his hand for me to give him five. When I did, he clasped his hand around mine, and our eyes locked. For the tiniest of instants, I considered what might happen if I kept holding his hand, if I took one step toward him, if I leaned in just a little. Which would have been absurd, since I hadn't even begun to mourn my separation and Parker was considering becoming a single dad. But the moment passed as quickly as it came, clearly nothing more than my imagination—and the wine.

"Plus," he said, breaking the tension, "I really needed a day off from work."

"And you did so much relaxing," I joked as he opened his car door. "But, seriously, I don't know how to say thank you."

He slid in the car and said, "You don't ever need to thank me, Liabelle. I'm always here for you." He smiled. "Sleep tight."

As I walked back inside the house, where dancing continued in the living room, I couldn't wipe the smile off my face. Even better, I felt calm again. I was going to be okay: I had severance, I had a résumé, I had references. I locked the door to my temporary room, pulled on my favorite cotton pajamas, and slid between the covers. The featherbed over the mattress felt like a cloud in heaven, and the slightest scent of lavender on the crisp sheets should have put me right to sleep. But I found myself thinking about the file of surrogates on my nightstand. And the emergency Reese's cups I'd hidden in the top drawer. I had filed for divorce today. I deserved some candy.

I put the first two candidates in the "no" pile and thought, *These are the women Parker finds suitable to carry his dead wife's baby?* Greer's journal entry peeked out from the back of the file. Digging into my emergency Reese's cups, I couldn't help myself. As I read about her embryos, her beautiful babies, I felt the tears streaming down my face.

Reading her words, I realized that, like it or not, I had become a part of their story long before. It was midnight, and the music was starting to die down, but I knew I would never be able to sleep now.

So I went to the kitchen, grabbed a gallon of milk, all the Girl Scout cookies, and my two new roommates, and said, "We have to talk about something. And it's really, really big."

"Oh my God! You *did* sleep with Parker," Sheree quipped, nearly sober now.

I smirked. "I did not sleep with Parker." I paused. "But I think I should have his baby."

Sheree swallowed her Peanut Butter Patty, put her hands over mine, and said, "Um, sweetheart. Unless something has changed drastically, you are sort of egg-release-challenged."

I took a deep breath. "You guys, Parker and Greer froze embryos before she died. And I accidentally found out they had been deemed abandoned. I set this whole crazy thing into motion by telling him, and now he wants to have his babies."

I had never seen those two speechless before. But they were most definitely speechless now. "I know. It's really big."

"And he asked *you* to carry them?" Sheree asked. "I mean, isn't that kind of a big thing to put on a person?"

I shook my head and plopped the file onto the breakfast room table, opening a new package of Thin Mints. "No, of course he didn't ask me. But these surrogates are not suitable."

Philip laughed. "They're not raising the kids. They aren't even donating an egg. They're ovens, Amelia. I wouldn't let it keep you up at night."

I handed them Greer's journal entry, and, three minutes later, Sheree was sobbing and Philip was clearing his throat repeatedly.

"That is literally the most heartbreaking thing I have ever read," Sheree said, handing the paper back to me.

Philip nodded. "I agree. And don't you kind of owe him your life?"

I thought back to that day on the beach. I did.

"So, are we on board? I mean, you're the other two-thirds of my throuple. You're going to be dealing with my mood swings and food cravings and crazy hours and morning sickness."

"Nothing new there," Philip said under his breath. Then he squeezed my wrist. "I'm kidding. I'm kidding." But he was only half-kidding: it didn't happen often, but when a doctor switched up my hormones or I couldn't refill one of them on time or my general dosage needs had just changed and took a while to get back on track, I was more than a little off. My friends knew that better than anyone.

Sheree shot him a look. "What Philip means to say is that we are here to support you in whatever you choose, no matter how absolutely insane it seems. But, Amelia, I urge you to take a few months to think about this. You just had the biggest two bombs of your life dropped on you. I don't think now is the time to make a huge decision."

I knew logically she was right. This wasn't the time to commit to something so monumental. But at the same time, I felt that tug that I had felt a lot lately, the one that meant I was ready for a new challenge. I wanted to do something more with my life. Something important. Greer McCann had left behind this whole huge legacy when she died at thirty-two. What had I done? How had I made the world a better place? And no, giving birth wasn't the most creative or brand-new way to change the world. But it was the best thing I'd thought of in some time.

"Oh, oh!" Philip piped in. "If you decide to go through with it, can I be there when you tell your mom? Please, please, pretty please?"

Sheree cringed. "Not me. I wouldn't touch that with a ten-foot pole."

They began imitating my mother, arguing over what they thought she would say. But I was somewhere else, wondering how Parker would react. And, for the first time in my entire life, I realized that, despite what I had always been told, I might, one day, feel a baby growing inside of me after all.

Parker

❦

SOUTHERN CROSS

IN THE BACK OF THE Uber after the party, I knew I was going to be exhausted at work tomorrow. I knew I should have left earlier. But I also couldn't stop doing something I hadn't really done in a long time: smiling.

The day, the dancing, the laughing. Had I imagined it? Or had there been a moment between Amelia and me as we said goodbye? Everyone in Cape Carolina knew I had always had a soft spot for Amelia—well, maybe everyone knew except for Amelia.

Once, I had believed that maybe she had a soft spot for me, too. Our mothers threw an epic end-of-summer party every year on the beach in front of the Oyster, the beach's oldest hotel. They invited all their friends, and they insisted that Robby, Mason, Amelia, and I be there every year.

But the summer after I graduated college, Robby was on

his honeymoon and Mason had wormed his way out by claiming he was sick. (Hungover was more like it.) So that left Amelia and me as the only two members of the under-fifty crowd.

We had exchanged hellos and caught up briefly. But then the sea of revelers wanted to ask me about my postcollege plans and to ask Amelia—much to my dismay—about potential wedding bells with her boyfriend. As it started to get dark and the tiki torches were lit and bonfires stoked on the beach, Amelia caught my eye across the party and gestured with her head out toward the sand.

I nodded, grabbed a bottle of champagne from the bar—the bartender protesting mildly—removed my shoes, and followed her down the beach, to a quiet spot away from the party. She sat down, wrapping her arms around her knees, and I followed suit.

"Don't get views like this in New York, do you?" she asked, smiling.

I shook the champagne just a little. As the cork popped and the bubbles exploded into the night, Amelia squealed. I handed her the bottle. "Ladies first."

She took a swig and handed it back to me.

I looked up. "There is nothing like a Southern sky," I said. I hadn't been alone with Amelia, this close to her, since the summer before I left for college. As I took a swig of the champagne and handed the bottle back to her, I told myself the jitters in my stomach were from the drink, not her.

"How's Daniel?" I asked casually.

She looked at me, rolled her eyes, and took another sip. "Between you and me?" I nodded. "Daniel cheated on me with the bartender at HMF."

HMF was one of the bars at the Breakers. "He did not."

"Oh, I assure you, he did."

"I'm assuming you haven't told your mother? Because from the talk around the party, everyone is expecting a proposal any day now."

She sighed, handed me the champagne, and lay down on her back on the still-warm sand, her arms behind her head. "Can I be honest with you?"

"Always." I looked over at her. Her serene face, her hair spread in the sand, the way the moon shone on her blue eyes, making them vibrant even in the dark . . . I had dated my fair share of beautiful women, but for me, there would always be only one Amelia Saxton.

"I felt relieved."

I laughed, looking out over the roaring ocean, raising the champagne to my mouth again.

"Why?"

"I didn't love him. My father loved that he was a scratch golfer. My mother loved his family and his job and how handsome he was. I *tried* to love him. I swear I did. But when I found out he'd cheated, I kind of felt relieved. He was crying and begging for forgiveness, and it was so easy to walk away. I realized I didn't even feel enough for him to shed a tear about it. Am I an awful person?"

I lay down beside her, twisting the base of the bottle in

the sand so it wouldn't spill. I turned my head toward her. "Amelia, you are a lot of things. Awful will never be one of them."

She met my eyes and smiled, making my stomach do that thing again that I could no longer pretend was from the champagne. Was she sending me a signal here?

She pointed up to the sky and said, "Is that the Southern Cross?"

I laughed.

"What?"

"Amelia, you can't see the Southern Cross from here. You have to be in the Southern Hemisphere. Occasionally you can catch it in Key West or maybe Texas, but never here."

She laughed, too. "But doesn't that look like a cross?"

I was pretty sure she had had too much champagne. "I've seen it," I said. "On my semester at sea."

"I'd like to see it," she said.

"I'd like to show you," I responded, feeling brave.

She turned toward me then, and the way she smiled, I knew what she said next was going to change my life. And it did. But not in the way I wanted. "Park, I have missed you. I don't think I realized it, but I have."

I couldn't breathe. My heart was beating out of my chest. *Is this actually happening?*

"You are the little brother I never had." She turned back toward the sky and said, "Is that the Big Dipper?" Then laughed. "Am I the worst amateur astronomer you've ever known?"

I tried to laugh, but *the little brother I never had* kept floating around in my head.

A decade later, as the Uber pulled into the driveway of my Palm Beach house, I realized that I had read that moment on that beach all wrong. So maybe tonight had just been in my head, too, something I had wanted to happen for so long that I believed things that weren't reality.

"Thanks, man," I said to the Uber driver, taking a moment to rate and tip him before I got inside and got distracted.

As I stepped in the back door, into the dark, quiet house, the smile left once and for all. *Greer.* What had I been thinking? I was Greer's. Always and forever. Nothing could change that. No moment, no dance, no fun day.

No one would ever convince me to move on from what I had lost.

Not even Amelia Saxton.

Amelia

A GREATER-GOOD ENDEAVOR

I FOUND OUT I WOULD never be a mother on March 17, 1996. Back then, I got upset about girls being mean at school or making a bad grade on a test or generally feeling flustered and afraid about life. I was a teenage girl, ready to cry on my mother's shoulder. But that's the day everything changed. Because the minute I heard the news, I knew somehow that it was going to be more difficult for her than it was for me. In the most ironic way, the day I found out I couldn't perform a core womanly biological function, I became a woman. I had to protect my mother. I would never cry on her shoulder again.

That moment split things open inside of me I didn't know I had. It was a single lightning strike that sank an entire ship. Minutes earlier, I'd assumed I would grow up, fall in love, get married, have children.

From the time I was born, practically, I had dragged a

baby doll around, and, as I got older, arranged my life around its fictional feeding times and diaper changes. I remember the doctor saying, "But with the advances in technology, you are perfectly capable of carrying a baby, Amelia. You'd just have to use someone else's egg."

I was fourteen years old, barely capable of understanding the reproductive process, and ignorant about anything related to sex. I had been horrified to even tell my mother that my period, which had arrived two years earlier, had suddenly stopped. And I was sitting in a paper gown in this cold exam room being talked to about things that I was entirely too young to process. *Primary ovarian insufficiency.* The word "insufficiency" bounced around in my head.

My mother could process these things that I couldn't. And that, I think, was why I had to be strong for her. Because my mother had had real babies. She had given birth to Robby and me. Carried us. Raised us.

Studying me on the examining table from where she sat on the rolling stool, her purse on her lap, she wore a look on her face that I had never seen before. When one is fourteen years old, it is really something to see a brand-new look on one's mother's face. That blankness, I know now, is the expression she wears when she has so many emotions she doesn't dare let a single one show. I give her credit for that. She was as strong as I had ever seen her. But that was because she didn't know what I was thinking.

As we got in the car together that day, I thought about Sunday school. I thought about what Mrs. Applegate said about God's will, about how he's always telling us what we need to know if we'll just be still and listen. God was sending me a message now.

"How about some ice cream?" Mom asked.

"Okay," I said. I turned up the radio. I was trying to act nonchalant, like the news didn't faze me.

Mom turned to me as she pulled out of the parking lot. "You can always adopt, you know."

I looked at her then and, without so much as a crack in my voice, I let the dream—the certainty, the platitude—that I would have children one day fly out the sunroof as I opened it. "You know, Mom, I think maybe this is a sign. I'm just not meant to be a mother."

I knew the look she gave me then. Shock. Dismay. Disappointment. Those were looks with which I was well acquainted. She patted my hand. "It has been a big day, darlin'. And you are only fourteen, after all. You have plenty of time to decide."

The cold of a Reese's Peanut Butter Cup Blizzard helped to numb my pain. When we got home, I walked straight upstairs, my mom calling, "I'm here if you need to talk." But I didn't need to talk. I needed to act. I needed to plot a new course. The first step? Pulling the giant Rubbermaid container of baby dolls, the Madame Alexanders and American Girls, the ones I'd been saving for my daughter, out from underneath the bed. I dragged them out, let the container drop, with a *thud*, step by step by step, down the stairs, and put them in the closet by the back door. That closet held all the things we never wanted to see again, which The Salvation Army dropped by four times a year to collect. By next month, all my dolls would be gone. I closed the door, brushed my hands off, and turned back upstairs.

Needing to take my mind off of the day, I opened the *Vanity Fair* magazine that Mom had left on my dresser. She always left her magazines for me, but I rarely read them. I was surprised to find myself lost in the pages, in the stories of Hollywood glamour, presidential scandal, the loss of a golden couple.

And, just like that, I had found my new calling. I was going to be a journalist. I was going to investigate what was wrong with the world and change it. My inability to have children wasn't anyone's fault. I was going to fix the problems that were.

I pulled out the little pink-and-purple journal that I kept between my mattress and box spring. Why I kept it there, I couldn't say. I didn't have any secrets—until now. In it, I wrote *Goals: 1. Become editor in chief of a magazine. 2. Find a man that loves me even though I can't have children.*

Then I went downstairs and asked Mom if I could get a subscription to the *Wall Street Journal*, to *Vogue*, to any publication that mattered. I started reading that day. I wrote my first investigative piece in September of that year about how the female lunch ladies deserved equal pay to the male janitor.

A mother died. A journalist was born. So how was it that reading Greer's letter had made an old flame flicker in me again, the one that thought maybe she wanted to feel those things she knew she never would?

•   •   •

After tossing and turning for hours, I must have finally fallen asleep. When I woke up, I picked up my phone and discovered it was nearly ten in the morning. I hadn't slept that late in years. As I yawned and stretched, it all came flooding back to me. The dance with Parker. The surrogates. My decision to ask him if I could carry his child. I could imagine the eyebrows I would raise with this.

My friend Martin, who I had met at a party six years ago and clicked with instantly, was the only one who would understand, so he was the one I called that morning. My other friends would pretend to understand, but they wouldn't really. They all wanted husbands and babies and traditional lives. They would say that I was ruining my chance at all that. They would view my choice as a response to my bad divorce, a bitter hangover that would clear—as soon as I found the right man. Martin really got what I was going through because his husband had left him for a woman.

So I was a little shocked when Martin—free-spirited, live-your-truth Martin—said, "Liabelle, have you lost your mind?"

Martin went home with me two years ago for Christmas, right after his separation, and still can't get over that my family calls me Liabelle. "I mean, maybe. Maybe I have. I guess after getting unceremoniously dumped from the job that has been my life for the past thirteen years and being traded in for

Chase, maybe I'm not doing all that great. So yeah, it's possible that I'm losing my mind."

"If you want to do something nice for Parker, send him flowers when the babies are born. Bake a casserole in an oven. Don't *be* the oven." Before I could say anything else, he said, "Look. Meet me at Café Boulud. Let's have a good omelette and a glass of wine and talk through this."

Café Boulud had always been our emergency spot. Martin was friends with the head waiter, so we always got the best table, in the center of the restaurant, where we could see absolutely everyone. With its perfect wineglasses and unforgettable food, it was a good place to go to forget your troubles.

An hour later, I was sipping a glass of rosé across from Martin, who was clad in fitted black pants, a thin black cashmere sweater, and a pair of Stubbs & Wootton smoking slippers. He said, "You know you'd have to give up booze for nine months."

I rolled my eyes. "Of course I know that, Martin. I'm not an idiot."

"And cheese and deli meat and sex and sushi."

I could feel my brow furrowing. "You don't have to give up sex."

He shook his head. "I'm sorry. If I'm paying you to grow my unborn child, I don't want some man's skanky sperm mixed in there with it."

"I don't sleep with people with skanky sperm," I said, realizing that I hadn't thought about any of this. "Plus, I'm not going to let him *pay* me." I hadn't even considered payment in this ill-conceived plan. But no, this was a greater-good endeavor, payback, a nice gesture to right my stance in the universe, which had seemed shaky as of late. I would not let him pay me. But I would let him give me a baller job.

Martin studied me. "Is there something more to this? Have you decided that you want to be a mother after all? Because you could adopt or have an egg donor or a million other things. I know you and Thad didn't want children, but you're allowed to change your mind."

I considered it briefly, but I didn't think that was it. Over the years, I had moved from simply coming to terms with not being able to have children, to embracing that that wasn't the life I wanted anyway. I shook my head. "I still don't want to be a mother. But this will be like the investigative piece of a lifetime. It's, like, the story you never think you'll get, and then it lands in your lap."

He put his hands on the table and said, "Look, I don't want to be the one to ask this, but it has to be asked." He looked at me inquisitively. "Are you in love with Parker?"

I had to put my napkin to my face to keep from spitting my wine across the table. "I mean, really? Parker is the annoying kid brother I never wanted. No. I am not and have not ever been anything resembling in love with him."

I looked out at the sun streaming on the bald head of Mac Montgomery, Mrs. Judy Lanham's paramour. Yes. Her paramour. Her husband was in a nursing home, and she had made no bones about moving on, whether her husband was alive or not. He was no longer available for the season's activities, so he might as well have been dead.

I handed Martin the folder. "Just look at this. He can't hire these women. They're strangers."

He flipped through the pages and said, "It's Greer McCann's beautiful, brilliant egg. Who cares about the surrogate?"

"But don't you think it has to matter? I mean, don't you think that somehow the woman who is growing the babies has to get mixed in there a little?"

He looked at me like I was deranged and held up the photocopy of Greer's words. "May I?"

I gestured, *Be my guest.*

A few seconds later, he dabbed his eyes and gasped. "You have to be her oven. You could be the hero that brings this great, dear, departed woman's dreams to fruition. You could give her the life she never got to have. You can give Parker the life he never got to have."

I rolled my eyes. "You change your tune really quickly. You know that, right?"

"Honey, you're just lucky you get to hear me sing my song."

If ever there was a time to mull, to consider, to make pro-and-con lists, this was the one. I was considering becoming pregnant, for heaven's sake, growing a baby inside of me and becoming attached to it and then not getting to take it home from the hospital. I was considering trading my taut belly and stretch-mark-free breasts to make someone else happy.

But, if I was honest, I couldn't remember the last time I

felt so sure, in my heart, in the depths of my soul, in all the places that really mattered.

So I didn't overthink it. I dumped out all the papers in Parker's folder, took a beautiful picture of me Thad had taken out of a frame in my bedroom, and put it in the folder. Who needs a picture of herself, anyway? I got in the car and drove toward Parker's feeling certain. Sure, my mother was going to have a stroke. But I was thirty-five years old, jobless, and untethered for the moment. What did I have to lose?

Parker

A SCENE

I LEFT THE OFFICE EARLY that day. I was exhausted, a little hungover, and, even though I knew it could never be, thinking about Amelia. I had planned to work from home, but when I got there, reading *Flappers and Philosophers* seemed more appealing.

When I heard a knock at the door, I assumed it was the yardman and called, "Come in!" I sat up, smiled, and said, "We have got to get better security at this place."

Amelia laughed. "Yes, this is a very dicey neighborhood."

My heart thudded. She had felt what I had felt last night. She was here to tell me. She handed me a folder. "I've decided for you."

I almost asked what she had decided, but I recognized the folder. The surrogates. The babies. *I'm sorry, Greer. How could I even think about another woman?*

I loosened the knot in the tie I had worn to work. I opened the folder. "This is a picture of you."

"Yes."

"It's a really nice picture?" I asked, raising an eyebrow.

Amelia sat down in a chair across from me, her forearms on her thighs, leaning in close to me. I ignored how her hair fell over her eye. I ignored how beautiful she looked. "I want to be your surrogate."

I laughed. She did not laugh. Neither of us moved. "Oh God. Amelia, you're not serious."

"I am serious."

"You can't. I can't. I mean, Cape Carolina. And our mothers. And paying you. And it's all too weird."

Hurt registered on her face, and I wished I could take it back. My instant response was that she couldn't be my surrogate. But why? *Because it's too complicated and then you could never be with her.*

"Oh God. No. Don't take this the wrong way." I paused. But I couldn't be with her anyway, right? I glanced at Greer's picture on the end table, rubbed my eyes, and got myself together. I would never move on from Greer. That much was clear. So why waste the chance to have someone I really knew and trusted carry my child? "I mean, let's back up. In your mind, how would this work? With the girls in the folder, it was just a straight business transaction. They give me a uterus, I give them money. That's it. With you, it'd be a totally different thing."

I saw the tears spring to Amelia's eyes, and I felt like a heel.

"I get it," she said. "It's all too much for you. I feel so stupid." She stood up and turned toward the row of floor-to-ceiling windows overlooking the terrace.

I sighed, got up, and followed her. Yes, it was complicated. But also, it felt good, I realized. I had serious reservations about choosing a woman out of a file to shepherd my child into the world. I knew Amelia would give this her all. I knew she wouldn't let me down. She wouldn't let Greer down. I put my hands on her shoulders and said, "Okay. Thank you."

She turned around, so close I could smell the cinnamon gum she was chewing. "What? I thought you didn't want me to do it."

"Well, of course I want you to. I don't want some stranger carrying around the most precious thing I'll ever have. I want to talk to my baby while it's growing."

She took my hands in hers, and I saw her eyes land on the wedding band I still hadn't been able to take off. "I don't want to complicate things for you, Parker. I really don't. I just was thinking about how much this meant to you and how I've known you forever and you saved my life and all of those things. I mean, yes, I'm kind of at a crossroads, but it feels like time that I thought about someone other than my-self."

"It really is." I winked at her. "So you'll move in here with me?"

"Um, no."

"Well, I'd want you to. Then you don't have to pay rent, and I get to watch my baby grow."

She scratched her cheek. "I was actually thinking about going home for a while."

I raised my eyebrow. Home. I loved Greer. I loved Palm Beach. I felt eternally tied to this house. But just the thought of home made everything inside of me that had been so uptight relax. Why hadn't I thought of this? I could go home. George, my boss and father-in-law, would understand. He would give me time off. I could work from North Carolina. He knew more than anyone that I had to do something to pull myself out of the murky puddle of depression I'd been living in. "Great," I said, as if we'd been planning it for months. "I'll get the back house repainted and ready to go, and we can live there."

The back house was a supposedly hurricane-safe structure that sat about a half acre away from my parents' house in a stand of trees. It had been on the property longer than the main house and had been home to many a wayward relative over the years. It also spent plenty of time empty and was the site of more ghost hunts than I could count.

Amelia looked confused. "Parker, I never mentioned us living together."

Suddenly, the thought of *not* living with her seemed the impossible part. I was so close to something like happy about this picture forming in my head. "But, Lia, that's the perk. Right? My baby gets to know my voice before it's born. I get to see your belly grow and know about your cravings and see what a pregnancy is like. It'd be such a gift." I paused, not wanting to seem desperate but not wanting to let it go. "Please."

"We need a contract," she said, sighing.

"We don't need a contract."

She looked me in the eye. "We need a contract," she repeated. "I need to know what you expect from me, what the rules are. It would make this much less messy for both of us."

"Kale," I said. "Kale should be in the contract."

"I eat kale. You can leave that out."

"Exercise, then?"

She snorted. "Right. Like I'm going to let my body go to hell while I'm growing *your* child."

"Money," I said.

"I don't want your money," she said immediately, ridiculously, since she had no job.

"I don't want you carrying the stress of a job while you're pregnant with my baby."

She nodded. "Kale and barre are expensive." She paused. "I have to ask you something kind of . . . awkward."

"More awkward than me watching you give birth?"

We both laughed.

"You know the story I'm writing about what people do with their frozen embryos?"

I felt guarded. I felt protective of Greer, of my baby. But Amelia continued.

"I've interviewed a couple who has donated their embryos to science, and I have a lead on a couple who might talk about why they decided to destroy them. But this angle is . . ." She paused. "This angle is extraordinary, Parker. I think it would be amazing to write about."

I felt myself relax. "Amelia, you're going to spend the next year of your life on this. How could you not write about it?" I took her hand. "Are you serious? Are we doing this?"

She hugged me. I'd take that as a yes.

"Our parents are going to die," she said into my ear.

I pulled away and said, "Let's go cause a scene."

◦　　◦　　◦

I knew when I saw their faces they all thought we were going to announce we were dating. Everyone knew Olivia Thaysden and Elizabeth Saxton's lifelong dream, from childhood—hell, maybe even from birth—was to have children who would grow up and get married. The truth was going to be a blow.

As I put my hand on the small of Amelia's back to let her walk through the front door of my parents' house first, I caught the conspiratorial smile that Mom and Elizabeth shared. Yeah, this was not going to be the dinner they were expecting.

It started out well. Mom had just had her kitchen redone and was excited to show it off. I don't know much about kitchens, but I knew it was nice. We never ever talked about money in our house, but I knew Dad was one of the top producers in the country in his field. I was proud of Dad for forging his own path, for taking a risk and creating a new life for himself. Now I hoped he would feel the same way about me.

We all had cocktails and appetizers around the kitchen island, which Mom was explaining was travertine. Amelia smiled at me nervously, and I noticed how quickly she drank her first glass of wine.

Fortunately, nerves had never affected my appetite, so I was fully able to enjoy the stuffed figs, pimento cheese, and flash-fried cauliflower.

We had agreed that I would take the lead. It was my news anyway, my life that was going to change. Before I put it out there, I had to be sure. Not pretty sure or almost sure, *sure* sure. I thought about going it alone, the all-nighters and the dirty diapers, the fevers and the doctor's appointments, my life no longer being my own. But then I thought about looking into the face of a child that was half-Greer, a child that we had imagined when she was alive. I would sacrifice anything to have her back. This was the only way that was ever going to happen. I was *sure* sure.

Greer had told me one day, with a scarf wrapped around her head, her face almost translucently white, not to do anything stupid when she was gone. The example she used was cryogenically freezing her in case she could be brought back to life. I tried to scoff, but it didn't quite take. That woman *knew* me. I had actually Googled cryogenic freezing the night before.

Besides, this wasn't extreme. It was normal. How many friends did we know who had done IVF? (Okay, one.) How many friends did we have who had had surrogates? (Again, one.) But that wasn't nothing.

I noticed that Mom had brought out Great-Grandmother's crystal and silver, which she only did on special occasions. As everyone sat down, I decided it was best to just get it out there, face the firing squad.

So I cleared my throat and said, "Um, you guys, I have an announcement."

My dad gave me the eye. "Don't you mean *we* have an announcement?" he said, gesturing toward Amelia.

She smiled nervously. "Sort of . . ." She trailed off and mumbled, "But it isn't what you think."

"Mom, Dad," I started, "I don't know if you remember, but Greer and I had embryos frozen before she died."

Dad took a sip of his scotch, and I could tell he had no idea what was coming next. Mom shifted her head. Her antennae were on high alert.

"Well, I just heard that those embryos had been considered abandoned . . ."

I trailed off, and Elizabeth said, "Oh, Parker, darling, that must be devastating for you."

Mom nodded in agreement. "So hard, sweetheart."

Dad and Mr. Saxton did not seem to share their emotions.

"Well, no," I said, realizing this train was going to go off the tracks quickly. "Actually, I have decided not to destroy them. I am going to have them." I cleared my throat again. "Using a surrogate."

Mom's face went white, Dad's scotch stopped midair, and total and complete silence fell over the table. It was horrible. But it was worse when they all started talking at the same time.

Mom was saying, "Parker, no. Absolutely not. That is ridiculous," as Elizabeth said, "I know it's a new day, but this is a little much," and Dad chimed in, "I think you've taken this mourning a little too far. Man up and move on," and Mr. Saxton was saying, "Son, you have no idea what you are getting yourself into."

Then they were all chattering wildly, more to themselves than to me, and all I could really catch was, "lost his mind?" and "no idea how much work!" and "babies need mothers."

Amelia and I shared a glance, and I wasn't sure what to do now. Should I interrupt? Slip out? While I was formulating an escape route, Elizabeth broke through the chatter. "So what does this have to do with Amelia?"

Bomb number two, ready for detonation.

"Well, Mom," she said quietly, "I am going to be his surrogate."

Elizabeth slammed her hand on the table and stood up so quickly her glass fell over. "You most certainly are not, young lady. I will not have it."

No one else at the table reacted, but I knew from five minutes' prior experience that that wasn't necessarily a good sign. At that exact moment—perfect timing as always—Mason bolted through the door, making a lot of noise, in a pair of gym shorts, a T-shirt, and filthy tennis shoes. He grabbed a plate off the sideboard, heaped food onto it, and, with half a roll stuffed in his mouth, said, "What? Is this a funeral or something?"

That was all it took to set them off again.

"Why is no one saying anything?" Elizabeth asked. "I can't be the only one who thinks this entire plan is lunacy. This is worse than when you two decided to free the trapped flies."

"Well, Mom," Amelia said, "it couldn't possibly be worse than *that*."

It couldn't be. There were flies everywhere that entire summer, like a plague had come down.

Elizabeth pointed to Mom. "Well, *say* something, for God's sake, Olivia."

Mom shrugged. "Well, it isn't ideal. But it makes me feel slightly better that it won't be some stranger carrying my grandchild. It will be Amelia. That's something."

Elizabeth crossed her arms. "Oh no, you're right. Perfect. Just let her sacrifice herself for *your* son. Who cares about her future, right?"

Now Mom was getting huffy. Lord help us all. Elizabeth and Mom had been best friends since birth, but that made them more like sisters than friends. So they fought like nothing you had ever seen—and about the stupidest things. Like the summer they chose to back different candidates for president of Garden Club, and they fought for months and almost drove Amelia, me, and our dads crazy.

Mom said, "No, *Elizabeth*. I'm not saying I don't care about Amelia. You know Amelia is the daughter I never had," she snapped. "I'm just saying that if Parker is dead set on this ridiculous scheme, then it makes me feel better to know that Amelia will be involved."

"Have you lost your mind?" Elizabeth asked, turning her fury back to Amelia. "Do you have any idea what it's like to carry a baby and then give it up? Do you have any idea how attached you are going to be to that baby, and how much it is going to break your heart to give it away?"

"But it isn't *mine*—" Amelia started.

But Elizabeth interrupted. "It doesn't matter, Amelia. It absolutely does not matter. Once they live inside of you, they are *yours*. It will kill you."

"I am totally amenable to your raising it with me," I interjected, smiling.

Amelia smirked at me. "That is not in the contract, my friend. If you'll recall, I have no interest in raising babies."

I had always thought she had no interest in babies because she knew she couldn't have them. Evidently, I had been wrong. Well, there went that idea. Back to interviewing nannies.

Elizabeth and Mom were glaring at each other. Dad and Mr. Saxton looked embarrassed, and Amelia looked on the verge of tears. This was my moment. I had to appeal to their emotions; this was my one shot, and it had to be good.

"You guys, look. I understand that it's unconventional. But I lost the love of my life. I have the opportunity to have a piece of her back, to make good on our promises to each other, even though she's gone. And Amelia coming alongside me in that journey is the greatest act of love I have ever seen from one friend to another." I grabbed her hand and squeezed it. Tears sprang to my eyes. "My life has been impossible without Greer. I have to find joy again. And I think this is how I can."

Mom and Elizabeth looked at me blankly. Dad said, "This is the craziest damn thing I've ever heard. When your life is ruined, don't come crying to me." Then he stood up and said, "Charles, shall we?" Mr. Saxton looked at Amelia and said, "Did you even consider what this would do to Robby's poll numbers?"

I'll admit, I had to stifle a laugh at that one as they retired to Dad's study, as usual. Mason grabbed his plate so quickly I was surprised the food didn't fall off, said, "Bro, you're on your own with this one," and ran off behind them. I'd figured this would be a lot for them—the two most hands-off fathers of all time and a man in his late thirties who still let his mom cook all his meals—to take in. But I didn't need their approval.

"Amelia, please," Elizabeth pleaded again.

She just shook her head. "Mom, look. I have spent my entire life thinking that I would never feel a baby growing inside of me. And now, here I am, single, alone, jobless, and, frankly, needing to find my place in the universe. I can't explain how I know I'm supposed to do this. I just do. I'm thirty-five years old, and this is a decision I'm allowed to make."

Mom and Elizabeth shared a look that wordlessly said we were both ill-behaved children.

This wasn't over. Far from it, in fact. I knew that. But we had done it. We had told the truth. I had taken a stand for my wife today. I had fought the good fight. And now it occurred to me that I had forgotten one major piece of this puzzle: I had told my family. Now I had to tell Greer's.

Greer

◈

JUNE 11, 2012

TODAY WAS, DEFINITIVELY, THE BEST day of my life. I had told Parker over and over again that I didn't want an elaborate proposal, just something simple and easy and us. And what I love most is that he knew me well enough to ignore me.

I was in New York to help him pack, and, while my father was thrilled that I had been there so much over the past fourteen months while Parker and I had been dating, he was already grumbling. *Now that Parker's moving to Palm Beach, you'll never want to come here anymore* and *Who's going to take over all your New York accounts?*

But I was so happy to have my love with me all the time that I couldn't even be upset by his grumbling. He looked down at his watch and said, "Well, I guess we aren't getting any work done today anyway. May as well not starve to death, too."

I smiled sweetly at him and said, "Why, yes, Daddy, I would love to go to lunch with you."

When we pulled up to Michael's, it hit me how long it had been since I had eaten there. Maybe even that lunch where my editor and I were talking about my first book deal. That lunch where I met Parker. I smiled just remembering it.

Dad said, "Hop on out, sugar. I need to talk to the driver for a minute."

As I stepped out of the car, Parker stepped out of a cab right beside me. He grinned at me, and I swear my heart stopped beating. The abs under that shirt were the only other thing that could do that to me. "Hey, babe," he said casually, taking my hand. He motioned with his head for me to climb back in the cab with him. The back seat was lined in twinkle lights, the part where there was usually a partition had been removed, and a little shelf had been added and was lined with flowers. That was when I noticed there was no driver. And it smelled remarkably un-cab-like, thank goodness. "Is this *the* cab?" I whispered.

Parker nodded. "This is the cab that changed my life. It's the cab where I picked up a phone and decided to track down a stranger."

"I love you, Parker," I said, overwhelmed.

"Do you know what I love most about you?" he asked me.

"Enlighten me."

"What I love most about you is that you have the most polished, perfect exterior I have ever seen, but, babe, you're kind of a mess."

I laughed. It wasn't the most romantic start to a proposal I had ever heard, but okay.

"You do things like leave your phone in cabs and forget one shoe in a hotel in Paris and lose your car in parking garages."

I nodded. "I do. I do lose my car in parking garages."

He smiled. "And that's good, because if you were as completely perfect as you seem, you wouldn't need me. There wouldn't be any room for me in your life. You aren't perfect, and neither am I. But when we are together, we are just right. We fit, babe. We fill up those empty parts of each other and make each other better."

I wiped a tear from my eye and whispered, "We really do."

He reached into his coat pocket and attempted to kneel in the back of that cab, which made us both crack up.

"Greer, I can't live without you. And I never want to. Will you marry me?"

I laughed and was crying in earnest now. I nodded. It was truly the easiest decision of my life. "Yes, Parker. Of course. Let's get married!"

He slid a ring on my finger, and we hugged awkwardly— we were in the back of a cab, after all—and kissed and then he said, "Let's get out of this gross thing."

I ran my finger across the black faux-leather seat, which was duct-taped in various places, and said, "What? I was hoping we could keep it."

He nodded. "Oh, we can. I had to buy it, so if you need a side hustle . . ."

We both laughed, and he helped me out of the cab. My dad and Parker's parents were waiting to cover us with hugs and kisses when we got into the restaurant. His mom was crying and saying, "I finally have a daughter."

And I said, "I couldn't have handpicked a better mother-in-law."

Even still, my insides burned like fire that my own mother wasn't there to see this day. All I can do is hope that somewhere, somehow, she is looking down on me. She knows I'm happy. And she knows that, someday, we'll be together again.

Elizabeth

SPUR THEM ON

SOUTHERN MOTHERS MUST MEDDLE. IT is in our DNA. We can't help it, and, for heaven's sake, who would want us to? Our meddling makes the world a better place.

In the seventh grade, Liv and I made a pact to have babies at the same time and do everything in our power to get them married.

It had worked out perfectly according to our plan. Almost. Liv had Mason, I had Amelia, and then Liv had Parker. We were certain Mason and Amelia would grow up and fall in love—especially the months they dated, until it all fell apart for my best friend and her son.

There were times we had discussed the possibility of Parker and Amelia, but the three-year age difference, during high school and college, seemed like a hurdle. But now, Greer was dead, Thad was gay, and three years was nothing.

What Southern mother worth her sherry wouldn't try to fix that situation—for the good of her *child*, of course? Liv and I were only ever thinking of them, which was what our useless husbands didn't understand when they made us promise to stop meddling. We promised. Just like they promised to quit smoking cigars.

When the kids had left and the men went to smoke and it was just Olivia and me alone at the table, I walked over to her new gold bar cart, grabbed the bourbon, and spilled some into each of our sweet teas. I tried not to be a little jealous of my best friend and all the beautiful updates she'd just done to her home. But I had made a choice. Liv had a newly remodeled home. I had a family estate, a legacy, and while, yes, all of our assets had to be tied up in it, that was the choice I had made.

Lately, I had begun to wonder if it was the right choice. For years, when the kids had been little and my darling husband had been young and strong and energetic, taking care of a massive working farm and a rambling estate hadn't been too much for us. But now it was.

I had decided to go back to work to help out with Dogwood's upkeep. It was paid for, of course. But it seemed like every time I turned around, the house needed a new roof or the water heater broke, or squirrels made a mess of the attic insulation, or a storm busted a few windows. But the day I went downtown to sell furniture, the police had come to get me in just four hours to say that Tilley was wandering down the street in a white negligee hollering for Robert. I couldn't have that. And a caregiver for her would cost the same as I was making. So that was out.

Truth be told, I wanted Charles to sell the farm. We had had large offers from developers pining for that waterfront property, not caring about the generations of men who had babied the soil, making it a hospitable place for crops to grow. But Charles felt the same way about those thousands of acres that I felt about Dogwood. They were his legacy. And, what's more, they were our living. I argued that selling the farm would be more than a living; it would be wealth. He argued back the very same thing about selling Dogwood. And I knew that, for him, it was so much more than that. He couldn't bear to see the land he loved become a cookie-cutter subdivision.

And so, there we sat, on opposite sides of the same fence, not angrily, I might add. We understood each other too well to be angry. It simply was what it was, and at some point, things would become dire, and either Charles would agree to sell a small portion of the farm or I would agree to sell Dogwood. But my secret hope was that one of my children would take it off my hands. Without the maintenance, Charles, Tilley, and I could live in a small house on the property, and Tilley's disability would cover a little help so we could have some freedom. But I knew it was unfair of me to burden either of my children with this behemoth of a house that I loved so dearly it felt like a part of my very soul.

I had hoped that, one day, when Thad inherited all that lovely money from his grandmother, he and Amelia would move back home, take over Dogwood, and fill it with children they'd adopted. Large homes do need to be filled with children, after all. It's their birthright, their singular point of pride.

But, right now, we had bigger fish to fry than the house.

"She offers to have his baby, he can't quit casually touching her the entire night, and they smile at each other like no one else is in the room." Liv stirred the bourbon into her tea with her knife and said, "How are we the only ones who can tell they are meant for each other?"

I sighed wearily. They did have a spark, those two. And, more and more, I noticed them sneaking off to the side at parties or family events, laughing and sharing private jokes. One could argue that they were good friends, but, in their presence, anyone could feel the current that ran between them.

Liv added, "So does this help the plan or hurt it? I can't tell."

I looked at her like she was dense. "Who cares about the damn plan? Can you even imagine the scandal of this? What is wrong with Amelia?"

Olivia motioned for me to sit down and handed me my drink. "Oh, Liz, everyone will be talking about it, but it's not really a *scandal.*"

I guessed she was right. Amelia had always been so strong-willed. I didn't know where she got it.

"And don't you see, Liz?"

I didn't see.

"Amelia will get pregnant with Parker's baby, and they will

be together all the time, and they will see what we have known for years."

I gasped. "That they're meant for each other." I paused. "So this is a good thing?"

"I think it could be, if we play our cards right." Liv got up and began collecting the linen napkins from the table.

I nodded furiously. "We need them here, where we can keep an eye on them, make sure they fall in love."

"Liz, it's too good. I'll make sure the guest quarters are perfect, and they'll be playing house and having this baby together, and they won't be able to help but see how beautiful a couple they make."

"But we'll have to protest," I said as she set the napkins on the buffet. They were beautifully monogrammed linen, but they had not been in her family for generations. I got another pang at the thought of letting go of my home.

"Oh, of course. I will have a fit about them living together, that kind of thing—"

"Which will only spur them on," I finished for her.

We shared a wide smile, and I took a sip of tea as she disappeared into the kitchen. Liv and I would be in-laws yet.

Parker

RUN OF THE MILL

THE LAST TIME I HAD been this nervous about going to talk to George, I had asked him if I could marry Greer. I knew he liked me, but there's a huge difference between liking someone and thinking they are a suitable husband for your baby girl.

George was a man much like the men I had grown up with. Large and imposing, he wore a suit and tie every day, chewed the end of a cigar, and used words like "acumen" and "acrimonious." Men of his generation were raised not to let people know what they were thinking. And George's parents had done a top-notch job, because I could never, ever tell what George McCann was thinking.

Greer would come home and tell me how over the moon her family was for me, and I would think, *Really? Even your father?*

George had had an incredibly difficult time with his wife's

death, and his pain was so palpable that you could almost smell it before you reached him. I knew that Greer's wedding would bring up a whole flood of emotions for him. A part of me wished we had just gone ahead and gotten married three months in so that Karen could have seen the wedding. She would have loved that.

Six years earlier, George had said stoically, "I'm not losing a daughter. I'm gaining a son." Then he slapped me on the back and poured me some scotch. But this talk was different. This wasn't something as run-of-the-mill as a proposal. This wasn't run-of-the-mill at all.

When I walked into his top-floor corner office that morning, George was, as always, behind his huge mahogany desk and the *Wall Street Journal*. I asked him one morning how he had time to read two newspapers every day. He had looked shocked. "Parker, how do you have time not to?"

Greer had taken his ritual to heart. She had read the *Wall Street Journal* and the *New York Times* every day, too, right up until the month she died.

He peeked over the top of the paper and folded it neatly when he saw me. He stood up and said, "What are you doing here, son? I thought you were in North Carolina."

I nodded and swallowed. George gestured for me to sit in one of the small black leather wingback chairs that flanked his desk.

"Well, sir . . ." That was a dead giveaway that I was nervous; I always said "sir" a lot when I was. "I need to talk to you about something."

He nodded knowingly. "Ah yes. I've been waiting for this. I've known it was coming for quite some time. And I want you to know that you have my blessing."

Known it was coming? How? Even I hadn't known it was coming. I studied his face as he said, "Parker, no father could have wished for a better man for his daughter. You stood by her faithfully in the worst of the worst, and I know firsthand what kind of fortitude that takes. So I wish you and your new gal well. I want you to find happiness."

Ohhhh . . . I almost laughed, but I cleared my throat instead. "Well, actually, um, no, sir. That's not what I'm talking about, exactly."

"Oh. Well, then just keep that talk in your back pocket for when the time comes."

I smiled. "I'm not sure that time will ever come, but I appreciate it. But this is about something . . . different."

He raised his eyebrow at me. "Will I need scotch?"

It was barely nine a.m., but, even so, I nodded.

He nodded, too, but didn't move.

"Greer and I had embryos frozen before her treatments," I started. "We had planned on having children together once she got well, but then . . ." I paused, looking down at my hands, the freshness of my pain this morning catching me off guard. I took a deep breath, not bothering to finish the sentence, because if anyone knew that Greer hadn't gotten better, it was her own father. "I have these pieces of her just sitting in a freezer, and I thought I might try to have one of them."

He looked positively confounded. "You've lost me, son."

"Well, I would get a surrogate. And then I'd raise the baby . . ."

He shook his head. "You mean to tell me that you are planning on having my late daughter's child, your child, with a surrogate?"

This was not going as well as the proposal chat.

I shrugged. "Well, I'm thinking about it." I nearly gulped. "Yes, sir."

That big bear of a man got up from his side of the desk. I got up, too, reflexively, defensively. He lunged at me, hugging me so tightly I thought I was going to lose feeling in my middle. He pulled back and wiped tears from his eyes, which I had seen him do only twice before. He grabbed me by the shoulders and said, "A grandchild would be just the thing."

I realized that mine wasn't the only life that had all but ended when Greer went. George's had, too. He needed me. I needed him. And he was right: a grandchild would be just the thing.

Amelia

WORST-CASE SCENARIO

LYING ON A PAPER-COVERED TABLE in Dr. Salter's tiny, old-fashioned Cape Carolina doctor's office, eyes closed to block out the glare of the inhospitable fluorescent lights, waiting for the procedure that would change my life, I felt, for the first time in weeks, completely calm. We were here. This was happening. It was real. I sensed eyes on me, and I opened mine, realizing that it was Parker's gaze I felt. When I smiled at him, he kissed my hand that he was holding in both of his. That was it, I realized. His being there was why I felt so calm.

Channeling my inner Greer, I had made Dr. Salter—poor Dr. Salter—take me into the lab before the implantation to see the embryos, which had been shipped to NC from Palm Beach for the occasion. We were implanting the two most viable ones: the teddy bear and the flower, as Greer had called them. They really did look uncannily like their namesakes.

"Hi, babies," I had said to the two of them—a boy and a girl. "I'm Amelia, and I am going to be growing you for a while until you're big and strong enough to come out and play. I have known your daddy, Parker, for a really, really long time, and I think he is going to be the best father in world. You two are extremely lucky babies." I paused. "So get ready to get sticky and stay inside me for the next nine months—or a little longer if you want." I touched my finger to the slide and whispered, "This is really important to a lot of people."

So, yeah, it's weird to talk to cells. But I wanted them to know that I was in this for the long haul.

I realized on the drive home how incredibly simple it had all been. All this buildup, all this worry. And, in a matter of minutes, it was over. It had happened. The actual process had involved little more than a tiny catheter and had been pretty darn easy. The mild sedative probably helped.

As Parker drove, unable to wipe the smile off his face, I, still blurry from the drugs, finally took a moment to reflect on all that had transpired the past couple of months.

While Parker and I were working out the details of this new arrangement—all while cohabiting at the octagon-shaped guest house on the Thaysdens' property—my childhood friends still thought I was going to change my mind. They figured that before Parker and I could get our IVF scheduled and legal paperwork signed I would go starry-eyed for some man. They kept shoving eligible bachelors in my face, and they were all *fine*. A couple were actually really great. But what they didn't understand was that it wasn't the men I didn't like.

All marriage was, it seemed to me, was one big competition. Who had a nicer car, who had a better house, who was
more in love, who had better jobs, made more money, went
on better vacations. I didn't think social media had helped
things much, but I thought the people who blamed it all on
Instagram were wrong. The world had been this way for as
long as I had been in it.

I had promised myself that I wouldn't get caught up in the
whirlwind when Thad and I got married. But I did. I couldn't
help it. I honestly did love him, so much. So why I felt the need
to have everyone see and comment on that, I'm not sure. How
I felt in my heart should have been enough for me. But when I
started planning dinner dates based on which restaurants
were the coolest and vacations based on what other people
would think, not what I really wanted to do, I realized that I
had become a person I never wanted to be. And then he left
me for Chase, and, well, if you want to talk about losing the
game, that was the way to do it. I had lost, once and for all.

The only way to truly stay out of the game, I thought, was
to remove myself from it altogether. Now, when my friends
talked about their awesome lives, I was sort of immune to it,
like a spinster aunt. No one was in competition with me. At
least, that's how it felt, already. I could ooh and aah over their
baby pictures and go to their showers and listen attentively
about their latest trips.

I was competitive by nature. In sports, in life. And now I
was out of the game, I thought again, as Parker helped me up
the steps and into my bed at the Thaysdens' little house. The

octagon house was nothing if not charming. With the tall, angular ceilings and leaf fans, I felt like I was somewhere in the Bahamas, not Cape Carolina. But when I looked out my window, I remembered because I could see the tree. And the tree was decidedly Cape Carolina. Live oaks grew all around our houses, with gnarled branches that extended up and out and sideways. They were amazing to climb. When I was in my prime tree-climbing years at seven, Parker was only four, but around our neighborhood, four was definitely old enough to be climbing trees. Only, I don't know why or how, but Parker just couldn't get the hang of it. He could take on bigger kids at basketball, hang in backyard baseball, and run with a wild abandon, but the kid couldn't climb trees. His shoes would slip if he had them on, but he'd get splinters if he was barefoot. And even when I hoisted him up, he'd only make it to the lowest branch. Then I'd scurry up to the top, and he'd look up at me and cry and cry.

So I went out to Daddy's workshop one day and got a bunch of boards and nails and hammered those scrap pieces one by one, climbing as I went. I knew I'd be in trouble later. Mom would be mad that I might have hurt the tree, and Daddy would be mad I'd taken wood without his permission. But Parker wouldn't have to cry over tree climbing anymore, so that would make it worth it. Sure enough, it worked. Parker climbed that tree for the very first time like it was nothing.

Light filled his eyes that day, like it did now, as he handed me a glass of water, sat down beside me, and said, "How are you feeling?"

I grinned up at him. "I feel great." I was a little crampy and a little nervous, but much calmer than I had felt before the in vitro. The "before" is so often the hardest part—that was definitely true of this process. I was lucky because I had heard and read a million times that egg retrieval was by far the hardest part of IVF, and Greer had taken one for the team on that one. We'd done a test implantation the month before so that the doctor could see exactly where the embryo was likely to implant. I'd taken a few medications to increase the chances of implantation, and the usual estradiol and progesterone I took each month anyway had been adjusted a little. But, overall, it had been pretty easy.

I was worried I would turn into one of those hormonal women you see on TV who absolutely cannot get it together, but I mostly just felt like I had PMS. Mom and Mrs. Thaysden might have caught the side effects instead. They had lain on each others' shoulders, clutching handkerchiefs and crying. Mr. Thaysden had muttered a bit about "real men," and my dad opened the bourbon. But, all in all, it could have been worse.

I mean, I had obviously had at least one full-on freak-out. I was becoming pregnant with my neighbor's baby. A freak-out was in order, right? It had started out quietly, as mine mostly do. I'm a serious internal processor, so I tend to keep things bottled up, which, as we all know, is *very* healthy.

I'd had some mounting concerns as implantation day got closer. And by "mounting concerns," I mean an endless supply of worst-case scenarios coursing through my mind on an endless loop. Fun thoughts like that I could hemorrhage and die or that God had made me so I didn't make eggs so I wouldn't have babies, and now I was absolutely going to die because I was bucking the plan. Or that both embryos would take and one of the babies die in utero and I'd have to deliver both of them and one was stillborn and the other one was way too premature. Or that both eggs would split a bunch of times and I'd end up on the cover of *Star* as the new Octomom. Or that Parker would freak out, change his mind, and I'd end up having to keep this baby I never wanted because it's not like I would just give it to a stranger.

Did I mention any of this to Parker? No. Of course not. Because keeping it all bottled up and not bothering anyone with your problems is a *much* better idea.

Two nights before the implantation, I was up panicking (this time because I hadn't gotten a good night's sleep in weeks and that was for sure going to keep the embryos from implanting). Nothing calms you back down and puts you right back to sleep quite like panicking about not sleeping. But finally I couldn't stand the gentle whir of the ceiling fan or the feel of the world's softest sheets and heaviest but also coolest comforter on my body. So I got up and walked out of the glass door in my bedroom, tiptoeing across the deck, across the yard, and to the end of our dock, which was closer than Parker's. I walked down to the end of the floating dock so I could submerge my feet in the cool water. I wasn't even pregnant yet, and already my feet and ankles felt a little swollen. I briefly envisioned a shark breaking the perfect silence and stillness of the night, soaring up out of the water, and chomping my foot off.

Parker and I didn't have a clause in the contract about whether I would still carry the babies if I'd had a recent dismemberment.

I heard a noise on the dock behind me and turned to look. Not a land-walking, oxygen-breathing shark. Just Parker.

"Oh, good," he said. "I didn't want to scare you." He sat down beside me and squeezed my knee. "I know. I'm freaking out, too."

I felt like I finally exhaled for the first time in about six months. "You are?"

"Are you kidding me? Lia, I've literally never held a baby. Not once."

I laughed. "Well, you seem very confident and unflappable."

"I have to. Can you imagine if I showed even an ounce of weakness to those vultures?" He pointed to the two big houses. "They would eat me alive. The *I told you so*s would be heard 'round the world."

I laughed. "I'm worried about everything, Parker. But, if I'm being honest, my biggest worry is that this isn't going to work, and it's going to be all my fault, that I got your hopes up and then dashed them in the ultimate way."

He squeezed my knee again, and I was suddenly aware that I was wearing striped flannel pajamas. Parker looked me straight in the eye and said, "Amelia, this is the first time my hopes have been up in more years than I'd like to say. If high hopes are all that comes out of this, that's enough."

I couldn't help the tears rolling down my cheeks. I wanted to say something about how between his brother and Greer he had been through so much. But I couldn't. All I could do was pray to God or the moon or the still, cool water or anyone who was listening that I got to give Parker Thaysden something to feel happy about.

"Are you sure you don't want to be involved in their lives?" he asked me for the thousandth time. But we had talked about this over and over again. It was even in our contract.

"Park, I just can't. My job here is to give birth to your children, help you get acclimated for a few days after and walk away. I'll see them. I'll be Aunt Amelia."

"And they'll know you gave birth to them," he added firmly.

"They'll know," I said. "Of course, they'll know. I gave birth to them, but Greer is their mother." I looked over at him, as he was looking out over the water. His cheeks were sunkissed from the boat and his hair slightly disheveled. I loved him most like this, in an old pair of gym shorts and Summer Splash and Fish tournament T-shirt, his guard down. The Palm Beach man in the suit was powerful and sexy. But this man was vulnerable and kind. I squeezed his shoulder, and when he turned to look at me, I nearly melted. And I allowed myself to envision, just for a moment, what it would be like if I stayed. . . .

Now, postimplantation, I was back to being sure that the only option I had was to walk away. It was too complicated otherwise. After a soft knock at the door, Trina, who had been waiting on the front porch of the octagon house to help me when we got home, walked in carrying a tray of steaming soup, while Parker fluffed my pillow for the tenth time. Everyone was treating me like I was sick, not potentially pregnant.

The doctor had advised twenty-four hours of bed rest, and then I was supposed to somehow figure out how to wait two entire weeks to figure out whether I was pregnant. It would be the longest two weeks of my life, even longer than the two weeks that my parents had shipped me off to a camp where you actually camped. Like outside. In tents. With no bathrooms. It was full-on atrocious.

"Your shoulders feel tense," Parker said, sitting down beside me on the bed, rubbing them, his strong, callused hands feeling manly and good through my thin cotton dress. I closed my eyes as his fingers ran up the back of my neck.

"This is my special, super-duper pregnancy soup," Trina said, making me open my eyes again. She had had three boys in three years, so I meant it when I said, "Seems like it works!"

She laughed.

Anything that might help me not let Parker down was fine by me. So, the memory of his touch on my skin lingering, I sipped the fertility soup. I think it was just chicken noodle, but whatever.

"I hope this works out," Trina said. "You would be such a good mom."

Maybe I hadn't been clear enough with Trina. "No, no," I said uneasily. "Parker is their dad. I'm just the surrogate. Nine months and my job here is done." I looked at Parker to make sure Trina's comment hadn't rattled him and saw a cloud pass over his face.

I gestured to the stack of books on the table. "Well, friends, I need to do my implantation meditation." (Yes. I was visualizing the embryos implanting. What could it hurt?) "And then I think I might dive into one of these amazing books and take a little nap."

Parker jumped up. "Can I get you anything? Are you hungry? Thirsty? Do you need the TV remote or anything?"

"Honey," Trina said, raising her eyebrow, "you'd better take him up on this while it lasts." She paused. "And trust me. It doesn't last long." I shooed them both out of my room. I closed my eyes, visualizing the babies implanting, the way my stomach would grow over the next nine months or so, how I would give birth to these two big, happy, healthy babies. As my visualization continued, though, Parker wasn't taking them home from the hospital alone. I was there, too.

I was feeding them and bathing them and putting them in their cribs. When Parker came up behind me, put his arms around me and kissed me as we watched them sleep, I sat straight up in bed. This wasn't a part of the plan. Not at all.

And I realized that, while my mind was visualizing what Parker and I had agreed on, my subconscious might be thinking of something else entirely.

Parker

ONE MINUTE

I HADN'T STEPPED FOOT IN a doctor's office since Greer's death, and now, in the midst of IVF, it seemed like all I was doing. I tried to bury it. But every time I walked through the doors of a doctor's office—even this small, hometown one that couldn't have been more different from the upscale Palm Beach ones—I couldn't help but think of her. My heart sank, but I smiled at Amelia as she climbed up on the brown table with the white paper sheet on top.

The only thing that Greer made me promise, when she agreed to keep living, was that I wouldn't let her get translucent and veiny and bald and allow people in to see her. When we had gone back to the doctor together after she found out the cancer wasn't responding, she had offered more treatments. Greer had said, "What are the chances that these treatments, which I assume will make me sick and bald, will work?"

The doctor had looked at her, resigned, and said, "Less than ten percent."

I was a mess, but Greer didn't skip a beat. She stood up, held out her hand, and said, "Dr. Taschel, I am most appreciative of your help. But I'm going to go home to enjoy the time I have left."

The doctor protested. "Even if you don't accept further treatment, we need to monitor the progression of the disease."

I agreed for some reason, like I needed to know, via a scan, when she was dying.

"I'll come back when I need hospice," Greer said.

Vomit rose up the back of my throat, and I ran out of the room to be sick in the hall trash can. Hospice. I still hadn't accepted that my bright, beautiful light could ever go out.

We made a pact on the way home to quit everything. And we did. We went to North Carolina. We went to Amsterdam. We went to Utah and Bali, LA and Bora Bora, Hawaii and Hong Kong. For almost an entire year, we traveled and sunned ourselves and made love and acted like we were on an extended vacation. I could pretend she was okay. But there were subtle changes—circles under her eyes, a change in her breath, the naps that she had to take in the afternoon.

The morning she woke up and said quietly, "Parker, take me back to Palm Beach," I wanted to jump out the window and end it. I couldn't bear the thought of living even a moment without her. I didn't want this part. I couldn't handle this part.

As Greer got sicker over those last few weeks, I kept my promise. Her beautiful hair had grown back and was almost to her chin. Her nurse—the same nurse they had hired for her mother only a few years earlier—did her hair and makeup every day so visitors could see the old Greer, not the dying one. That was maybe the worst part for me, because, even though she was leaving me, when she was made-up, she barely looked sick. I could sit across from her on the couch and pretend things were fine, that this was just a bump in the road.

To watch the person you love more than yourself suffer is hell on earth. But even then, I couldn't be wholly sorry. Because we had one full, memorable year.

A year had never felt faster.

And now two weeks had never felt longer.

Every day I wavered between piercing fear that the embryos hadn't taken, overwhelming joy that they had, and crippling panic over either.

Amelia swore she didn't need an appointment to tell her what she already knew. She was nauseous and bloated and moody. She was positive she was pregnant. She had been cooking up a storm for the past couple of weeks. I tried to take her out, but she insisted that the babies needed an organic diet. She had a little calendar on the fridge where she was keeping tally of the fruits and vegetables she ate daily to make sure she got at least ten servings. That seemed like a lot to me, but I was unendingly grateful for the time and attention she was paying to my future child or, if things had gone really well, children. And we had gotten into quite a rhythm with our cooking. I'd play one of her Spotify playlists over the house's sound system and pour a glass of flavored sparkling water in a wine glass for her, an Old Fashioned for me, on which Amelia insisted upon burning an orange rind. I knew already that I would never be able to drink it any other way now.

She would hand me vegetables and instruct me to dice or chop or whatever, and she'd get going on the fish or chicken. Sometimes she'd send me out to the grill. Amelia was a great cook, but that wasn't what I loved about those nights. It was the talking, the sharing of secrets and laughter, the way we'd dance around the kitchen when a favorite song came on.

Living in fifteen hundred square feet with someone bonds you fairly quickly. I loved the smell of her shampoo wafting through the house after she showered, the taste of the decaf coffee she'd added a pinch of cinnamon to, which we'd share on the porch at sunrise, the sound of her humming while she wrote, lost in one of several freelance pieces she had landed. The feelings I was developing toward her should have set off alarm bells. But they didn't. They felt simple. They felt right.

We read books together and discussed them, a hobby I had never shared with anyone else. Greer loved to read, but we had different tastes. Amelia tore articles out of *The New York Times* and left them for me and turned down corners of stories in *The New Yorker* she thought I'd like.

One night, I said, "It seems like you're really into the New

York–based publications these days. Any reason?" I was teasing, but the thought of her in New York made my heart race uneasily.

She smiled noncommittally. "I guess I'm just thinking that I love Palm Beach, but I don't have my own home and I don't have a job, and while I'll miss my friends, they've all moved on, too, you know? After being a managing editor at *Clematis*, I feel like I can certainly get a writing position at a New York publication. I used to be a little scared of New York." She laughed ironically. "But certain events of the past year have made me braver."

My mind was racing with ways to keep her in Palm Beach, with me, even as I said, "Lia, I told you already that you can have any job you want at McCann Media." I paused. "You're having my baby, for God's sake. You're carrying the heir to the McCann Media empire. I'd say it's the least I can do."

I knew what she would say before she even said it: "I appreciate that, and I will certainly come to you if I need help, but I feel like I have to do this on my own."

On my own . . . on my own . . . The words rolled around in my head as I paced nervously around the tiny doctor's office. We were waiting for the results of Amelia's blood test, and she was lying back on the table, doing some sort of intense deep-breathing exercise. I assumed she was visualizing, but it seemed a little late for that. Finally, I sat down on the swivel stool beside her and took her hand. She looked at me with one eye. "I'm breathing here," she said.

"Yes. And you're doing it very, very well."

She smiled at me.

"I just need you to know," I said, "that this has been the most amazing thing that anyone has ever done for me. I am so honored."

I looked into her eyes, and she looked into mine, and if a third person had been in the room, they would have felt it, too—the tension between us, like something seriously romantic might happen at any time. But was it just in my head, like it had been before?

"I think the hard part is getting ready to start," she said. I could tell she was trying to keep things light, defuse the intensity of the moment. But she couldn't. "Thank you," she whispered, biting her lip.

"For what?"

"For this. I've spent my whole life feeling so inadequate as a woman. I was scared, and you pushed me, and . . ." She paused, putting her hand on her stomach. "I know now what it's like to feel life growing inside of you."

She was so sincere and so beautiful and uncharacteristically vulnerable. I felt myself leaning in closer to her. As the hair fell over her face, I put my hand to her warm, smooth cheek, pushed her hair back behind her ear. She turned her head toward me, and our faces were mere inches apart.

The door flew open, and the doctor walked in.

Saved by the bell. Or not. It depends on how you think about it. Saved, I decided. I could never do that to Greer.

Dr. Salter sat down on his rolling stool and said, "Kids, I wish I had some better news for you."

My heart sank, and I prayed, *Let the news be that there's only one baby*.

When he said, "We can't detect a pregnancy," Amelia, who was now sitting up, said, "That's impossible. I feel so incredibly pregnant."

He held up a piece of paper. "It might be bloating from all the produce you're eating, if your food log is to be believed."

Suddenly white, Amelia looked at me, and all I wanted to do was console her. I was the one who had lost my babies—or had never had them. But I couldn't stand the tears rolling down her cheeks.

"It's my fault," she whispered.

"No, no," Dr. Salter said soothingly. "You know we confirmed all that, Amelia. It isn't your fault. There's nothing you could have done. Sometimes it works and sometimes it doesn't." He paused. "You can always try again. You have two more healthy embryos."

In that moment, I realized I would do whatever she wanted to. Even though they were my embryos, and it was my life that would change, I was going to let her decide. All I wanted was to see her smile.

She had been so sure this was going to work out that she had made me sure, too. We had both been wrong. It was over before it started. My children. My link to Greer. And now, as it felt, my link to Amelia, too. It was all crumbling around me as Dr. Salter said, "I'll give you two a minute."

A minute. One minute everything was great and the next it was terrible; one minute Greer was breathing and the next she wasn't; one minute Amelia and I were having babies and the next we weren't. I hated minutes.

All I knew was that, as bad as this minute was, I didn't want it to be over. Because I had come to depend on Amelia. I loved waking up to her making eggs in the morning, seeing her curled up with her book and herbal tea at night. When this minute was over, she was going to be gone.

"I can't," Amelia said through her tears.

And I realized that, even though I had sworn I would never be with anyone else, even though I felt in my bones that Greer was the only woman for me, Amelia was a part of my heart. She always had been. And when she walked out that door, the part of me that had come back to life with her was going to die all over again.

·   ·   ·

My saving grace was that I had driven us. I had a sickening feeling that if I hadn't, she would have gotten in the car and left, maybe forever. I could imagine how she was feeling. Truly. Because I was feeling it, too. A sense of loss and helplessness and wondering whether you would ever get what you really, really wanted. But what I hadn't predicted is when she broke the silence in the car by saying, "I failed you, Parker. I am so sorry."

I slammed on the brakes and pulled the car over like my dad used to do when Mason and I were fighting in the back seat. "Amelia, you could never, ever fail me. How can you even say that?"

She looked incredulous. "Of course I failed you. I had one job. I can't even do something most women can do by accident."

I had to wonder then if this had more to do with her inability to have children of her own than with this loss—or at least if her grief was split. I wondered if this loss also emphasized all the other ones this year: Thad, her job. I could feel her world crumbling. I wanted to put it back together for her, but I didn't know how. And even if I did, would she want that?

She put her head in her hands, crying. "Parker, you were so happy. So, so happy. I hadn't seen you smile like that since I put the boards on the tree so you could climb it."

I laughed then, remembering being four years old and the goddess Amelia paying attention to me. That was all I had ever wanted.

"You got to the top of that tree, and I have never seen you so happy, Parker. It was the best feeling in the world. And I thought I would give that feeling to you again, but this time, I couldn't get you to the top of the tree."

I knew then that she wouldn't try again; it wouldn't be fair of me to ask her. This situation was so complicated; how much more complicated could it become if we had actually had the babies? I thought back to my file of surrogates. I wondered if, knowing what I knew now, any of them would ever be enough. The thought of one of those strangers carrying my baby made me feel so alone.

I took Amelia's hand in mine and nudged her face with

my finger so she was looking at me. "That day with the boards and that day you had the embryos implanted, I wasn't happy because of the end result—or the potential end result."

She looked confused. "You weren't?"

I shook my head. "I was happy because the girl whose attention I had always wanted, the person I had always thought was the queen of the universe, would do something so huge for me." I paused. "Amelia, then and now, you made me feel like the most important person in the world. That's why I was so happy. And that's why I'm still so happy."

That wasn't strictly true. I wasn't *happy*. But that she would try to do this for me helped. I put the car in drive and made the way back to our house, hoping that I had satisfied her. I was afraid that she was going to leave, that this adventure was going to be over.

I thought of Greer again. I thought of her pain that last night, how rigid her body had been but how she relaxed into my arms when the nurse gave her a shot of morphine. She slept. I held her all night, didn't move, wouldn't have dreamed of getting up, wouldn't have dared to fall asleep. In her last moments, I knew I should be feeling something like relief for her.

But I would never, ever get to a place where I could feel like my wife, my beautiful, perfect, vibrant wife, being gone was okay.

I felt her breathing get shallow and fast. I recognized that it had stopped. But still, I lay there quietly, knowing that this was the last time I would ever hold her in my arms. Who she was lying there was different from the woman she had been. I don't know if it was because I had mourned for so long already, or if she was with me then, but I felt preternaturally calm.

I got up, kissed her on the forehead—the lips felt wrong—and said, "Goodbye, my girl. You are my only love, and I will spend the rest of my life honoring that."

The only thing that gave me the courage to tell the nurse that she was gone, to leave her there in the bed we had shared, was the knowledge that the person lying there wasn't my wife. That was just a shell.

As the paramedics started to arrive, I sat down in the hall and, just like that night almost eighteen months earlier in the shower, sobbed. Only, this time, Greer wasn't there to tell me it would be okay. And that's how I knew it never would be.

Every day since then, I had longed to hold her in my arms again. When I found out about those embryos, I really thought I had found a way. But as I watched Amelia pack her bags, I knew that Greer was, definitively, gone. I would never get her back. I would never hold her in my arms again. Not even half of her.

"Do you have to go, Amelia?" I finally asked.

Tears standing in her eyes, she said, "You're trying to have your dead wife's babies, Parker. How can I stay?"

She was right. I had been holding on to the past so hard that I couldn't even imagine the future. But if I could, if I was ready, would she still walk away? I wanted to ask, but the words wouldn't come.

Until she told me otherwise, a part of me could wonder— maybe even hope—that, by leaving, Amelia was opening a window for the possibility of us. Or, better yet, a door.

Amelia

CLEAN SLATE

AS I PACKED MY BAGS in my room at the octagon house, the view of the sun glinting off the water so bright that I had to squint, Parker watched me quietly, sitting in a chair in the corner.

I had let myself do the unthinkable: I had let myself feel something for Parker. Not just in a neighborly way, but in a loving, warm, maybe-we-could-be-together kind of way.

And now I had failed him. I was mortified. Oh, the way I had gone on and on about knowing that I was pregnant. What an idiot. This year had been nothing but one huge failure after another, and I just needed to go. I needed a clean slate.

Parker could never, ever know what I had been thinking, how I had envisioned a future for us. He was Greer's and Greer's alone, forever. Anyone could see that. I had thought for a moment that maybe we could open up to each other, that the love of a really good man could heal my heart. But now that I had crushed his dreams in the biggest possible way, I couldn't stay here. I couldn't face his pain and know that I had caused it.

One of my goals this year was to be bolder, braver, to take more chances. This was a big chance, but, really, what did I have to lose? Worst case, he wasn't interested, and I could go home, nurse my wounds, and move on.

I wasn't going to confess my undying love or anything. I just wanted to ask if he felt what I felt or if it had been the hormones. An hour earlier, right after we had gotten home from the doctor's office, I walked quietly down the hall into his room, where I could see him standing, his back to me. When I saw what he was doing, I knew that there wasn't a chance for us. In his hands was a picture of Greer. He had told me over and over that she was the only one for him, but I hadn't quite believed it. But, of course, it was true. He had done all of this for her. I had been the one to crush his dreams.

She would never be just a memory, and I could never play second fiddle to a dead woman. If I ever let myself move forward, I wanted to be first in a man's heart. I hadn't gotten that with Thad.

Now, in my bedroom, folding the final few items to put into my suitcase, Parker looked at me expectantly, like maybe he was going to say something, like maybe there was something else to say. But even I knew there wasn't. I was defeated, humiliated, and ready to go find my real life, whatever and wherever that was. I couldn't believe that just a few hours ago I had been prancing around here declaring how pregnant I knew I was. Really, it had just been gas from too much produce. What kind of woman couldn't tell the difference between gas and a baby?

The weight of it all hit me so hard that I sat down on the bed. I made the critical mistake of saying, "I'm so sorry, Parker," which was all it took for the tears to start flowing down my cheeks.

He sat beside me, put his arm around me, and consoled me, like I knew he would. He pulled me close and said, "There is nothing to be sorry for, Liabelle. We took a chance; we rolled the dice. So we didn't win this time. It's okay. It isn't your fault."

He pulled away and looked at me expectantly, trying to discern whether he had mended my broken heart. He had not. Nothing could. But, on the bright side, I had an interview at *Sea & Sky* the next week that I would nail and get the job and all this would be a blinking light in my rearview mirror.

I made the mistake of looking into his eyes. I remembered those eyes when he was a child, how wild they had been, how blinking and shining and full. His face still looked young, like someone who could just as easily have been doing keg stands with his fraternity brothers as mourning the loss of his would-be children. But his eyes? His were eyes that had seen things, that had known things that eyes that age should not know.

It was those sad eyes that had made me want to do this in the first place. And now, instead of making those sad eyes bright again, I had only contributed to the very real longing that stood, plain as day, behind their oceanic blue.

A part of me—a very small part—wondered if I should offer to do it again. But the real me, who wasn't as brave as she thought she was, knew that wasn't a possibility. I couldn't take those eyes.

I squeezed Parker's hand, smiled at him bravely, and said, "Goodbye, Parker."

He didn't say a word. What did that mean? I turned to walk away, feeling sad and empty.

When I got to Dogwood, my mother was on the living room sofa with Aunt Tilley, who was wearing normal clothes for the first time this entire trip. I knew it meant she was having a good spell, but, even still, I missed her silly Victorian dresses. Mrs. Thaysden was across the room. They were all sipping out of tiny teacups.

"Darlin', don't go," Aunt Tilley pleaded.

"Yes, please don't," Mrs. Thaysden added. "Having y'all back home has been too wonderful for words. We don't want to go back to just us old ladies."

"Well, you'll still have Parker for a while," I interjected as cheerily as I could muster. *And Mason.* But I had a feeling no one wanted to be reminded of that. I tried to keep the tears from coming to my eyes. I knew Mom would see them, and I didn't want her to. I wanted to be brave. I wanted to be strong. And I felt neither right now.

"Parker's going back to Palm Beach right away, sweetheart," Mom said. "Didn't he tell you?"

Now I felt even worse if possible. He had to go back there and tell his father-in-law that there wouldn't be a baby. Poor Parker. The man truly couldn't catch a break.

Parker was going back to Palm Beach. I was going to New York, to a fresh start, a new life. I had run from Palm Beach. Now I was running from Cape Carolina. And it occurred to me that, pretty soon, I was going to be all out of places to hide.

Greer

DECEMBER 15, 2012

IN JOURNALISM, AND IN LIFE, you must always know who your competition is. You have to study the competition, make sure you're staying a step ahead. I have never met Amelia Saxton, but, judging from the way Parker talks about her, I'm realizing that maybe I should. Or, at least, that I should work very hard to make sure Parker isn't around her. I'm actually a little relieved she can't come to the wedding. He can say what he wants to, make jokes and fun, but men are the most transparent creatures in all the world, and it isn't hard to see that he has the hots for her.

And, yeah, he's probably right that she was just always the older girl next door, that she would never give him the time of day. And maybe it's the phenomenon like how once you want a house—even if it's been on the market for five years—suddenly everyone starts wanting it. Or, at least, you're paranoid that everyone wants it. But now I am certain, totally sure, that every woman in the world wants my man. Why wouldn't they? He is perfection.

I know that Parker only wants me. Or maybe Amelia and me. But, either way, I will be watching that girl very, very closely.

Elizabeth

TRUMP CARDS

"WHAT IS WRONG WITH YOU two?" Tilley hissed as soon as the door closed behind Amelia. "I thought you had a plan. I thought this was all worked out."

"Well, we thought it was, too," Liv said. "Obviously."

Tilley stood up, an impassioned rant coming on. "Those two gave me something to look forward to again. Babies. Weddings." She cocked her head to the side. "In the wrong order, of course, but even still, they did. They made me feel like life was taking a turn for the better."

I sighed. "Tilley, for heaven's sake, sit down. We know. We wanted it to work out, too. But they're not children anymore. This isn't like the cotillion; we can't force them into it. They have to come together in their own time." I paused and took a sip of tea. "I have to believe they will."

"Or . . ." Tilley interjected.

A wicked smile popped across Olivia's face, and she said the phrase that kept my stomach in knots, the one I hoped she wouldn't. "Or we play the trump cards."

I sighed. The trump cards: the big, monumental things that Liv and I kept in our skirt pockets in case we ever needed them. We'd joked a lot about those two ending up together, and I have to say that, on this trip, I was convinced they might. A woman does not offer to have a man's dead wife's babies out of the goodness of her heart. That is a thing that one does only out of pure, unadulterated love. But my trump card was one I did not ever want to have to play. Not now. Not ever.

"You play yours, Olivia. I'm not ready."

Tilley rolled her eyes. "It's a new day," she said. "People don't look at things the same way. She won't blame you."

And that's what I had worried about all these years, right? Being blamed. Everything somehow being my fault, like I had secretly suspected. Amelia not understanding. I looked Tilley in the eye, wondering if maybe she wasn't having as good a day as I had thought.

Olivia locked her gaze on me. "Liz, it's not fair to make me play mine if you don't have to play yours."

"But you have to," I disagreed. "Eventually, Parker has to know. Amelia never does."

She sipped her tea. "I suppose that's true."

"Let's give it a few months," Tilley moderated. "They will have had the chance to sort through these very strong emotions and perhaps the truth will come to light all on its own, no meddling necessary."

I nodded optimistically, but I had to say that that very real possibility—that the truth would come to light on its own—haunted me night and day.

Parker

❧

GROW UP

THE DAY AFTER AMELIA LEFT, I knew I needed to leave, too. She was gone. The dream was gone. I went over to the house to say goodbye to my mom. She was nowhere to be found, but Mason was in the kitchen, eating cereal in his boxers. For a minute, it took me back to the days when we sat at that bar together, eating Cap'n Crunch, watching cartoons, and feeling the freedom of childhood Saturday mornings that can never be replicated. Mason was my hero. I wanted to be just like him.

I hadn't seen my brother more than a handful of times since I'd been home. He kept odd hours, sleeping during the day, going out all night. Basically, everyone else had grown up while he had stayed eighteen. I tried not to think about it, especially because it was at least partially my fault that his life had turned out this way. Sure, there was the whole bad-things-happen-and-can't-be-controlled argument. But I had controlled a large part of this. I was the reason that my brother, the next Babe Ruth, had never spent one single day on a professional baseball field.

"Oh, good. There you are," I said, as though I had been looking for him this whole time. "I'm heading back to Palm Beach."

He looked up at me. "Why?"

"Um. Because I have a job."

"I thought you were here having a baby with Amelia or some shit."

I sighed, angry and annoyed. I wanted to scream, *Grow up! Move on! You think your dream died? Well, mine did, too, brother.*

I felt a familiar sickness creeping inside of me. Sometimes I thought losing Greer was some sort of karmic retribution for taking Mason's great love away from him. Only, I hadn't meant to. I couldn't have seen how it would play out when I set it all in motion. Yeah, I had been jealous. But I had also been proud. I wanted the best for my brother.

"It was my baby with Greer, and Amelia was going to carry it, but it didn't work out. The embryos didn't take."

He put his spoon down and stopped chewing. "Bro, I love you, and that is why I'm saying this to you. You've got to get over it."

I laughed ironically. He'd fired me up good now. "*I've* got to get over it? *Me?* I lost the love of my life, Mason. You're sitting here in your parents' kitchen at thirty-six years old eating cereal in your boxers. Maybe you're the one who needs to get the hell over it. News flash: you wouldn't still be playing baseball, no matter what."

He didn't seem fazed, which annoyed the hell out of me. "Dude, Greer was hot and all that, but you act like she was perfect. She wasn't perfect. She didn't appreciate you enough. She took over your life, and you let her."

I didn't even think. My bag was off my shoulder, and I was lunging at my brother, throwing him off the stool, onto the floor. I landed on top of him before I could even consider controlling myself. My arm was reared back to punch him in the face, and the terror that flashed in his eyes thrilled me.

But I was the one who should have been terrified. Mason might have been lazy about work and life, but he hadn't taken a day off from training, as though he was going to be in the major leagues next week, since he was fourteen. Which is to say, he could have killed me swiftly, easily, and probably not even left any blood.

Instead of punching him, I said, "I do not ever want to hear her name come out of your mouth again. Do you understand me?" In retrospect, maybe I was taking everything that had just happened out on my brother. It wasn't fair. But sometimes brothers do that.

As I looked into Mason's face, I had a moment of pure clarity. Greer was gone. She wasn't here to fight for herself, so I had to fight for her. But that didn't mean that, while she was here, she was perfect—or even that our relationship was perfect. We had problems like everyone else, only it seemed unfair of me to remember those now. But maybe it wasn't unfair. Maybe Mason was right. Maybe it was better. I loved how strong-willed she was, but, sometimes, I wished she had been softer with me. I loved how decisive she was, but, often, I wanted her to factor me into her decisions a little more. I loved how put together she was, but, every now and then, I needed to be reminded that she could fall apart.

Mason put his hands up. "Dude, I'm sorry, okay. I'm sorry."

He was right. My brother was right. I couldn't say it yet, but, truth be told, I was sorry, too.

Greer

AUGUST 17, 2011

I HAVE ALWAYS BEEN A writer, sure, but I had never imagined writing a book. Especially a book about *myself.* Now I'm upset that I have taken this on. My mother is sick as a dog but trying very hard to hide it, and I've signed this damn contract. I mean, sure, I could get out of it or an extension or something, but Dad spent the better part of a lifetime teaching me that we honor our commitments. My name on that dotted line is as good as my blood. I can't stand the thought of having a book out in the world without my mother getting to at least read the first draft—especially since she has always been my role model and my inspiration for everything.

Between Mom and the company and the newspaper column and the podcast and Instagram and this book, the world feels like it's spinning too fast. I want to get off the ride, but I also don't want to disappoint anyone. Not my dad, not my mom, not the 2,167,493 women (as of an hour ago) who follow me. And, most of all, not myself.

This is the one thing that I feel like Parker and I can't talk about. He just doesn't understand. He wants to tell me how to fix it, who I could hire, how I could optimize this or automate that. I know he comes from a good place, but this is seriously the biggest fight we have. I'm not a problem to be solved. Sometimes I just want to vent and feel understood.

Of course, I can't say any of that in the book. I can't tell people how my relationship isn't as perfect as it seems on Instagram or how sometimes I feel like I'm falling down an elevator chute. No one wants to read about my weaknesses. And, quite frankly, I wish I didn't have any to write about in the first place.

Parker

A PERFECT PAIR

I WAS SITTING AT MY desk in my bright office, chewing absent-mindedly on a pen cap when Brian, my assistant, walked in and handed me a stack of magazines. The July issues. Had it really been almost four months of back to normal? Well, the "normal" in which Greer was gone, the embryos hadn't taken, and Amelia had left? He looked a little rumpled, like he had just rolled out of bed. But he could return emails with more efficiency than I had ever seen, so I let it go. "So, what's the deal with McCann acquiring *Sea & Sky*?" he asked.

I jerked my head up. "I'm sorry. What?"

"Did you not know?" Brian paused. "Well, then maybe it's just a rumor."

I shook my head, my mind racing. After Amelia had gotten a job there, I had looked into the magazine and been extremely impressed by how well it was doing. Circulation and ad sales were both up during a critically difficult market, which was really saying something. The word on the street was that they were looking to sell, and I had mentioned it off-handedly to my father-in-law, but I didn't know he was actually considering it. And now that he was, I was beginning to have second thoughts. I would obviously have to make sure that Amelia wasn't fired again in another McCann Media takeover. In fact, I would make sure she got a promotion. Yeah. That would make her happy.

I picked up a copy of *Parenthood*. I still thought every day about the way Amelia had said goodbye. It wasn't a *See you soon!*

I thought that being unable to get that goodbye out of my head was a sign I should try to say hello again. But I didn't have the nerve to reach out. And, even if I had, I wouldn't have said all the things that were on my mind. I knew we'd both be home for the Summer Splash and Fish. At least, I assumed that she would be. I hated how excited I was to see her. I hated how the idea of looking over and seeing her sitting on the end of her dock, hair blowing in the breeze, made me want to kiss her like I had wanted to do for so long.

But then there was Greer. Was moving on dismissing her memory? So I said, "Hm. Keep me posted on that. I have a lot of ideas I'm going to want implemented."

Brian saluted me. "Will do, boss. Will do."

I glanced down at *Parenthood* again and noticed that the couple on the cover was telling a story of how they'd adopted out their frozen embryos. I thought of Amelia. I wondered if she'd ever finished that story.

I got a nostalgic feeling when I thought about the weeks we'd had together and remembered sitting beside her on the boat, puttering through the creeks and canals around the beach.

When I asked her to ride with me, she had said, "What if all that motion isn't good for the babies?"

I had barely been able to get her out of the house all week, and, while I appreciated what she was doing, I didn't want her stressed out or feeling stuck.

"We won't go fast. Promise."

As we made our way out of the marsh we both cherished, I glanced over at the serenity on her face. I loved the way she looked in moments like this, when it was just the two of us, the wind blowing her wavy hair, her skin bare and sun-kissed. She was so effortlessly beautiful. Greer was gorgeous. No doubt about that. But a lot of care and concern went into her appearance. It was a very different thing to be living with a woman who took five minutes to get ready in the morning.

"Thanks, Park," she said, interrupting my thoughts. "You're right. This feels so good."

I was convinced that there was nothing in the world better than the sun, the salt, and the fresh air to cure anything at all. Of course, I hadn't done too good of a job curing myself. . . . But, as Amelia nestled closer to me on the bench seat and looped her arm around mine, I realized that the pain was fading rapidly.

"Thad never understood this," Amelia said. "The perfection of being out on the water, of spending a day with your toes in the sand without making it a social event."

"Greer didn't either." Immediately, I felt like I had betrayed her.

"Want to anchor at Sand Dollar Island and look for shells?" I asked.

She looked down at herself. "I don't have a bathing suit on."

"I'll get you to shore." I winked at her.

She held the wheel, while I threw the anchors and jumped in the chilly but invigorating water. It was only to my thighs, but would have been to Amelia's waist.

She stepped to the back of the boat and said, "So what are we doing?"

"You're getting on my shoulders."

She laughed. "Oh Lord. Okay."

I held my hands up so she could steady herself, as I walked through the water. On the beach, I steeled myself and kneeled down so she could climb off. I was out of breath and we were both laughing. I was trying to look tough and like it hadn't been hard for me, so I turned so she couldn't see me panting. And when I did, I saw the most perfect conch shell in a soft, weathered gray. I wanted to show it to Amelia, but she was already several yards away.

"Park!" she called, her hand in the air. "Look what I found."

I walked to meet her in the middle, and she, too, had found a whole, weathered gray conch. I held mine up. "A perfect pair," she said, her eyes meeting mine and holding my gaze for a moment.

Then, looking down at her stomach, as if remembering, she said, "We should save them for the babies. We can teach them to put their ear to them to hear the roar of the ocean."

Back in my office, I smiled, remembering. Maybe not being alone anymore had just felt good. Maybe it was being with someone who had known me forever; I got to skip all the small talk and sob stories.

Being with Amelia had reignited a flame inside of me. And that's when it hit me: I needed to extend some sort of olive branch to her before the fishing tournament. I skimmed the article about the couple who'd adopted out their frozen embryos. If they would talk to her, it would definitely help her with her story.

I flagged the article with a sticky note, retrieved a piece of stationery from my top drawer, and scrawled.

Thought this might help with your article. Let's discuss at Summer Splash?

Best,
Parker

Too formal. It was like a memo I would send to an employee. I threw it into the tiny wastebasket.

Thought this might be a new lead for your frozen embryo
story. Happy to help in any way. Can we discuss at the
tournament?

Love,
Parker
P.S. Want to have another lemonade stand? Maybe with
vodka this time?

I chuckled. Yes, this was much better. And it would make
her laugh. Some twenty-five years ago, we had gotten the notion to create a traveling lemonade stand in the back of Amelia's small boat. It would have been a great idea except that the
first large boat that passed us nearly capsized our vessel, the
lemonade dumped over, our signs were soaked, and we were
out of business before we started.

Next I texted my Mom, Can I have Amelia's new address?
She responded, Sending her flowers? ;)
You wish.
I sort of wished, too, actually.

While I waited, I sent a memo to my father-in-law. He
only worked down the hall, but we tried to limit our conversations during the day because a simple exchange could turn
into an hour and a half. He still liked to get handwritten
notes. I scrawled off:

I'll meet you at the Tattersalls' cocktail party next week
at 7. RSVP'd for both of us. Can we discuss the Sea & Sky

acquisition? I'd love to know your thoughts and I have
some as well.

—P

P.S. Are you wearing your velvet slippers? I don't want us
to be twins.

I teased my father-in-law mercilessly about the gold-trimmed velvet slippers that he wore to cocktail parties. They were atrocious.

I closed my laptop, stood up, slipped my wallet in my back pocket and my phone in my front, and waved bye to Brian as I walked out the door.

I was meeting a potential new hire for lunch at Sant Ambroeus. She had just finished graduate school at UNC, and the dean had personally emailed about her interest in our digital media position. That had been Greer's pet project, and since she had left, we hadn't been able to find anyone to suitably fill her role. Or maybe it wasn't that they weren't suitable. Maybe it was that they weren't Greer . . . I wasn't sure.

The job listing specified at least five years' work experience, but Lindsey Underhill didn't let that deter her. When she sent her résumé, I deleted it right away. When the letter came from the dean, I dragged it over into my "Potential Résumés" folder. When I hadn't contacted her after a week, Lindsey called, and I politely said, "I appreciate your enthusiasm, but you don't have the experience we're looking for."

She called back the next day. And the next. And the next.

And, while it was annoying, it was also kind of impressive. I wasn't sure I'd ever had an employee who wanted a job quite that badly. And after five interviews with five perfect-on-paper candidates who'd fallen completely flat in real life, I thought, *Why not?* I still didn't think Lindsey Underhill had enough real-life experience to be able to take on such a high-level position. But I figured, if she wanted to work for McCann that badly, maybe I could find another job for her.

I liked to be earlier than my interviewees, but I had missed the boat on that end. The maître d' pointed me toward my usual table, the corner booth by the window, and as I approached, a blond girl in her early twenties wearing a red dress stood up to shake my hand. She was as tall as I was, and I was over six feet. After we had made our introductions and sat down, she said, "I know what you're thinking."

I smiled, amused. She was confident, no doubt about it. I motioned to the waiter for a black napkin instead of a white one so I wouldn't go back to work with lint all over my pants, and said, "Please enlighten me, Lindsey. What am I thinking?"

"You're thinking that I don't have enough experience for this position."

I pulled a piece of bread from the basket and buttered it. I nodded, glancing down at the résumé she'd slid in front of me. "Wow," I said. "Mind reader isn't on your list of skills." I paused. "Although I've told you that no fewer than a dozen times, so it's not really a stretch."

"Look, I know I haven't had years and years of job experience, but I think that's a positive. I have ideas. I can bring a fresh perspective. I can do things differently." She paused, searching my face, as if deciding whether to forge ahead. "I can shake this position up like Greer did."

No one, ever, in the history of the world, could do things like Greer did. My face must have changed, because she stumbled.

"I mean, no. Not *like* Greer did. I don't mean I could re-place her or anything like that. I just mean that she brought a fresh vision to McCann Media, and I have a new perspective that I could bring, too."

She was clearly flustered, and I almost felt sorry for her. The waiter came to the table, and I ordered a bottle of wine, something I rarely did at a meeting. I felt the smile come back to my face naturally. I had forgiven her already.

She put her hands to her face and said, "I'm mortified. God. This is not how I thought this was going to go."

I shook my head. "It's going fine," I said softly. "No one will ever be Greer, but, unfortunately, we all have to move on."

It was like the words were coming from somewhere else. The phrase rolled around in my head: *We all have to move on.* I almost wanted to stand up on the chair and shout, *WE ALL HAVE TO MOVE ON.* I hadn't moved on an inch in the past three years. Not a centimeter. Everyone and their brother had told me that. But Lindsay's faux pas—plus, I had to admit, Mason's unexpected wisdom—had made me see it.

We both ordered the catch of the day, and we talked about Lindsey's ideas. Her face changed when she talked about McCann Media. "Greer is the reason I went to journalism school," she said. "I followed her career for years. I reread her books every six months. I admired her, not just as a journalist, but as a woman, more than words can say. She inspired me so much."

"She inspired me, too." In everything. I sat across the table and looked at this person whose charm must have gotten her a lot of what she wanted in life. It was going to work for her again. I took a sip of wine and said, "You know what, Lindsey? I might regret this, but I'm going to give you the job."

She looked shocked.

"Greer would have liked you," I said. "I don't know how I know that, but I do. If she were sitting here beside me, she would say, *Look, Park, yeah, her résumé isn't the best one we've seen, but she's smart and she has passion. And sometimes that's enough.* And so I'm going to give you a three-month trial. But I want to be wowed, Lindsey." I wrote a number on a sugar packet and slid it across the table. "If you make it past the three months, this will go up."

She nodded. "Wow. Just, wow. Thank you for taking a chance on me. I know I have a lot to learn, but I promise I will learn fast. And I will transform your digital media for a new generation. I swear I will."

I believed her. I paid the check and walked Lindsey to her car.

She turned and grinned at me, saying, "See you on Monday, boss."

As I smiled and shook her hand, I realized this lunch had been the first time in four months that I'd been immersed in work, the first time in four months I'd gone more than an hour without thinking about Amelia.

Amelia

THE GREAT UNKNOWN

NEW YORK WAS MY FAVORITE place. I couldn't imagine how, why, and again, how I hadn't realized how fabulous it was a long time ago. The restaurants, the theater, the people, the job . . . I mean, yes, going from managing editor to reporter had felt like a step backward. But I was only thirty-five, for heaven's sake. I had plenty of time to prove myself at a new publication and work my way back up the ladder. I ignored the fact that doing so had taken me twelve years at *Clematis*.

I was sharing a small but bright two-bedroom with Martin, who had decided he needed a fresh start, too, and, in true BFF fashion, had joined me in my life change. My secret nest egg was funding the venture, but, even still, Martin was footing more than half of the bills. I had protested, but he had insisted. And, much to my surprise, I had given in. He was right. None of the places I could actually afford were suitable for our swanky new start.

As the captain of all things fabulous, Martin was connected to the coolest people. He was the reason I was having so much fun, the reason I didn't feel lonely. And he was the reason I was going on this damn date tonight.

"Please, Amelia, please," he had begged. "Do this for me. I promised Harris a smoking-hot date to the premiere." Harris was Martin's boss at the PR firm where he was now working, the sister company of his Palm Beach firm. The job was part of the reason that he knew all the fabulous people. The other part was that his soft hair and megawatt smile simply attracted everyone to him like moths to a flame. He was handsome and generous, and he had the best stories—which were at least thirty percent true.

Like the one he was telling now in the back of the car while Harris and I smiled shyly at each other. I thought it was sweet that Harris could smile shyly because he was forty-two, graying right around his temples, and a total fox in the most gorgeous custom suit I had ever seen. My heart actually started pounding when he stepped out of the car, took my hand, and introduced himself.

"And the craziest part about the entire thing," Martin was saying, "is that after she confessed that she was pregnant with her lover's baby, after he killed himself on their kitchen floor, her husband *still* wants her back."

Harris smiled at me and said, "No!" I could tell he'd hired Martin ten percent because he was brilliant and ninety percent because he was the most damn entertaining person in the world.

"Yes! Can you believe it?"

Harris squeezed my elbow and said, "I can't. Can you, Amelia?"

I grinned at him. Was he flirting with me? I liked it. I liked him. Right away. Martin had been right. "Why would he do that?" I asked.

"He wanted to keep his family together."

It was the first time in an hour I had thought of Parker and the family—albeit the unconventional one—that we had almost had. It still stung. But it stung a little less as Harris took my hand and helped me out of the car in front of the Paris Theater. The producer of this advance screening was the firm's client, and I was happy to be there to support him. I readjusted the fitted black dress I was wearing and was glad I had gone with the stiletto boots, because Harris was tall. *Tall* tall.

Inside the theater, we were handed Moscow mules and cute, retro boxes of popcorn. I put my hand inside the crook of Harris's arm when he offered it to me. "I think you're really going to like this film," he whispered in my ear. Now I was positive he was flirting with me. Was this really so shocking? Was I that out of practice?

The movie wasn't really my kind of thing. A sort of action-adventure film with a lot of boat racing and some stolen diamonds and some sex scenes that were, quite frankly, a little raunchy and very uncomfortable, especially while you were sitting beside a boy you kind of liked. Okay, yeah. I knew Harris wasn't a boy. But when you're in the movies and you can't concentrate because you're wondering if he might try to put his arm around you or hold your hand, he's a boy and you're a girl. In a lot of ways, life never moves beyond seventh grade.

I must not have understood the movie, because afterward Harris and Martin absolutely fell all over their producer client, plying him with compliments. Martin deemed it "a sure box-office hit" and Harris agreed that "fans are going to go crazy."

But when we were in the privacy of the car again, Harris exhaled long and slow and said, "Well, we better start working on a strategy."

Martin groaned. "How do we even begin to defend that? That piece of trash is going to bomb."

"I don't know," I said hopefully. "Maybe you're underestimating how base the American population has become?"

"Even Americans won't go for that drivel," Harris said.

I could feel Harris's mood begin to shift from lighthearted and fun to agitated. And I got it. I really did. Nothing could sour my mood like a perfectly good project gone wrong. My mind turned to the notes from my frozen embryo story, still sitting in my desk drawer. I hadn't been able to stomach them, for obvious reasons.

But I was super bummed about what the shift meant for my night. I was hoping for a nightcap, a kiss at the stoop, a promise of a second date. New York Amelia was fresh and fun and open to, if not love, at least a handsome man to escort her about town.

Martin cupped Harris on the shoulder and said, "I've got your back, man." It was very reassuring and very . . . straight.

"You always do," Harris said, as though they had been working together for decades, not months. "I'm just going to leave it all to you."

I could tell he meant it because some of his stress seemed to dissipate in that moment. Not all of it, unfortunately. When we got back to our apartment, Martin took off down the sidewalk, claiming he needed to grab something from Duane Reade. I was still hoping that Harris might suggest a drink, but there was no question that his mind was somewhere else.

He took my hand, kissed my cheek, and said, "May I call you some time? Take you out on a proper date that doesn't involve a movie high school boys will be streaming on repeat soon?"

When I said, "Please do. I would really like that," Harris squeezed my hand.

Then he turned, got back in the car, and, with a final glance, was gone. It made me feel wistful and wanton. And I was confident that he felt the same. He would call tomorrow. He wouldn't be able to wait. I just knew it.

Only, after three days of silence, I was beginning to feel like he either hadn't been interested or I hadn't laid my cards on the table obviously enough.

"So he hasn't said a single thing about me?" I prodded Martin, yet again, as he shook martinis. Our apartment might have been shoebox tiny, but Martin—and my mother—had made sure it was fabulous. The entire thing had a very Holly-wood Regency vibe. It wasn't the comfortable, classic look I normally went for, but this was a new life, a fresh start. I needed something different than normal. And this high-glam vibe was perfect. Plus, the egregious number of mirrors made the space feel slightly bigger.

While my mother had made sure the apartment was dec-orated to the nines with furniture she had stashed in the attic from Aunt Tilley's first apartment decades ago, she had also made sure to tell me how cramped the apartment was. She asked if it'd be nice to go back to Palm Beach. Or maybe come home? I had quipped, "Why, Mom? One family member in the attic just not enough for you?"

I found myself very amusing. She found me less so.

Now, Martin said, "Liabelle, what do you want me to do? The man is my *boss*."

Now I was suspicious. In classic Martin fashion, he hadn't directly answered my question. "But has he said anything about me?"

Martin shrugged coyly, and I reached for the martini he was delivering to our chic slipper couch, which was covered in a high-shine, low-pile velvet the exact color of a pink Akoya pearl, and gave him the evil eye.

He sighed, dramatically folding himself into one of the beautiful Lucite creations, trimmed in gold, that Mom and Aunt Tilley had procured from a thrift store in—where else?—Palm Beach in the '70s.

Every thought of Palm Beach was a reminder of Parker, of that spark I felt and, maybe most of all, of the way in which I had failed him. The Summer Splash was coming up, and, normally, I would have been excited to go home for days of parties and croquet and tennis and, obviously, fishing. But this year I had told Mom I couldn't do it. I couldn't face Parker. I couldn't be reminded of all the pain I had caused.

"I just told him that you hadn't done much getting back on the horse since Thad, and that I didn't know if it would be that easy to convince you."

I was *aghast*. "Martin! I liked him. You knew that. I at least wanted to go on a proper date before I wrote him off."

He looked shocked. "Well, that's not what you've been saying for the past five months."

He wasn't wrong. "Well," I sputtered. "You're my best friend. You should be able to read my mind."

He smiled at me wickedly, and, as though he had conjured it, the doorbell rang. I figured it was a new neighbor dropping off a casserole. I had obviously forgotten momentarily that I was no longer in the South, where casseroles were social currency.

I looked at Martin. "I thought I was living with a man so he could protect me in situations when unexpected strangers ring the doorbell." He crossed one leg over the other and sipped his martini. I was on my own.

I got up and crossed the room, noting that I did feel impossibly glamorous in my mirrored apartment, holding my martini. Martin had even insisted I get a blowout today to lift my spirits. I wasn't exactly financially secure at the moment and hadn't wanted to part with the money, but it had been worth every penny.

I opened the door to an unspeakably devastating Harris, in a tux, holding two dozen red roses and a bottle of champagne. He grinned. "Martin suggested that a text might not win me another date."

I laughed, even more grateful my hair wasn't in a messy bun. "Come in, come in."

Now Martin stood up, taking the flowers and the champagne. "Well played, boss. Well played." Then he paused. "Oh God. There isn't some heinous limo waiting downstairs, is there?"

Harris laughed, the kind of laugh that took over his entire body. Everything about the way he moved seemed effortless. Even for a girl who had sworn off men, it was intoxicating. "Just the town car."

"Um," I said. "If we're going somewhere fancy, I'm not sure I'm black-tie-ready."

"Check your bed," Martin said coyly.

I put my hand on my heart. "I retract my previous statement. You *can* read my mind."

I gasped when I saw it, recognizing the dress right off the bat: a vintage straight sheath Chanel gown in a vivid emerald green. I had seen it on Martin's grandmother in the photo of her on our end table, and it was effortlessly stunning. I'd had no idea he even had it. It was very me. Well, me if I had ever been able to afford Chanel. Which I could not. I slipped it on, Martin zipped, and it was official: I felt like a princess.

"So, where are we going, exactly?" I asked Harris.

"That's for me to know."

"Do you think I'm safe with him?" I mock-whispered to Martin, realizing the martini had made this all quite a bit more fun.

"Don't worry," he whispered back. "I put a dime in your purse in case you have to call me from a pay phone." He winked.

We made our way down Fifth Avenue, and stopped in front of the Viceroy. For a moment, I was nervous that he was taking me to a hotel room, which would be about the seediest thing that could happen. But when the elevator opened, he pushed the button that would take us to the Roof, which was, in my very limited opinion, New York's best rooftop bar. Martin must have filled him in on that.

As Harris opened a door, I could already picture how crowded it would be, but, instead of the throngs of people I was expecting, the Roof was completely empty, save one table, two chairs, and a ton of candles.

"Am I on *The Bachelor*?"

Harris took my hand. "It's a new concept. A cross between *Survivor* and *Bachelor Pad*."

"Harris, honestly, this is a hair extravagant."

He nodded. "Oh, I know. Next date is pizza and boxed wine." He grinned as he popped the cork of a bottle of Veuve.

I didn't think of myself as a girl who was swept up in romance. In fact, I could hear myself speaking with disdain about this very thing. But I couldn't help but be. Here I was with this man I really liked, on a stunning rooftop with a peerless view of Manhattan, in a vintage gown, holding a glass of champagne.

Harris raised his glass and said, "Here's to diving headfirst into the great unknown." He paused and added, "Again."

We both laughed and clinked glasses. And I had to hope that my second foray into the great unknown this year would turn out a little bit better than my first.

Parker

─────※─────

ALL RIGHT

THE TATTERSALLS LIVED IN A historic Palm Beach stucco home that was completely invisible from the road, obscured by mature bougainvillea. They had been the McCanns' best family friends since the beginning of time, it seemed, and when Greer lost her mother, she turned to Kathie Tattersall for comfort and advice. I think losing Greer had hit Kathie almost as hard as it had hit George and me. Or maybe it was that Greer's death had compounded Karen's death.

I thought back to those failed embryos, and I realized that I understood how that felt. That second loss had compounded the first.

Greer had loved this time in Palm Beach—"the season." She loved the parties and dressing up, loved that the population doubled. Over the past three years, going out without Greer on my arm, where she had been for so many years, had felt impossible. But, little by little, my father in law had asked me to attend functions for some business purpose or another and I had agreed. He had lost his wife and his daughter, and his other daughter, who was not close to the rest of the family, was all the way in California. It wasn't fair to make him face the world alone.

Kathie greeted me at the door. All the ladies in Palm Beach marveled at Kathie's agelessness—although no one credited her good genes. Everyone had a half-dozen plastic surgeons on speed dial. But plastic surgery was like cologne: easily overdone. Kathie always stayed on the right side of that line, or so they said.

Greer always said that no one did Palm Beach chic decor better than Kathie. I never knew exactly what that meant, but I knew it was a very nice, colorful house with a great dock. As I pulled away from Kathie, a tall blonde caught my eye. When she turned, locked eyes with me, and smiled, I realized it was Lindsey.

George leaned in. "You're right, son. *Sea & Sky* is the perfect move. I've made an offer, and I think they'll accept." He winked. "Or they will if they know what's good for them." He was wearing the ridiculous slippers.

"Great news." This meant I was going to have to go to New York. I'd have to tell Amelia. I didn't want her to be ambushed again.

But I couldn't worry about that as Lindsey sashayed over to me, her heels so high I didn't know how she walked in them, in a green dress. She put her arm in mine and said, "Let's get you a drink, boss."

"Not until Monday," I quipped.

She smiled at me disarmingly. "Are you saying that you might change your mind?" She laughed like that was completely impossible, and I realized that she was right. I couldn't wait to see what she could do.

She steered us to the bar and said, "I'll have a glass of rosé, and Parker Thaysden always has an old-fashioned with one ice cube."

I laughed. "How do you know that?"

She shrugged. "I do my research."

"What are you doing here?" I asked, noticing that the crowd skewed decidedly older than me and certainly older than Lindsey.

"My parents and the Tattersalls have been friends forever."

Oh. Of course. "So why didn't you just have Kathie call George or me when you wanted the job?"

She shrugged. "Because I knew I didn't need to cheat. Eventually you'd see how perfect I was for the job and make the right decision."

I turned and caught my father-in-law's eye. He winked at me. Could he think that I was interested in another woman? He raised his glass to me, and I raised mine back. I thought back to our embryo talk in his office, and I realized that George McCann, mogul, titan, and father-in-law, had just given me some sort of blessing to move on. But he was reading this one all wrong.

"So, do you enjoy these things?" I asked.

"Not usually," she said breezily. "But I presume I will feel differently about this party."

Because I was here? I wanted to jump in and save her feelings. I couldn't count the number of times I had said, *Look, I'm flattered, but Greer was the only woman for me*, in the past three and a half years.

But then she said, "I have a thing for Tanner Prescott, and he's here." She smiled at me and said, "Your arm is a ploy to make him jealous."

I laughed, suitably humbled. "You always have a plan, don't you?"

She nodded and stepped away from me, handing me my old-fashioned and taking a sip of her rosé. "You have to stay a step ahead," Lindsey said. "It's a gorgeous night. Want to go out by the pool?"

"If we're by the pool, Tanner won't be able to see you." I was very amused by this.

"Oh, he'll follow me," she whispered. "Just you wait and see."

"We're excited about your first day at McCann," I said, following Lindsey outside and sitting down on the end of one of the chaises, pulling up my pants legs to accommodate the low position. Couples and small groups were scattered around the white pool deck, cocktails in hand.

"So am I!" she practically squealed.

"Tanner will be very impressed," I joked.

She grinned. "So what about you?" she asked, sitting on the chaise beside me. "Any leads?"

"On stories?"

She sighed and looked at me, exasperated. "On women, Parker. Seriously?"

I shrugged but didn't say anything.

"I have a girlfriend you would really like . . ." She trailed off.

"I don't think I'm ready for all that."

She looked into my eyes. "Forgive me if I'm overstepping. But she'll always be there, won't she? Do you think you'll ever really be able to be with someone else without thinking of her?"

Before I could answer, Tanner Prescott, as promised, was heading in our direction. Lindsey did an above-average job of pretending she didn't notice until he reached her.

Then she was gone. But her words lingered. My mind flipped immediately, out of habit, to Greer. But it terrified me to admit that Lindsey was right: I wasn't thinking about tonight or this party or these people at all. My mind was up the coast, in the city that never sleeps, with the one that, I was now realizing, most certainly got away.

•   •   •

Three days later, I was on a plane to New York. I was going to sign paperwork and brief the office on the details of the new acquisition. But it could have waited. The papers could have been faxed; I could have sent someone else. I was going because I wanted to see Amelia.

I didn't have a plan. I knew what I had always felt for her had resurfaced and I knew the loss of the babies would make things strained between us. And then there was a huge part of me terrified that if I tried to move on, I would only think of Greer.

Were it some other woman, we could date. We could say we'd tried. But if things went awry with Amelia, there was no coming back from that. We would be in each other's lives forever.

And so, as I hailed a cab into the city, I decided that I wouldn't tell her anything. Not yet. This meeting would be strictly professional. I looked at my watch, 7:13 a.m. I would be in the city before she left for work.

The cab smelled distinctly like eucalyptus. Maybe a little cinnamon. Peppermint? About halfway through the ride, caught up on email and tired of being inside my own head, my curiosity got the best of me. "What is that smell?" I asked.

I could see the driver's smile in the rearview mirror. "Essential oils."

"Why do you have them in the car?"

"Makes it smell better—and it's supposed to promote good health."

Good health. Those two simple words were all it took to catapult me backward, to staying up all night Googling Ayurvedic treatment centers, stem cell transplants, holistic therapy. When Greer opened her eyes that morning, I was filled with adrenaline. I was sure that one of these three packets I was about to present my wife held the cure. We would go to India or maybe just California or even the mountains of North Carolina. Three options. She could pick the best one.

But when I told her, she put her hands on my face. "My mother died of ovarian cancer, and now I am, too. It's okay. It's okay to just accept it, sweetheart. It doesn't make you less of a man to admit when you have lost a fight."

In the dark of night, I had been so sure this was the answer. This was going to save my wife. As I climbed in bed beside her, I realized that I hadn't lost the fight, because it wasn't my fight to win or lose. It was Greer's. If this was what she wanted, then I had to take it like a man. Because it was her cancer. It was her choice.

Standing in front of the door to Amelia's apartment that early morning, after that cab ride, I still wasn't sure what I would say. But I guessed that, like Greer, I had a limited amount of time. And maybe I should get on with living.

One thing was for sure: I missed Amelia. I missed her face. I missed her smile. I missed the way she looked at me like she understood me even better than I understood myself. I was going to lead with my heart.

I was about to knock when the door opened, seemingly of its own accord. It wasn't Amelia. And it wasn't Martin.

I was getting ready to say that I must have the wrong apartment when Amelia appeared in her bathrobe.

"Parker?" she asked. She looked confused. "What are you doing here?"

Now I was racking my brain. Was this guy with Martin?

"Um," I started. "I wanted to talk to you."

She raised her eyebrows.

The man in the suit stood awkwardly in the doorway and then said, "Well, I'll call you, Amelia."

"Okay. I'll look forward to it." Amelia smiled giddily, and I wanted to punch this guy. He was definitely not with Martin.

He shook my hand and smacked me on the back. He had declared war.

Amelia tightened her robe string and put her hands up like *What in the world?* Then she gestured for me to come in.

She shut the door behind me and led me over to a Lucite table with a gold base and two chairs. Jesus, this place was gaudy. "I was just getting ready to make some coffee," she said, ignoring the elephant in the room.

"Sure," I said. "With—"

"Two sugars, Parker. I know."

Her tone wasn't angry exactly, but it wasn't friendly, either. It was a tone I had never heard from her. Like a stranger.

"Did I just walk into something here?" I asked.

She turned to me, leaning on the small expanse of counter, and bit her lip almost guiltily. That was when I noticed how hot she was when she had just woken up. Bedhead suited her.

Before she could answer, Martin's voice preceded him into the tiny kitchen. "Good morning, beautiful people!" he trilled.

He was already in his suit and perfectly coiffed. He stopped when he saw me. "Oh. Not the beautiful person I was expecting."

I stood up and hugged him.

"What are you doing here?" he asked.

I nodded my head toward Amelia. "Just came to talk to this one."

"Ah," he said, looking almost embarrassed for me. It was not my favorite look on him.

He kissed Amelia on the cheek and said, "Actually, I think I'm going to grab my coffee on the way."

I saw him mouth, *Call me*, to her.

She poured boiling water over a funnel/strainer combination filled with grounds, which was way fancier than my Nespresso.

She stirred in my two sugars and said, "Not to be rude, Parker, but I need to get ready for work."

I shook my head. "No, you don't. I mean, you do, but it's okay if you're late."

She raised her eyebrow and sat down.

"McCann acquired *Sea & Sky*."

Her face went red, and she said, "If you are here to tell me I'm fired again, I swear to God, Parker—"

I laughed and then cut her off, taking her hand from midair, bringing it back down to the table and putting mine on top of it. "You're not fired, Amelia. In fact, you're promoted. To whatever you want. I was thinking executive editor this year, maybe managing editor in another year or two?" I paused. "Not that you aren't clearly suited for managing editor. I just wasn't sure if you wanted all the pressure right away."

She visibly relaxed, and I moved my hand, feeling sorry as I did.

"So I don't need to get ready because you're my new boss."

I shrugged. "No. Not really. But also yeah. I won't be in the office day in and day out or anything, but I wanted you to hear it from me this time."

She nodded resolutely. "Well, thank you. I appreciate that. And I'm excited to be working for a McCann company. Despite firing me, I think you guys make some really responsible, positive changes in your acquisitions."

She was so robotic toward me now. The smiling, flirtatious Amelia of my past seemed to have been replaced by this other woman, whose hair was falling seductively out of her messy bun but who refused to reveal her real inner power.

"Is that why you got on a plane at four thirty in the morning? So you could tell me that?"

I took a beat before I responded.

"The thing with that guy. Is it serious?"

I could tell she was trying not to smile. My stomach sank all the way to the floor. "It's new," she responded shortly.

It was new. All the hairs on my body suddenly stood on end. I wanted to tell her that I couldn't stop thinking about her. That she was the first woman in a long time who had made me feel alive.

"But we aren't," I said, getting up and walking to the door. I wanted her to confirm that my feelings weren't one-sided, that this wasn't all in my head. But I couldn't sit there while I waited.

I noticed the article I had sent sitting on a small table by the door that housed a stack of mail. I wondered what it meant that she hadn't responded.

"Parker . . ." she started. I turned, ashamed of how expectant I must have looked. She smiled and shrugged.

I picked up a copy of *Southern Coast* that was in her mail pile and held it up, attempting to cover my pain with a joke. "No non-McCann publications allowed, young lady."

She smiled. "If you want me to quit reading non-McCann magazines, then you're going to have to buy *Southern Coast*."

Greer always used to say that, too. Greer and Amelia. Two very different women. One a product of the luxury, pomp, and circumstance of Palm Beach and New York, the other raised by the simplicity of a small slice of Southern shore. But they both loved *Southern Coast*. And, as was becoming clearer by the minute, I loved both of them.

Amelia

GOSPEL TRUTH

I HAD NEVER REALLY SEEN Parker in his element. Well, I mean, I had seen him in his element surfing or fishing or hunting or making good grades. But I hadn't seen grown-up Parker in his custom suit, standing before an entire magazine staff—editors and all—announcing that a big change was about to come their way. To be honest, he wowed me. In fact, I could barely focus on what he was saying, just that he seemed so powerful in front of this room, so commanding, so effortless, delivering what—let's be honest—wasn't going to be good news for everyone. And, weirdly, his accent was incredibly neutral, professional, like he could have been from anywhere in the country. I actually kind of hated that part.

My new coworker Lucia, who was quickly becoming my work friend, leaned over and said, "New boss is a hottie. Wonder what his policy on workplace relationships is?" She winked at me from underneath her curtain of luscious eye-lashes, and a jealous heat rose through me. I knew she was kidding, but I sounded entirely too stern when I said, "They're frowned upon."

I snapped back to Parker as he was saying, "One of McCann's fortes is seamlessly interlinking print and online presence. So I'd love to hear your ideas about how we could do that. This is your magazine, after all." He paused. "And if those ideas increase revenue, well, then so much the better for all of us." A light chuckle wafted through the room, and my hand went up.

"Yes, ma'am," he said, pointing at me, his Southern drawl finally shining back through in the most adorable way. I guessed he couldn't say my name because it would intimate that we had a relationship, which would immediately put him—and me—at odds with the rest of the staff.

"I've been assigned the monthly home features," I started. So, no, it wasn't investigative, but I did get to do interviews with some of the most famous designers in the country—and their A-list clients—that were interesting and fun. Creating a compulsively readable story that combined the feel of the family, the expertise of the designer, and actual factual infor-mation about the decor fulfilled me in a way that surprised me. It was a new challenge, and rising to it was thrilling. "I was thinking that when I write the monthly home features, we could make the images shoppable online, so that people can actually buy the pieces in the room, and we could make an affiliate commission."

He smiled at me. And it wasn't a new-boss smile. It was a Parker-and-Amelia smile, one that warmed me to the tips of my toes. "Genius. I love it. Anyone else?" He glanced at the other end of the table, pointed to Dan from marketing. While Dan was talking, Parker smiled at me.

I leaned back in my chair, satisfied by the praise, happy that I had looked competent in front of my new-ish coworkers. Parker and I were in this together. And I couldn't help but notice that we made a terrific team.

◆　◆　◆

"I do not understand," I was saying to Martin, two days after Parker's impromptu visit, "why my mother insists that I come home every year for this fishing tournament. I don't even like to fish."

He spread himself dramatically across my bed. "Well, your daddy likes to fish, and he likes for you to be there, so maybe it's more about that."

I zipped four sundresses into a hanging bag, knowing that I absolutely loved the Summer Splash. I was just in a *mood*.

"You said, like, a million times that you weren't going to this thing this year. What made you change your mind?"

I shrugged noncommittally. So, yes, maybe, just maybe, it had something to do with the fact that I hadn't been able to get Parker out of my mind since he showed up on my doorstep two days ago and shone in that board room, damn it. I saw him in a brand-new way, one that combined the charm of our history with fresh feelings for a real man at the top of his game, one who could command a room but also listen, who could make rules but also take criticism. I had known Parker was cute and smart and all that. But it had eluded me that the man was a *catch*.

But Parker meant baggage. He meant backstories. He meant mothers who were best friends. Most of all, he meant living in the shadow of a dead woman, because Parker would never get over her. And I wasn't willing to put myself through that.

Fortunately, Martin either didn't notice my pause or simply decided not to press me on it. "Traveling with a hanging bag seems like a nightmare," he said.

I rolled my eyes. "It is. It totally is, but Mom will be mad if I'm wrinkled." I sprayed the perfume that Harris got me in the air and walked through it, feeling my annoyance dissipate. "I owe you big-time," I said, turning back to look at my friend.

He nodded. "I know. And don't screw this up. If you throw him out like last week's garbage, it will not do great things for my career."

I smiled. "I won't," I said. And I meant it. I couldn't count the number of times over the months since Thad and I had split that I had said I wasn't going to move on, that I wasn't going to get serious with anyone. And, while Harris and I weren't *serious* per se, we were heading in the direction of serious at a rapid clip. "I think I'll probably stay at his place tonight," I said. "That okay?"

Martin groaned. "Is it okay not to have to sleep with my noise-canceling headphones on? Yeah. I'd say that's okay."

I gasped, flushing, and put my hand to my mouth.

"I'm kidding, I'm kidding," Martin said, even though he wasn't.

I bit my lip and said, "Well, let's just say if I had slept with Harris a little bit earlier, I would have realized a lot of things about my marriage sooner."

I looked at my watch. Five fifteen. I couldn't wait to get to my date, but Harris wasn't meeting me until eight thirty. There was something decidedly less pleasant I had to do first.

I checked my hair and lip gloss in the mirror and adjusted the high waistband of my pants. Martin said, "Are you sure you don't want me to come with you?"

"Of course I want you to come with me. But I think if I have you there as a crutch and a decoy, I'd just be delaying the inevitable."

Martin stood up, kissed me goodbye, and said, "You look fabulous. Knock 'em dead."

As I walked outside, I realized that I still mostly felt like a tourist in New York. And that was a good thing. Every little detail still seemed magical and new. The world was a different place than it had been; I was a different person than I had been. My thoughts wandered to Cape Carolina and to Parker. But I pushed him out of my mind, as I had been doing more and more these past few days.

It distracted me so much that I almost walked right past the Plaza. Abruptly adjusting course, I made my way up the steps and through the revolving gilded door with the pristine *P*s. And as I entered the lobby, my eyes fixed on the intricate, gilded ceiling. I passed a giant arrangement of peonies on my way into the Palm Court. I thought I was cool, calm, and collected, but when my eyes met his across the bar, I realized that, sex or no sex, great dates or not, seeing Thad again, here, in what was my town now, felt like a sucker punch. At least he was alone.

When he saw me, he stood up, ever the gentleman—except, of course, when he was sleeping with other people while we were married. He pulled me to him, and I felt his body go limp against mine, the way it used to, even after everything, even after all of it. We weren't in love. I knew that now. But our bond hadn't disappeared overnight.

When I finally pulled away, he wiped his eyes, and I realized the shoulder of my top was wet. I climbed up onto my bar stool, and Thad followed suit. He took my hand and said, "I just miss you so much, Amelia. Every day."

I made eye contact with the bartender and said, "I'll have whatever you'd make for Eloise if she was all grown-up."

He laughed, and Thad sniffed and laughed, too.

"I miss you, too, Thad. I really do. I'm angry at you, but I'm happy for you. And I hate going through what we're going through, but I love you for all the things you taught me about myself." I paused. Then I finally asked, "Why are we here?"

When Thad had called and said he'd be in New York and asked to meet, I couldn't imagine why. Our divorce was all but done. The papers would be filed next week. In Florida, they get the job done quickly.

He smiled nervously, which made me nervous. I was

grateful a martini glass appeared in front of me with something that tasted like pink lemonade. Cute. This was what a grown-up Eloise would drink for sure.

"First, I wanted to apologize for everything with Kitty that day in our apartment."

I couldn't help but smile. "Yeah. What in the world was that?"

He shook his head. "I feel guilty saying that it has been hard for me because I know it has been hard for you. But I didn't come out. I didn't plan or prepare for it. I was just sort of pushed out with no warning. My entire life changed in one day, and I wasn't ready."

I wanted to say—snarkily—that we were both pushed with no warning, to ask him if he thought my entire life hadn't changed.

"I wasn't prepared for Kitty being so upset, and you know I can't stand it when Kitty is upset."

I nodded, trying to hide my smile. I had never seen a grown man love his grandmother so much.

"She wanted me to stay married to you," he went on. "Maybe have Chase on the side. And, at the time, she convinced me that everyone would be happy. Kitty would be happy because I would appear to be what she wanted. You would be happy because we weren't divorced. Chase would be happy because nothing would change." He shook his head. "About an hour after you left, I realized how ridiculous that was. Everyone wouldn't be happy. No one would be."

I reached over and squeezed his hand. I could tell this was

hard for him. "How are things with Kitty now?" I practically whispered. I knew that losing her might be even harder for Thad than losing me.

"She is happy, happy, happy." He paused and looked at me intently. "Her friends accepted Chase and me right into the fold, and, well, she's also thrilled because we're adopting a baby."

I almost spit out my Eloise martini.

Then he added, "Well, no. Not a baby, probably. Maybe a toddler or a teenager or anything in between. We don't know."

I shook my head about a million times. So. Many. Questions. First: "I thought you didn't want kids. We talked about how we didn't want kids like a million times. Hell, I wrote an entire *New York Times* piece about it."

A reasonable person would have realized that Thad's being gay was why he left me. But in five seconds flat, I had spiraled down into a place where he had left me because I couldn't have children. It was ridiculous, obviously. We could have adopted or a million other options. But in that moment, no one on earth could have convinced me otherwise. It irritated me. Hadn't I made my peace with this like twenty years ago, realized that a biological function didn't define me?

"I know. I didn't think I did. But Chase really does, and the more we talked about it, the more I realized that this was a new chapter for me and what I wanted had changed."

"Well, that's obvious," I said more snarkily than I had meant to, but damn. I signaled to the bartender that I needed another. "And Chase? Really? I thought Chase didn't know we were married. I thought Chase was mad."

Thad scrunched his nose. "Well, I think Chase was a little bit worried about losing all his clients who were team Amelia."

"Traitor," I whispered as the bartender inserted another glass into my hand. We were speaking the same language here. "Unbelievable."

I felt like I was in the ocean, trying to get out past the breakers, but the waves kept hitting me in the face, knocking me to the sandy ocean floor. Every time I got my bearings and tried to swim again, another one just toppled me.

"Amelia, I didn't want to hurt you, but I didn't want you to hear it from someone else."

I realized I was a teeny-tiny bit drunk. And I suddenly felt incredibly tired. I knew tonight was going to end in a giant emotional scene, and Martin seemed like a better person to fall apart with than Harris, so I texted Harris. I'm not really feeling up to a party tonight. Rain check?

He texted back immediately. I'll send the car to get you, and we can order in.

That didn't solve the problem, but I really wanted to see him. Surely I could do that without making any stupid remarks or decisions. Plus, my little double bed in our lipsticked apartment was cute, but Harris's giant, plush, king-sized mattress with its ten million thread count sheets and remote-control blackout shades and meditative surround sleep sounds were impossible to resist. I put my glass down, looked at the bartender, and said, "Don't give me any more alcohol, no matter how hard I beg." He laughed, and a water appeared seconds later.

I looked at Thad. "I'm not sure what I'm supposed to say to you right now."

"Well," he said, looking down at his lap, "I guess I was hoping you'd be happy for me?"

I could feel the amazement written all over my face. "Okay. Yeah. Sure. I'm happy for you." I paused. "No. I tell you what: I am happy for the kid, because every child deserves a great home, and you will be a fantastic father. But I am not quite happy for *you*. Not yet."

I got up and walked out, feeling only a tiny bit hazy, with Thad calling behind me. I wasn't sure exactly what I was going to do, but Harris's car was already waiting for me on the curb. As I slid into the back seat and said, "Hi, Tom. Thanks for getting me," I could feel tears sliding down my cheeks. I wasn't so much sad as I was furious. I felt betrayed, like he'd known I had this one huge insecurity—that I couldn't have children, which I had proven quite handily this year. And now he was rubbing it in my face. I tried to make small talk with Tom and seem normal, but it was pretty impossible to seem normal in front of Harris when I arrived with my tearstained face and shaking voice.

And as he pulled me into him, making me feel so safe and secure and happy, I couldn't help but fall apart. Maybe I hadn't done that enough over these past months. But, boy, did I ever do it then. I fell apart about my marriage and my family's disappointment and not having Parker's babies and breaking his heart all over again and breaking my own and knowing that, as much as I tried to push it away, I felt something for him that he could never feel for me. (I didn't say that to Harris, obviously.) And I hated myself the entire time because *this* was what I had been trying to avoid. I liked Harris. He was handsome and laid-back, and, when we were together, I was the cool girl who didn't have to talk about the future or "what we were." Now I was ruining that with all these emotions.

Despite my better judgment, I allowed a rich, expensive cabernet to soothe my hurt feelings when Harris handed it to me. And when "Moon River" came on and I said I loved that song, I let Harris fold me into his arms and lead me around his kitchen-turned-dance floor, feeling so in sync with him that when he changed the foot he was leading with I didn't even step on his toes. And I ate a delicious, thick steak, which made me feel full and warm and soothed inside. Sitting on Harris's plush couch with a bottled water, the roaring fire feeling warm and good even though it was hot outside, I caught myself off guard saying, "I just want to stay right here forever."

He shocked me by saying, "I wish you would."

I looked at him wide-eyed, my buzz wearing off. I didn't want to make too big a thing of it, so I laughed casually.

And he said, "No, really. I've been thinking about it. I know it's early, but I want you to move in. Here."

The vulnerable part of me wanted to eagerly take the bait that had been offered. But something was holding me back.

"After my giant scene, you still want me to move in with you?"

He laughed. "If *that* was your idea of a major scene, then yes, I want you to move in with me even more."

"I don't know what to say," I said.

"Don't say anything," he said, waving it away. "This has been a big night for you. I know a lot is happening. Just think about it." He paused. "I think we want the same things," he said. "I don't want to be married or have children. You don't want those things, either. We have a great time together. We get each other. This feels like the real thing to me, Amelia."

"It feels like the real thing to me, too," I said.

It startled me to realize that, just a few months ago, all those things he had just said had been the God's honest gospel truth. But then I imagined Parker beside me in that doctor's office, holding my hand, how devastated he seemed as he'd walked out of my apartment just a few days earlier. How I had held myself back from telling him the way I felt when he was around, how everything had seemed right when we were together. In just a few weeks, everything I wanted had completely changed. But I couldn't admit that yet. Not even to myself.

Parker

A REAL CATCH

WHY IN THE HELL DID Amelia have to bring this Harris guy here? I bet he got seasick. I bet he'd never fished a proper tournament in his life. I bet Harris knew not the first thing about the Cape Carolina Summer Splash & Fish, and yet here he was.

Now he'd be fishing with me and my dad and Amelia's dad, and they'd get to be all chummy. Don't get me wrong. I liked the guy. But I couldn't get Amelia to fall in love with me if her rich, handsome boyfriend was around. This nonsense had me off my game, which is the only reason I could figure my mother tricked me into stringing lights in the town square.

"If you can, lift that strand just a little higher, Parker, dar-lin'," Mrs. Stack said, breaking me out of my thoughts. All I could think about was that, when we were in middle school, we called her Mrs. Stacked. She'd been the subject of every Mrs. Robinson fantasy in Cape Carolina. Now the memory makes me cringe.

But lucky for her, we all started volunteering for the Summer Splash around the age of twelve, and, looking around and seeing that Watson, Spence, and even useless-ass Mason (who hadn't been out of bed this early since last year's Summer Splash) were here helping, it seemed like, no matter the original reason why, the action stuck.

I gave Mason credit: he was a bigger man than I was. Watson, Spence, and I were the reason the 2000 number one draft pick was living at home with his parents. I was still pissed at him for what he said about Greer last time I was home, but I was trying to let it go.

"Mace!" I shouted to my brother, who was on another ladder about twenty feet away from me. "Catch!" I threw him a strand that I had secured in my tree branch and he secured it to his, then threw it to Spence, and so on and so forth. After twenty years, we pretty much had this whole situation down.

I couldn't see my mom or Mrs. Saxton or Trina. But I could hear them. Mom and Mrs. Saxton were continuing in the legacy of their mothers, the charter members of the Cape Carolina Garden Club, and Trina was the next generation to carry the torch. After four years, they'd finally gotten the town's approval and raised the money to install a gazebo by the pond, and they were making sure that the flowers around it looked perfect. Or, well, actually, Robby was. Poor guy. He'd drawn the short straw. We'd all been there, though. Because the Cape Carolina Garden Club didn't plant or prune; they pointed. Today, they were pointing at Robby.

By tomorrow, the entire square would be transformed with lights and flowers, food and wine, and, in the middle of it all, a dance floor with a band where the whole town gathered. Grandchildren danced with grandparents and neighbors with neighbors, couples and singles. Everyone had fun. I never got nervous about dancing because I'd been doing it my whole life with my mom and my grandmother, Amelia's aunt Tilley, the girl with the pigtails in my third-grade class, and, yes, even Mrs. Stacked. Stack. Force of habit.

But the first time I brought Greer here, I danced only with her. I could see only Greer, in her long yellow dress, a flower in her hair. The night she died, I closed my eyes and thought about her under the twinkle lights that I had hung on the dance floor at the Summer Splash. That's how I wanted to remember her: free and alive.

My stomach rolled as I thought about the possibility of dancing with Amelia tomorrow night. Right then, I realized something: there was room for two great loves in my life. I could remember Greer. But I could also love Amelia. In a way, I always had.

"That's all, boys," Mrs. Stack called. "Thanks for your time."

She winked at me as I climbed down the ladder and said, "Save me a dance, Parker."

Twenty years ago, that would have given me bragging rights for months.

"You fishing with your dad tomorrow?" Watson asked, coming up beside me.

"Yeah. You?"

He nodded.

"And Amelia's new paramour," Mason said, walking up. I had to control my eye roll. "But not for long," he added.

"What does that mean?" I asked, my heart racing. Had he heard something? Did she feel the same way about me as I did about her?

"Oh, I saw the way she was looking at me last time she was home. I think I've got a shot."

"Yeah," I said under my breath. "She's just dying to get back with you after how well you treated her last time." It was unfair, but the thought of Mason going after Amelia had me rattled, especially after my new realization.

He got up in my face. "What did you say to me?"

"Hey, man, chill out," Spence said, running up behind us now.

"I said you don't have a shot with Amelia," I said, getting closer to him now. "What are you going to do about it? Are you going to tackle me in the town square? Make Mrs. Stack call Mom? We're in our thirties, man. Grow up."

The flash in his eye told me that Mason was furious, but, much to my surprise, he didn't tackle me in the town square. But could he seriously want Amelia back? She'd never get back with Mason, right? The thought of my brother with the only woman that made me feel like I could move on made me sick.

"I hate to break your heart, man," Spence interjected as we all started walking in the direction of home again, "but I'm pretty sure you're not the Thaysden brother that has a chance with Amelia."

Mason looked at me like I was dog shit and said, "Ass face couldn't convert the point if his life depended on it." But then he slung his arm around my shoulder in a brotherly way, so I assumed we were fine. He was quick to anger, but he was also quick to forgive, thank God. Otherwise there was no way we'd all be standing here together right now. "I'm just giving you a hard time, little bro. You got this."

I wanted to act cool in front of my friends and my brother. That impulse never changes. But I needed support. "Do you guys really think I should go for it with Amelia?"

"She tried to have your baby, man," Spence said. "If you're waiting for a sign, I think that was it."

Spence's wife, Christina, stepped out of the gazebo, and their toddler daughter wriggled out of her mom's arms and ran down the brick sidewalk, squealing, "Daddy!" as he lifted her up into the air.

Watson was saying, "You've got to get back out there."

Watching one of my oldest, best buddies hold his daughter, I realized that Amelia wasn't all I wanted. I wanted to be a dad; I wanted to be a family.

"You're just getting started," Spence chimed in.

Walking down the brick sidewalk with two of my oldest, best buddies and my brother in the town that raised me, I couldn't help but wonder if maybe Spence was right.

Amelia

— ❦ —

WISTFUL AND ROMANTIC

"I PROMISE YOU THAT THEY'LL teach you," I lied for the millionth time.

"But what if I throw up? What if we have a huge fish, and I'm trying to reel it in and I lose it, and then they lose the tournament because of me?"

Harris and I were watching fishing videos on YouTube, and I truly couldn't decide if I was doing the right thing. I mean, yeah, I was feeding Harris to the wolves. In 2045, I would be hearing about the time they had to take that pretty city boy on the boat and he nearly drowned or some other hyperbolized account of how unmanly Harris was. I had never seen him the least bit vulnerable, and it made me like him even more. I felt such an outpouring of compassion for him in that moment that I leaned over and kissed him.

He smiled. "Are you going to tell your parents we're moving in together?"

I grimaced. "I think I'll just keep paying for the apartment indefinitely and pretend I live there."

He laughed. "You're not honestly telling me that they are going to be scandalized by their thirty-five-year-old daughter living with her boyfriend?"

I didn't say anything, but he had no idea. My mother would not care that her friends' children had all lived with significant others before marriage. She would not care that I was old enough to make my own decisions, that I liked Harris and I loved the agreement about our lives that we—as grown-ups—had reached. She would only care that she had not raised me to live with a man I wasn't married to and that I was directly defying those orders. "Maybe we should tell them at Christmas?" I smiled encouragingly.

He laughed. "Amelia, that's, like, six months away."

"Oh! Oh!" I said. "Maybe we could make up an elaborate story about something horrible that happened at my apartment and you are sacrificing and lovingly taking me in, as a friend, and letting me live in your guest room."

My new favorite thing in life was going to Harris's after a long day at work and making dinner together with soft music playing in the background and drinking sophisticated wine and talking about everything—the new story idea I had, how far I had gotten into my research, his funny miscommunications with a new overseas client, the state of the environment and the world, and our separate friends who were quickly becoming our mutual friends. I really, truly, solidly looked forward to doing those things without having to pack an overnight bag. But did I *love* him? I couldn't tell. I felt like he was a good friend that was also super hot and who I liked to sleep with. Maybe that *was* love. *Stupid Thad*, I thought. I couldn't even tell if I was in love anymore, for heaven's sake.

I looked at Harris again, studied the lines in his forehead, which were deeper when he was being sincere, the boyish sandy blond of his hair, how adorable he looked lounging in his Peter Millar athletic wear.

"Babe, look," he said. "I get it. The South is different, your parents are old fashioned. Maybe I don't understand it completely, but I'm trying to. All I know is that we're good together. We want the same things. I can tell them with you, if you want, but it would be a shame to ruin something great over some outdated idea of what a relationship should look like."

Maybe the salt air made me feel wistful and romantic, or maybe it was how sincere he was. But in that moment, I decided firmly that being with him—in the way that worked for us—was worth the scrutiny of my family. I was thirty-five years old, for heaven's sake. "I'll tell them now," I said. I could give them time to get used to the idea of us moving in sometime, pretend it existed in a hazy and far-off future.

He picked up my hand and kissed it. "You still have a tan line where your ring used to be."

That was true. "I know. I should probably get something to fill up the space."

I didn't love how that sounded. And I had to wonder if filling up space was exactly, precisely what I was doing with Harris.

* * *

Three hours later, I was kissing him goodbye, saying, "Are you sure you're okay if I go? I feel just terrible leaving you here."

Harris had a conference call in China that couldn't be rescheduled, so he was going to take a Benadryl, go to sleep now, at seven, so he could get up at two, take the call, grab a quick nap, and be on the dock at five. Bless the man's sweet heart. I felt awful. But he had to go fishing. Even though the ridicule would be significant, it was nothing compared to what would happen if he didn't go. I had left out the part about how the prize money, depending on the size and number of the fish caught, could be upwards of a million dollars. He was nervous enough when he just thought this was for fun.

I kissed him gently, marveling that I had brought a new boy home to meet my parents. Lo and behold, Mom and Daddy—who sighed and rolled their eyes and made considerable fuss about why I couldn't find a nice Southern boy—really loved Harris. In fact, he kind of made Mom swoon, which was a real plus.

Daddy wasn't a huge fan of the Summer Splash, and he wasn't going, which I thought made him a bad sport, but I didn't say so. Instead, I took Mom as my date. As she climbed in the passenger side, her yellow-and-white-striped shirt-dress's full skirt swishing around her calves, toned from her Pilates regimen, I said, "So, Mom, what do you think?"

She looked at me very seriously and said, "I was prepared to hate him. I *wanted* to hate him. But, darling girl, that man is a doll. He is perfection roaming the face of the earth."

I was doing my best to back out of the very long driveway when she said, "And what's more, he is madly in love with you."

I glanced at her as I turned onto the road. "You think?"

She nodded and pursed her lips. "Anyone could see it, but he told me so himself."

I laughed out loud. "Then why on earth hasn't he told *me*?"

"He thinks he'll scare you off. After the whole Thad debacle." She paused and let out a low whistle.

"It will no longer be a debacle as of tomorrow," I said.

"They get it done in Florida, don't they? Time flies when you're having fun." She paused and winked. "With Harris."

I laughed again. "I've already signed. I'm just glad it's over." I paused. "But, like, what do I do tomorrow?"

"Do about what, darling?"

"Well, I mean, do I call Thad? Do I text him?"

She gasped audibly. "Call that two-timing life destroyer? I very much think not. After what he did to you . . ." She trailed off, and I could tell she was trying to calm herself down. That woman could work herself into a frenzy.

"It's just weird, you know. Like, he was my best friend, and now it's all over." I paused. "He and Chase are getting married. And adopting a child."

When we entered downtown, I pulled into the first parking spot I saw on the side of the street. We would have to walk a couple of blocks, but I was surprised to find a spot at all. As I opened the door, I could already hear the band playing. It made me smile. The simplicity of it all.

"That is just the worst betrayal yet. How could he do this to you?" Mom said.

I shrugged. It was strange because I couldn't even really work up to feeling mad. But that wasn't fair because I had been mad. And devastated. And jealous. And insecure. All the things, I think, that are natural to feel when the person who is supposed to love you most betrays you. I'd had time to be all those things and let them pass, but this was brand-new for my mom. We walked down the sidewalk, making our way toward the party.

"Hi, sweet Amelia." Mrs. Abrams, my kindergarten teacher, waved. She was walking past, presumably on her way to the dance, too.

"Hi, Mrs. Abrams," I said, basking in the familiarity of home. It was special, this place. This town. Every time I was here, I had a pang for my old life, where everyone knew me, where I belonged.

Larry walked by, pushing an old-fashioned ice cream cart. "You want anything?" he paused to ask us. Larry was a veteran who decided when he retired that he needed something to keep him happy and in shape. So he bought an ice cream cart and walked it around five days a week, giving away free goodies to every kid and a lot of the adults in town. It was an undeniably generous calling—and, ironically, it kept him in great shape. He said he'd never cared much for ice cream.

"No, thanks, Larry. Maybe later?"

He nodded. "You know where to find me."

He didn't even have to ask my mother. I wondered if she'd ever had ice cream in her entire life.

"You know, Mom, I think I've made my peace with it."

She put her arm around my waist and bumped my hip with hers. "Finding a Harris will do that for a girl."

We shared a smile, and Walt, our preacher, grabbed my mother away from me and pulled her onto the dance floor. The Summer Splash had begun, and everyone, it seemed, was ecstatic. I ignored how my stomach flip-flopped when I spotted Parker across the room. In his navy shorts and his blue-and-white-checked shirt with the sleeves rolled up, he was taking his mother for a spin around the dance floor. It was positively darling. His dad didn't like the Summer Splash, either. And both our dads were, no doubt, sitting somewhere together, drinking bourbon and strategizing about the morning's fishing.

I was about to sit down on a park bench on the perimeter where I could see the action, feeling a small pang that Harris wasn't here with me—we hadn't had an occasion to dance together in public yet—when Parker came up next to me and said, "Miss Amelia, might I have this dance?"

My heart raced when he took my hand. I couldn't very well say no. But, roles reversed, I wouldn't want Harris dancing with a woman who made his heart beat a little too fast.

Parker put one hand on the small of my back. I had danced with him before, sure, that night in Palm Beach in Philip and Sheree's living room. But that had been drunken and wild. That had been before I had so cavalierly offered to have his baby, before I hadn't made good on my promise. I was trying to forget. But being with him now, sober and sincere, made me remember.

"I've missed you," he said into my ear.

It was so simple yet so cryptic. He'd missed me. Missed me how? He'd missed me like you do an old neighbor? Or a good friend? Or he'd missed me like you miss a woman you've pined for? There was so much gray area there. And I knew I shouldn't care. But I did.

"I've missed you, too," I replied honestly.

He pulled back and studied my face. "Really? I'm surprised you've had the time, as busy as you've been with your new boyfriend."

I rolled my eyes, but I wasn't sure why. Was it because I was home, in the arms of a boy I had known my entire life, and that was the exact reaction my fifteen-year-old self would have had? Or was it because my heart knew something that my head didn't?

"I'm thinking about moving in with him," I said nonchalantly, as though we hadn't all but decided what our future would hold, as if I wasn't planning on packing boxes next week.

"Do you have to?" he replied without skipping a beat.

I laughed. He'd caught me off guard. "I mean, no. I don't *have* to, but it seems like a good idea." I paused. "Right?"

"You could move back to Palm Beach," he said teasingly.

"And do what?"

He pulled me closer and said in my ear, "Whatever you want."

If I thought my heart was racing before, now I was certain. Whatever I wanted. Did I want to be with Parker? Why, when I pictured a life with Parker, did it all seem so clear? What about his perfect, untainted memory of Greer? I could never compete with that. I was alive and imperfect. We would fight. We would be messy. We would have a real life together, and she would always be there in the background. Things with Harris were just simpler. They were grown-up. They were uncomplicated.

Before I could respond, Elayna, this nightmare of a girl I went to high school with, danced up beside us with Ray, her high school boyfriend-turned-husband. "Hey, girl," she said, elbowing me, "I hear this one's straight. You might want to hold on to him."

I knew she was trying to be funny. Probably. And it was clear she was a little drunk. But, as okay as I had been seconds earlier, that didn't sit well with me. Parker must have sensed it, because he took my hand and led me off the dance floor. Suddenly, all those warm and fuzzy hometown feelings were gone. Now I wanted to be anywhere but here. Sure, Elayna might have been the only person tacky enough to actually say that to my face, but that didn't mean everyone else in the brightly lit town square wasn't thinking or saying the same thing. I looked around for my mom and, when I didn't see her, said, "Park, could you take me home?"

"Sure," he said. He hadn't let go of my hand, and no, I hadn't made an attempt to get him to do so. I would grapple with that later. For now, instead of making me feel loved and a part of a community, the music filling the air and the sounds of chatter and laughter were making me feel even more alone.

It wasn't until Parker and I were in his car, by ourselves, that I began to feel, once again, like all was right with the world.

Parker

STUCK

NEEDLESS TO SAY, I COULDN'T sleep. If Elayna hadn't interrupted, what would Amelia have said? Would she have wanted to give us a shot? Could we have finally broken through this gray area to the truth?

I knew that Amelia saw the loss of the babies as a failure, could tell that it was weighing on her. And I was now more convinced than ever that I wanted to be a dad. Sometimes I still considered hiring a surrogate for the last two embryos. But what had seemed like such a great plan months ago, now only made me feel lonely.

I finally got up and went to the window, opening the drawn curtains and looking out onto the water. I wondered where Greer was now, what she could see, if heaven was as beautiful as this part of earth.

And then I saw her. Not Greer. Amelia. I couldn't help but

smile. How many times had I watched her out this window? How many nights had she taken to her kayak with nothing more than the light of the moon as her guide? I double-checked to make sure she was alone, that Harris was nowhere in sight, then I opened the door of the octagon house we had shared only a few months ago, and made my way down to the Saxtons' dock, where their kayaks were in racks.

I pulled one by its top handle. She had been able to lift this by herself? The stillness and cool of the night was refreshing, the way the moon painted a trail onto the water hypnotic. I watched as Amelia paddled lazily, turning left into the "maze," as we used to call it, into a tall patch of marsh grass. The path through it changed often. It was one of our favorite parts of childhood to try to navigate it in a new way, sometimes successfully, sometimes getting stuck in the oyster beds below.

The kayak made a small splash as I dropped it into the water and slid in myself, holding a paddle in my left hand. I pushed away from the dock, realizing that there was almost no current tonight, and made the box with my arms that Mason had taught me almost thirty years ago. I slid the paddle in smooth, nearly silent strokes, marveling at how it could seem so dark and then—once your eyes adjusted to the brightness of the moon on the water, to the vividness of the stars—so incredibly light.

I reached the entrance of the maze quickly, expecting to paddle furiously to catch up to Amelia. But when I turned, she was sitting right at the edge, as though she was waiting for me.

I was behind her, and even though she couldn't have seen me, she said, "I didn't want to get stuck out here alone."

The weight of her words struck me, heavy and poignant. What did she not want stuck, her kayak? Herself? Maybe both. And what about me? Did I feel stuck? I decided, as I paddled right up beside her, yes. These past three years I had been a kind of stuck I never could have imagined. Everything that used to be in color seemed gray. My job. My house. My life. Even my friends in Palm Beach. Everything around me was covered with the scent of Greer, the feel of Greer, the memory of Greer. It was only now that I realized that while, yes, it had helped me remember her, maybe some things are meant to fade, maybe some things have to fade in order for us to quit feeling trapped. Because that's what I was. But the thought of moving out of that house, of resigning from my position at her company, made me feel light-headed. It was too hard. It was too much. And, yeah, I guessed I knew she was never coming back for me. I had known that the entire time. And that made letting go of the life we had shared that much harder.

But then Amelia came back into my life, and everything seemed light again. At first, it was the prospect of having the babies, of having a piece of Greer back. But then I realized that it wasn't about Greer. It was about Amelia, about the way she made me laugh, the way my heart sped up when she smiled at me, the way she made me realize that my ability to love didn't die with Greer.

I turned my head to look at Amelia, shifting slightly in my

kayak. She turned, and her eyes met mine. We were so close. "I was okay with being stuck out here alone," I said. "I'd made my peace with it."

She nodded.

I looked down at my hands, afraid of what I would find in her face when I confessed, "But I'd rather be with you."

And suddenly, the silence, which had been so peaceful, became deafening.

When Amelia pushed away from me and started paddling, I knew I had blown it. I shouldn't have said all that, shouldn't have put her on the spot. She had a boyfriend; she was planning a future. But how could I not say it? How could I continue to live a life where she didn't know? I sighed, paddling behind her. There was nothing else to do. I wanted to hang back, but my desire to help her get her kayak up on the dock was even stronger than my desire to save face.

I paddled up ahead of her and jumped out, pulling my boat out of the water. She bumped the dock, and I leaned down to take her paddle and then her hands. I pulled her up, my fingers on her skin feeling electric and jolting. Just as I noticed the way the moon glowed on her beautiful face, she wrapped her arms around my neck. I leaned down, pausing to take it in, the flowery smell of Amelia and the earthy smell of the marsh, the sounds of the night making this patch of earth feel alive and thrumming, the moon bathing us in its light, the stars conspiring to give us this swept away feeling. My lips met hers, slightly salty from the air and the water and, as I kissed her and kept kissing her, never wanting to stop, as I pulled her in tighter and closer to me like I would never let her go again, the bullfrogs silenced, the cicadas stopped singing, the world quit spinning. Everything faded away except for Amelia, me, and this one moment that was so perfect, so right, I knew for sure that neither of us could ever deny it again.

Elizabeth

THE FABRIC OF FAMILY

I KNEW OLIVIA WAS GOING to be furious. Positively furious. I wanted to wait until the morning to tell her, but when she showed up at my door with a bottle of chardonnay in her hand and her best scheming look on her face, I knew I wasn't going to be able to put it off. She was grinning from ear to ear. I was in trouble.

"He loves her," she said, her voice gleeful.

I pulled her in the front door, putting my finger to my mouth.

"Harris," I whispered, pointing upstairs.

Olivia rolled her eyes. Her cheeks were flushed. This is awful to say, but I loved her so much more at times like this, when she had about a half glass of wine in her. Not too much. But my best friend could be terribly serious, and she was so much more fun when she loosened up just a touch.

But tonight, I knew I was going to take the fun down several (hundred) notches.

I almost broke down and cried right then and there. How many more times would my best friend walk through my door like this, like she had thousands of times since our childhood? Just before Amelia came back to town, Charles and I had had a very real conversation about our future, and, much to my surprise, I had finally acquiesced. No, we weren't old yet, but we were getting too old to take care of such a large house. It didn't make sense, financially or otherwise. Charles felt suffocated by the place that made me feel warm and protected. Robby and Trina weren't interested in dedicating their lives to a house like Charles and I had. And I wasn't sure how Amelia was even paying her rent right now.

Charles tried to console me by saying that we could live in the cabin behind Dogwood, that we would still be on our same land. Liv would still be right next door. Nothing would change.

But everything would change. The mere thought of leaving this beautiful home where I had carved my initials in the banister, where my great-grandmother had given birth to my grandmother upstairs, where my grandparents had hosted black-tie affairs and dinner parties that I had watched from the top of the staircase, where my children had taken their first steps, where my sister and I had pulled off the biggest secret of our lives . . . This wasn't a house. It was the fabric of my family, woven thread by thread, memory by memory.

I couldn't share any of that with Liv, I decided. Not yet. Not now. The sorrow was too big to digest. Pulling her into the kitchen and pointing to a stool at the island, I produced a wine opener from the drawer, got two glasses, poured, and handed her one. Then I sat down beside her, and we both swiveled so our knees were almost touching, the same way we had done since we were barely toddlers.

"How do you know he loves her?" I whispered.

Her eyes were glittering. "Did you see them dancing tonight? The whole town knows they're in love now."

"I don't want to tell you this," I said.

Her face darkened.

"But I think she loves Harris."

Elizabeth made a skeptical sound and said, "Oh, please. They have nothing in common. It'll never work."

But I knew that they did have quite a lot in common. They both loved books and art and music. They both loved New York. She smiled a lot when Harris was around, and, well, that was good enough for me. Not that I was abandoning my dreams of my best friend and me being sort of related. I wasn't. But I was willing to put my daughter's happiness above that, I'm happy to report.

I shrugged, and Olivia crossed her arms. "Do you mean to tell me that we have done all of this—*all* of this—for nothing?"

Olivia is a dreamer, a talker. She will talk, talk, talk about something, and when it doesn't magically materialize, she is flabbergasted because, even though she has done absolutely nothing to help the situation on its way, she feels like she has. I usually think it's hilarious, but tonight it didn't seem funny at all.

"I don't know, Liv. I could be wrong. I have been wrong before. I think I'm just so happy to see her smile again."

She took a fortifying sip of her wine. "I am, too. Obviously. But I want to see him happy, too, Liz. It has been years, and I'm just afraid that he'll never find joy again. He lights up when Amelia is around." She shrugged. "He always has."

Now I was torn. I wanted Amelia to be happy. But what if she could be happy with Parker? We had thought she could be happy with Mason, but that was before, well, everything. And I felt grateful that she hadn't gone down with his sinking ship. A lot of girls her age would have. And I was grateful that my friendship with Liv had recovered. A lesser friendship never would have survived.

"You know what, Liv? I think it's time for you to tell him."

She nodded stoically. "Are you sure?"

"She might settle down with this Harris. And I'm okay with that. But this also might be the last chance, if Parker really that way, for him to tell her."

She took the last sip of her chardonnay and stood up. I stood, too, and tried to hand her the bottle back, but she waved it away.

"Nothing to do now but let the chips fall where they may," Liv said. Usually, I had an idea of where I wanted the chips to fall, but, on this point, I was a little torn. I said a silent prayer for it all to work out. Whether she chose Harris or Parker—or simply lived out the rest of her life alone—all I wanted was for my daughter to be happy again.

Amelia

ASPARAGUS

I KNEW THE FISHING TOURNAMENT had gone even worse than I'd expected as soon as I saw all their faces. And that's saying a lot because I expected it to go truly terribly. Maybe he had thrown up. Or maybe he had let a fish get away.

"Cool boyfriend you have there," Mason said, under his breath, as he slid by me.

I glanced up at Parker, who rolled his eyes and shook his head, but then flashed me a tiny, secret smile that made my heart race—and my guilty conscience surge. Dad had gone straight upstairs, which was a good call because they all smelled horrific after a day of sun, wind, sweat, beer, and, yes, fish guts.

I took Harris's arm and guided him protectively up the stairs. "What on earth?" I whispered.

"Well, for a second, I was the hero. I hooked a marlin, it

trailed the boat for almost thirty minutes, and I did it. I reeled that sucker in. It was the biggest rush of my life. I had no idea what I was doing, but it was just instinct. My hunter-gatherer ancestors were taking over. I was in it. I was in control. It was man versus animal, and man would prevail. Everyone was yelling and high-fiving me. For, like, two hours, I was in."

I wanted to say something, but I didn't know what. I held my breath.

"And then," he said, like it was a full sentence.

"And then what?" I asked, pulling him into my bedroom and closing the door behind him, motioning for him to sit down on the bed.

"Did you know that every person on a boat has to have a fishing license?"

I gasped and put my hand over my mouth. Oh my gosh. He didn't have to say anything else. Every person on a boat had to have a fishing license. It didn't matter if you were in the galley flipping pancakes when the fish came in. I was sure they got a ticket and had been disqualified from the tournament. All that beautiful prize money and all those bragging rights just gone, in an instant. I was so used to everyone I knew receiving a lifetime hunting and fishing license when they were born that it hadn't even occurred to me. Shouldn't Dad have thought of that? Or Parker? Had they set him up?

He rested his head on my shoulder, and I stroked his cheek, bathing in guilt that I had brought him and, even worse, that I had kissed Parker. No, not kissed Parker. Made out with Parker like a teenager for much longer than I would like to admit, totally unable to pull myself away from him. "Poor baby. I am so sorry. This is my fault. I should have known."

"We won, Amelia. They won. All that glory, and poof! Just gone."

"I know, Harris," I said soothingly. "But it's okay. It isn't the end of the world."

He sat up and looked at me seriously. "They will hate me forever now. I will never be a part of your world the way I want to be because of this stupid, stupid thing."

"No, no," I lied. "They'll all forget about it." They would never, ever forget about it. And, unlike the other scenarios I had imagined, it would take a long time for any of them to treat this like a funny anecdote. Yeah, maybe it was stupid that a fishing tournament was so important to them. But it was. Yeah, the loss of nearly seven figures worth of prize money hurt. But I knew it was the loss of the bragging rights of a lifetime that bothered my dad and Mr. Thaysden most of all.

⋆   ⋆   ⋆

Later that night, I finally convinced Harris to show his face. Harris; my friends Sarah, Jennifer, and Madison; Parker's friends Spence and Watson; Robby and Trina; and, of course, Parker were milling around the Thaysdens' porch. It was a tradition of sorts, that the "kids" gathered for dinner at the Thaysdens' after the tournament and the "adults" gathered at Dogwood. Our hometown friends were all married now, but the spouses that weren't Cape Carolina natives had politely bowed out after the first year. This was an old-school Cape Carolina tradition. It was awkward when other people joined in. But we couldn't very well tell Harris to stay in my old bedroom.

We had all gotten the routine down over the past two decades or so: Parker cooked the steaks on the grill, Sarah was in charge of twice-baked potatoes, I handled the asparagus, which couldn't have been simpler—olive oil, lemon, salt, pan—and Spence made his famous sangria. We had garlic bread if Watson wasn't so drunk from fishing all day that he burned it. It hadn't happened yet, but we were holding out hope.

I was feeling mightily uncomfortable, not only about my boyfriend ruining half the lives in that room, but also because of the night before with Parker. I stole a glance or two at him, looking so competent and strong in his apron at the grill. He wanted to be with me. The night before, I had been more than certain that I wanted to be with him too. But then there was Harris and the fun we had and the plans we had made. . . . So I avoided it. I sat here on a teak bench overlooking the marsh, with my friends gathered around drinking their beverages of choice, as Trina said, "So, of course, the teacher says, 'Well, Robby Jr. was calling a girl at school 'butt face,' and when I told him he couldn't call her that anymore, he started calling her 'poopy-pants.' And it's awful, and I know it, and she is so serious, and what do I do? I burst out laughing. And she looks at me like, *No wonder your kid is a delinquent.*"

And then we all burst out laughing because, well, it was funny, and also Trina was so animated and adorable as she told the story that you just couldn't help but join in the fun. Harris's arm was around my shoulder, and he squeezed me to him and kissed my temple right as Parker caught my eye.

So I did what any woman in my position would do: I finished off the rest of my beer and reached down into the cooler beside me to get another one. The fact that this was my fourth beer was perhaps not totally ideal, which I realized as I stood up for dinner.

I have plenty of friends who are the good kind of drunk. You know, the ones who get really quiet so as not to make fools of themselves? Well, not me. I am the kind of drunk who doesn't exactly realize that she's totally wasted, instead finding herself more charming and adorable than ever. So I just get louder and tell more stories, and everyone else is laughing their heads off, partly because they're drunk, too, thank God, partly because they actually think I'm funny, and partly because I'm embarrassing myself so badly.

After I served the asparagus on the fine china, I sat down at the head of the table. And who was to my left and right? Why, Harris and Parker. Charming. Comfortable. So now I was drunk *and* nervous, which made me drink more and talk more, which is the only reason I can possibly imagine that I said, through my second bite of dinner, "I'm lucky that my pee never smells like asparagus."

Spence, from the other end of the table said, "It's not that your pee doesn't smell like asparagus. It's that you don't have the gene to be able to smell it."

"Wait, wait, back up," Jennifer said. "So what you're saying is that everyone's pee smells like asparagus, it's just that only some people can smell it?"

"Exactly," Spence said, looking very self-assured.

"I can't smell it," Trina said.

"Me neither," Robby chimed in.

"Oh, I can," Parker said. "Definitely."

"Me too," Harris said. "Just a little fun fact about the man you're moving in with."

Everyone around the table was chattering loudly, and I was finishing my beer, which is the only reason I can imagine that I said, "I want to see if my pee actually smells like asparagus. Who will smell it for me?"

The table quieted down, I think sensing that something pretty exciting was happening at our end, and, as Harris said, "Gross, Amelia. No way," Parker chimed in, very seriously, "I'll do it."

The drunk version of Amelia who believed she was charming said, "Oh, yay!"

And then I proceeded to stand up and teeter down the hall to the master bathroom, Parker on my heels.

As he closed the door behind him, I think I sobered up just enough to realize that this was crazy and also inappropriate. So I said, "Oh, Park. You don't have to smell my pee."

He laughed. "Lia, if the past thirtysomething years haven't

proven this to you, there is nothing that I wouldn't do for you. I will even smell your asparagus pee."

Even though he laughed as he said it, I knew he was serious. And it felt so heavy, that statement.

"Hey, Park," I said, "if my trying to have your baby didn't prove it, I'd do anything for you, too."

I leaned back against the vanity, the edge cold and hard through my sundress. I glanced over at the silver tray Olivia kept perfectly organized with makeup. When I was little, Mom never let me play in her makeup. But Olivia always did. I almost wanted to pick up one of her softer-than-air brushes and swirl it in powder just to feel it on my face.

Parker took a step toward me, and that's when I realized, once and for all, that I wanted him to keep walking toward me, that there might have been a man out there who was handsome and smart and strong, but when I thought about love, how it felt, it wasn't him that I thought of. It was Parker. Spending time with him again was the first time my guard had really been down since . . . since, well, ever. My entire life I had these walls up when it came to men, when it came to actually really, truly loving someone in a way that could shatter my world. I had gotten the exact type of love I had given, guarded and self-protective. And I had received the type of love I had believed I deserved. But I was starting to see that maybe I could have more.

He took another step toward me, this time with more intention, and ran his hands down my arms. My breath was shorter now, and I suddenly felt very, very sober. I leaned toward him, my lips almost grazing his, the kiss that I had craved all day so close to happening.

As the bathroom door flew open, he jumped away as though I had bitten him. "So, what's the verdict?" Madison trilled.

I laughed nervously, trying to pretend that nothing had happened, nothing was happening. "Oh, um . . ."

"It smells like asparagus," Parker jumped in confidently.

Trina appeared at the door. "Pee sniffer! There's a new one for Robby Jr. to try."

We all laughed, the tension breaking. As Parker caught my eye, making my heart race, I briefly considered that maybe everything that had happened between us was colliding in this moment, conspiring to bring us back where we belonged.

Parker

CONNECTED

I WAS MORE THAN A little bit surprised when I got home after midnight after a very eventful dinner to see that my mom was sitting on the back porch. I didn't want to talk; I wanted to sit alone with my thoughts about Amelia and me and analyze every inch of it. But I slid open the back door, and she said, "Sit down, honey."

I took a seat beside her on the sofa, noticing how loudly the bullfrogs were croaking. The winds of the morning had calmed to a gentle breeze and the marsh grass blew, the moon highlighting the water that ran through it.

I noticed an envelope in Mom's hand as I sat down beside her, trying to appear sober. She took my hand in hers, and my heart started racing. Not in the way it had when I was alone in that bathroom with Amelia earlier. But in the way it did when I was afraid. Something was wrong with my mother. In the seconds before her next sentence, I decided that she had terminal breast cancer, that she had been fighting it for months, maybe even years, without letting me know. Because that's the kind of mother she was. I had to call Dad and grill him about once a week because my mother was so damn secretive.

The splash of a fish that I couldn't see jumping out of the water broke me out of my thoughts, and I finally got my nerve up to say, "What's the matter, Mom?"

She smiled at me, and I had the most vivid memory of being four years old, of falling in the driveway and skinning my knee. Mom had run out from the kitchen and knelt down to pull me into her lap and kiss me, and she had given me this same smile, one meant to bolster but that also held undeniable pity.

She put her hand up to her white blouse, her plain gold wedding band catching the light. "Darling, I have tossed and turned over whether I should say this to you. You know I believe in letting my boys run their own business." She paused and looked at me thoughtfully. "But, well, I believe that you love Amelia. And Elizabeth believes that she loves Harris. And while I'm not saying that she doesn't, I have to wonder if she knew how you felt about her, she might change her mind about him."

I thought about the night before on the dock. I thought about that horrible day in the car on the way home from the doctor's office when all I wanted to do was make it better for Amelia.

"I think about it, Mom. I really do. But then there's Greer, and I loved her so much that I worry I might not ever be able to move on. If I try and fail, I've lost Amelia forever. We will always be in each other's lives because of you and Elizabeth."

Mom nodded. "It's a big step to put yourself out there like that, to say something that huge that you can never take back. I'm not saying that you should. I can't make that decision for you, darling. But I can tell you that I hope with all my heart that you don't let what you lost keep you from what you could have. I don't mean just with Amelia. Life is short. Love is precious, and it makes living so worthwhile."

"What if Greer is looking down on me, and knowing that I've moved on breaks her heart?"

She looked out over the water and said, "You know, sweetheart, Greer made me promise that, when she was gone, I would take care of everything. So I did. I took care of her funeral plans and accepting the casseroles and writing the thank-you notes and getting the death certificate and dealing with the estate. I made good on my promise—except for one thing." She paused and looked at me. "I haven't taken care of you, though God himself knows how hard I've tried."

"Mom—" I interrupted. I wanted to tell her that I wasn't her responsibility, I had to take care of myself. But if she heard me interject, she didn't let on.

"Greer gave me something for you. It has sat for three years between the sock that holds my mother's pearls and the sock that holds my grandmother's earrings. All of my most important things are, as it turns out, stored in that humblest of drawers." She turned to me, and my mouth went dry. "Greer had said I would know when it was time. And I do. I finally have to take care of the one remnant of Greer's life that matters most."

She handed me the envelope she'd been holding and, when she turned it over, I saw it. My name. In the scrawling cursive that only belonged to one beautiful woman.

Mom kissed my cheek, and then she was gone. I put my finger to the sharp corner of the thick paper envelope. I flipped it over to reveal Greer's engraved return address. Our return address. The letter was written on our wedding thank-you cards, the ones that I had spent two hours at the stationer's over, while Greer and her aunt hemmed and hawed. They had landed on simple ecru stationery engraved in gold. I knew when I opened it I would find *Greer and Parker Thaysden* at the top of the card. It was the simplest thing, yet a million decisions, conscious and unconscious, had gone into it—kind of like love.

Greer and I had fit together so seamlessly, it felt like, but there *had* been a million decisions that had gone into our love.

Then I slid my finger underneath the seal of the envelope, imagining her licking it shut. Part of me wanted to rip into that letter, to read and reread it all night. But I didn't. I sat with it, staring at her handwriting as if it could bring her back from the dead, for far longer than I would like to admit.

I took a deep breath, got my nerve up, pulled the thick card out of its envelope, and read.

Greer

‿❦‿

July 19, 2016

Dearest Parker,

    Everything changes when you know it is the end. Even three months ago, the idea of you with someone else made my insides wrench and my heart feel so hard and heavy I could scarcely breathe. But three months ago was not now. Two months ago was not now. Today, I can finally accept that I am going to be gone. It is sort of odd to imagine the world without yourself in it. I hope that doesn't sound conceited, and if so I don't mean it that way. It's only that once you are gone, so is the specific part you played in the world, making it different in some ways.

    I tell you this because it is only today that I can, with all my heart, ask you to move on, to move forward with your life. Don't forget me. Don't stop loving me. I could never do that if the roles were reversed, and so I won't ask something impossible. But, Parker, please don't waste your life pining for me, crying over someone who, no matter how hard we both wish, can never come back.

When I closed my eyes this morning, I saw you with someone new. I saw you with two babies and a smile on your face. And, Parker, it made me glad. Even then, as happy as you looked, I felt the way that you carried me in your heart, the way that I am always a part of you, just as you are always a part of me. But please don't let me be the only part.

I love you so much that I want you to be happy might sound like a martyr's plea. But it honestly isn't. It's selfish, in fact. I can't leave this earth content knowing that you might never experience all the good things life has to offer. We aren't meant to be alone, my love. I know that now. So when you find that woman, the special one, the right one, the one that is worthy of all that you are, don't be afraid to tell her how you feel. You won't be sullying my memory. You will only be making a new one.

Parker, you have been the kindest, most heroic man I could ever have hoped to meet. The way that you have taken care of me and loved me and never skipped a beat through the worst ordeal imaginable is the stuff of fairy tales. You are my knight in shining armor. You are the love of my life. I know that, for a time, I was yours, too.

Our story didn't end as planned, and I regret that wholeheartedly. But please, Parker, please: don't let the idea that our story ended badly keep you from writing a new one.

With all my love and all my heart, forever, until the end of time,
Greer

Amelia

A SHORT ROPE

WHEN GREER CAME TO MY apartment in Palm Beach that day, almost five years ago, face ashen, my first instinct was to worry about the mess in my living room. Piles of magazines on the coffee table, bills strewn about, a bed pillow on the couch, the couch pillows on the floor, two Diet Dr Pepper cans, half-drunk, on the end table.

"I'm sorry," I said as she walked in, my mind rushing with excuses, beyond that I had been really lazy the past couple of days.

But as she sat down on top of a copy of the *Wall Street Journal*, I realized that Greer wasn't worried about what my apartment looked like. She was . . . somewhere else. I'm pretty sure I went white, too, then.

"Greer," I said softly, sitting down beside her. "It's too late. It has gone to press. There's no way I can get the story back now."

But then she looked up at me, eyes big and round and tear-filled. "It isn't about the story," she whispered. She looked down at her hands. "I can't do it," she said.

My heart started to race, but I wasn't sure why. "Do what?"

"I have to ask you for a favor."

Why was she whispering? We were all alone. My eyes locked on hers.

Getting that story back from the printer, making 350,000 copies of one of the country's premier magazines disappear, felt simpler than what she said next.

Now, years later, I lay awake all night at Dogwood in my childhood twin bed with its monogrammed duvet cover and tiny canopy, thinking about Greer, about the bond we shared after that night. Was that bond holding me back from Parker? Did it feel like a betrayal to Greer? Or was her coming to me that night somehow a way of giving me permission?

For me, one worry always begets another. That night with Greer had come back to me after I realized that this could be one of the last times I ever slept in my bed, in my house, in the place that signified security and happiness and everything simple and good in life.

In my drunken state postdinner, I had come home to find my mother dozing in the chaise lounge beside my bed. In the dim, uneven lamplight, she told me the news about Dogwood, that it would be sold. She felt confident she could squeeze out a little more time. But it *was* going to be sold.

The blanket of the alcohol made the news seem manageable, palatable even. It was sensible. It was right. I found myself consoling my mother, regaling her with details of our new traditions of Christmas in Paris and Easter at the Breakers. I think I made her feel better. I also think I was overestimating how far the amount of money they would get for the property would stretch, but it soothed both of us in the moment.

But as the hours passed and the news set in (and the alcohol wore off), a deep, longing sadness took over. I couldn't count the number of nights, cold and ornery, I had cursed this house, prayed that God would bring a couple to the door to buy it, so we could move somewhere smaller, where every room could be warm and cozy.

The farm had prospered. Things had gotten better. It just wasn't enough to maintain this beast of a house that, even in my lovelorn state, I knew was running my family dry. Even though it was terribly unfair, I hated my mother in that moment. Why hadn't she sold Dogwood way back when it was just a family home, not a symbol of all that had been good in my life?

The sun rose on that sleepless night, lifting some of the stress the blanket of darkness had intensified. Harris was inside drinking coffee with my mother, reassuring himself that she loved him best, that he was first and foremost in her heart despite the fishing fiasco, which left me to load our luggage into the car—and contemplate whether he was first and foremost in *my* heart. And, if so, did I tell him about the kiss?

As I was throwing a bag into the trunk, I smelled cigarette smoke behind me, and when I turned, Mason was walking toward me in a rumpled polo shirt and a pair of Patagonia shorts that I think used to be navy and were now a faded co-balt.

"My bags are packed, I'm ready to go," he sang.

I smiled at him, squinting into the morning sun behind his head.

"Isn't this kind of early for you to be up?"

He laughed. "Oh, Amelia. Always with the jokes."

I used to say that Mason and I were technically still to-gether. We'd never actually broken up, after all. We had been dating, if you could even call it that. It was more like, we'd hung out mostly with other friends and by ourselves a few times.

When he had his accident, though, it was like he just dis-appeared. No call. No letter. No explanation. Romantic com-edy over. I spent more time than I'd like to admit wondering what could have been between us. What if he'd accepted that his baseball dream was over, gone to college, gotten a job? For months, I expected him to just show back up in Cape Caro-lina, kiss me passionately, thank me for waiting for him. But that was all very, very long ago.

"What's up with you and my brother?"

"You jealous?" I retorted, winking at him.

"Hell yeah, I am."

"I'm a little old for you," I said as he lifted the other suitcase into the back of the car. The entire town marveled at Mason's ability to continuously date twenty-year-olds, but I didn't think it was a mystery. They were the only ones who didn't know better.

"You gonna just keep pretending that you don't know my brother's in love with you?"

I smirked at him and leaned against the car, crossing my arms. He took a final drag of his cigarette and stomped it out.

"Parker's heart will always belong to Greer." I shrugged. "I'm not trying to spend my life in the shadow of a dead woman. There are plenty of living women whose shadows I can be in."

Mason scoffed and squinted at me. "Parker has always had the hots for you."

I eyed him curiously.

He eyed me back and sort of half chuckled. "Oh my God. You don't know."

"Know what?" I wasn't just playing coy. I really didn't know. And I was morbidly interested to find out.

"The fight."

Those two words took me back to the smoky Tackle Box. We were all underage, but no one cared. Mason was royalty. I was the royal girlfriend—or well, the royal girl of the week, at least. Parker was the royal brother. All the other people in town were subjects. I remember thinking that Parker, Watson, and Spence were a little too fired up that night, a little too rowdy, more than a little too drunk. But Mason had just pitched his last game at Cape Carolina High, a complete shutout. I had been the girl who had run out on the field to congratulate him, the one he looked for, the one whose lips he kissed for the whole town to see. I was the one whose ear he'd whispered into, as we walked off the field, "This is how it's always going to be, babe. Big wins. You and me." The glare of stardom will blind a girl, especially a seventeen-year-old one.

I never really knew what happened, only that one minute I was dancing barefoot by the bar with my girlfriends, basking in Mason's victory as if it were my own, and the next minute, Watson, Spence, and Parker were in a pile on top of Mason, and he was screaming in a way that made the ambulance, the arm broken in three places, and the surgery less of a surprise. But, still, what happened was unthinkable.

And then everything was over for Mason. His career. Our relationship. It was worse for him than for me, of course, but to just be abandoned like that . . . The way he threw me out of his life without a single word changed me. I longed for him the way only a teenaged girl truly can, spent nights crying myself to sleep and days moping around. I promised that I would never mourn for a man like that again. I sulked for a couple months of my senior year. Then I went to college. And, well, in the fun and the freedom and the buffet of boys, I forgot about Mason. I realized that we didn't really know each other, that we had nothing in common, and that what we'd had wasn't real. I'd never looked back. And I'd never let a man do that to me again. Not even Thad.

But I also couldn't help but wonder if maybe refusing to truly let yourself fall in love all the way wasn't really a way to live.

"I said that maybe now that I was graduating I could finally nail you," Mason said, breaking me out of my thoughts after lighting another cigarette. "Then I'd throw you back into

Dogwood and move on to all the hot chicks on the road." He visibly winced as he said it. Then he whispered, "Sorry. I was a stupid kid."

That night was almost half my life ago, but even still, it stung. But his contrition helped ease the sting a little. Maybe, somewhere, way deep down, Mason had felt something for me, something that was creating a small bit of remorse now.

"Lovely," I said. But I still wasn't sure where he was going with this.

"Parker got up in my face and said, 'If you ever say some-thing like that about her again, I will end you.'" He shrugged and looked down at the ground. "I wasn't worried about it; I didn't care. My punk-ass little brother wasn't going to take me down. After that no-hitter, I was flying as high as I had ever flown in my life. I shouldn't have kept at it. I honestly don't even remember what I said. But it was about you—and it set him off." Then Mason looked back up at me, the pain in his eyes so sharp and prescient that I had to look away. "And he did. He ended me. For you." He took a drag of his cigarette and half smiled.

I felt sick all over. My stomach, my head. Mason's life had been ruined because of me. Parker had ended his brother's career to defend my honor. That broken arm had changed his life. I wanted to say something to make it better, but there wasn't anything to say. Yeah, he'd been an ass, but even an ass doesn't deserve to have his life ruined because of a stupid in-sult.

"Look," he continued. "I know he didn't mean it. We were

all drunk, and when I took that swing at him, all those boys just came at me. I shouldn't have said it." He paused. "And I shouldn't have disappeared on you. It just seemed easier."

Mortifyingly, his words put back together something that had been broken inside for nearly half my life. But I just shrugged.

"At the time it didn't seem to matter much what I did," he said. "But now I've had a couple decades to think about it, and I've realized that the way we treat people is really all we have. Either way, yeah, my brother ruined my life. But his got ruined worse in the end. He was defending you with his life even way back then." He smiled cockily. "And I do mean his life. Because I could easily have killed him with my bare hands. I just thought you should know he always thought you were the one for him."

Then he literally turned and sauntered away, taking the last drag of his cigarette and flicking it into the bushes with a practiced hand, the same way I had seen him do about a million times as a teenager. Dropped a bomb and didn't even have the decency to run.

Harris chose the perfect time to come down the front steps, Mom on his arm.

"You ready, babe?"

"Amelia," Mom said, looking into my face. "You look like you've seen a ghost."

How could I possibly make her understand that I had?

Parker

THE SHALLOW END

AS THE DOUBLE SLIDING DOORS of the airport opened, I tapped my Fly Delta app and clicked "ticket change." I don't know what it was about that moment that convinced me, but I knew I couldn't go back to Palm Beach. At least, not without Amelia.

I had been so sure that she would come talk to me before she left, that she felt what I felt, that we were finally on the same page. But she hadn't. I had decided this morning to let it go, to move forward. Now, I had undecided.

The next flight to New York wasn't until five p.m., which would put me in the city about eight. Amelia and Harris would arrive back in the city by two. That gave her six hours to forget about Cape Carolina and me and that kiss. It gave her six hours to start packing, to put wheels in motion toward a new life, a life that didn't include me. What if I was too late?

I sighed. Maybe it was fate. I almost gave up, decided that it wasn't meant to be.

But then it was like I could actually hear Greer in my head, telling me that she wanted me to be happy.

So, what the hell? Amelia might reject me. I might fall flat on my face. But I'd lived through worse.

I raced to the ticket counter and said breathlessly to a stern-looking woman with orange-red chin-length hair and a Delta-blue uniform, "Have you ever seen *Love Actually*?"

She raised her eyebrow. I would take that as a yes.

•   •   •

After an hour of infuriating, nearly stopped traffic, six blocks from Amelia's apartment, I said, "Just let me out here, please."

"No, no, a few more blocks," the cabbie replied.

"Yeah, man, I know. But I want to get out here." I tossed him cash and jumped out, running down the sidewalk, my wheeled carry-on behind me, everyone on the street looking.

My heart was pounding both from the fact that I hadn't actually run in far too long and because I was panicking. I was doing my dead-level best to get there, but what if I was too late? Not that moving in with someone was saying marriage vows or anything, but it was big. And it was messy.

It wasn't until I got to Amelia's door, out of breath and, I'm sure, red-faced, that I realized I didn't have a clue what I was going to say. Certainly, some grand profession of love would scare her off. But a lukewarm *I know you're moving in with a man you love, but I think I might like you* probably wasn't going to be compelling enough to make her want to walk away from the future she was creating with him.

Before I could decide, the door opened, and I was face-to-face with Martin. As I leaned over, my hands on my knees, trying to catch my breath, he said, "Ew. You're so sweaty."

I looked past him into the living room and stood up again. "No boxes?" I practically panted.

"Lord. Come inside and sit down," he said. "What is going on with you? You are a mess." As I sat down, he said, "Ohhhhhh. You're a mess because your second one true love is moving in with another man. Poor baby."

"Where is she?" I was finally catching my breath, and the room was coming into focus. Amelia wasn't here. I had *Love Actually*ed my heart out, but I had still been too late. Well, actually, as Sharon, my new BFF at Delta, had informed me, it was less *Love Actually* and more *The Parent Trap*, because I was trying to beat the woman I loved home. It didn't seem nearly as romantic to me, but I had acquiesced because I thought doing so would get me on an earlier flight. I was right.

"Her flight was delayed. She isn't even home yet."

I sank back on the sofa.

But then the door flew open and Amelia walked through it in jeans and a T-shirt, which she looked amazing in, I might add. She looked from Martin to me and said casually, "Whatcha doin'?"

Now I looked at Martin, like he was going to help me out of this situation.

"Where is my boss?" Martin asked, throwing daggers out his eyes at Amelia.

"Oh, um, home, I presume. Or, if he is to be believed, at a bar somewhere, trying to forget that I exist."

Martin sighed dramatically and stood up. "This is why you don't set your boss up." He waved his hand, pulled out his phone, and said, "Well, I'd better get on Find My Friends and fix this mess you've made. Thank God I'm a fixer for a living." He pointed at Amelia and said, his voice laced with annoyance, "I'll deal with you later."

She smiled weakly and looked at me again, a little nervously. I wouldn't say that I necessarily knew Amelia better than anyone else in the world, but I knew her well enough to know that that face meant she was scared that I was here to make a grand confession of love. Which I was not.

I stood up and took her bag from her. She stepped inside her living room, and I said, "Are you okay?"

She nodded. "I just didn't see any point in moving in when we want different things."

I stepped closer to her. "And what do you want?"

"I don't want marriage or babies or any of that, but I also don't love the idea of it being completely taken off the table. It feels so . . . final." She shrugged. "Park, what are you doing here?"

I weighed my options. I could tell her. Or I could be cool. And she had likely had a very emotional day. So I decided on cool. "Well, we never discussed that article I sent you."

She crossed her arms and smirked. "Uh-huh. You flew to New York to talk about an article?"

"You know how serious I am about literature."

"I read it," she said. "I thought it was fascinating. I love that the couple adopted their embryos out to friends. I have an interview scheduled with them next week, so thank you for that. I think I can finally put this story to bed."

I smiled. I knew she would like that. "What was your favorite part?" I asked.

A slow grin spread across her face. "When they introduced their children to their new biological siblings, who had different parents but would grow up right down the street."

Now it was my turn to grin. "I love that line where she says something about how when she looks back on her life, that's how she'll always remember her children. Her son and daughter meeting these new baby twins, the awe of that moment, the serendipity of it all."

Amelia looked at me for a long moment. I couldn't quite read her expression.

"When I think of you," she finally said, "it isn't as a baby in a bassinet or as the annoying neighbor kid who squirted me with the water gun. I mean, I can think of you all those ways, of course, and I love that I can. But it's that day when you were lying over me on the beach and the water was dripping off your chest onto me, and all of a sudden you were grown-up. And you said—"

"'You're okay, Amelia,'" I interjected softly. "'I'm not going to let anything happen to you.'"

If only she knew how many times I had thought about that moment. I moved closer, my eyes on her eyes, testing the waters. I touched her cheek, dipping my toe into the shallow end. I was in that moment all over again, all those years ago, my face so close to hers, our breaths in time.

It'd be the simplest thing to lean into her, let my lips touch her lips. But I didn't. Not now. Not yet.

"Hey, Lia?"

"Yeah?"

"Want to go to dinner with me?"

She smiled and nodded. I reached out my hand to her, and she took it. It was perfect. It was a start. And if anyone needed a fresh start, it was us.

Amelia

FALLING TOGETHER

PARKER AND I HAD THE best dinner ever. We had finally taken this spark between us out on the road, and it had been as electric as I had dreamed. I'd been charming, effervescent even. He had been as handsome and adorable and as sweet as any romantic hero. And then he walked me home, our fingers intertwined, his hand strong and steady and capable in mine, fitting there so nicely that I wondered why we hadn't been doing this the entire time. And then we were standing close together inside the doorway of my apartment, and I knew what was going to happen next. My mind was racing with thoughts of us on the dock, the heat between us, the urgency.

Then he leaned over and kissed my cheek. Not my lips, not my neck, not any part of me where he wouldn't have kissed his great-aunt Emily. And all that old self-doubt, all that insufficiency, started creeping in.

Parker had said he would never move on from Greer, and I should have believed him. He obviously hadn't. Worse still, I could tell myself whatever I wanted to, but I hadn't moved in with Harris because of Parker. I mean, sure, yes, I'd wanted to leave myself open to the possibility of love, but, come on. I had wanted to leave myself open to the possibility of Parker.

As he put his hand on the doorknob, I thought that I'd made a mistake. Maybe he just didn't see me in that way. Maybe the kiss was a fluke. Well, this was humiliating. It was defeating. But I still had manners. "Parker," I said. I was going to thank him for dinner, for making my night out so nice. He turned back to me and, before I could say, *Thank you*, before I could even think about it, his lips were on mine. I can't say whether I kissed him or he kissed me, but I think it was more like a magnetic pull took over and we were together, the way we were meant to be.

His hands were in my hair, and our clothes were in a scattered trail from the front door to my bedroom. And I realized that I hadn't stopped smiling for a single moment. Not one. The thoughts would flood in later, the concerns, the questions. But, for now, having Parker Thaysden as close to me as a man had ever been felt like coming home.

*   *   *

It must have been four a.m. that I woke up in a panic. And then I realized that the hand on me was Parker's. And he was shirtless and beautiful in my bed. I kissed his chest, which was in close proximity to my face, savoring the manly smell of it and the real, unwaxed chest hair. I kissed his neck as I buried my head in, and then I sat straight up, realizing what the panic was for. I loved him. I was in love with Parker Thaysden. It wasn't a fling or a crush or a one-night stand or, arguably, the best sex I had ever had. This was real. And I realized that my fear wasn't the fear that I'd get attached and he'd leave me like with Thad or even Mason. No, I was afraid because I loved him so much I couldn't bear to be without him—and he was never going to love me as much as he loved her. He was never going to be able to give his heart to me like I had given my heart to him. And I hadn't even known I was doing it.

"Lia?" he asked sleepily. Now he sat up, too, rubbing his eyes. Then he kissed me and was smiling, and he looked so happy that I thought I should just let it go, play it as it came. But it was only delaying the inevitable. If I thought I loved him now, imagine after six months of dates and memories and future plans. But I think, ultimately, it was the way my heart was beating out of my chest in panic that made me say, "I can't do this, Parker. I just can't. I can't be in her shadow. I can't be second best."

He sighed and kissed my bare shoulder. "I will always love her, Lia. Of course I will. Forever. But I love her like I love her. And I love you like I love you."

I laughed out loud. "Parker Thaysden, you do not love me." But I knew he did.

He nodded at me very seriously. "Oh yes, I do. Of course I do. I have for . . ." He looked up to the ceiling like he was calculating. "Seventeen years."

I couldn't help but smile. "That's all?"

He nodded. "You remember that AP World History project we got assigned to do together? The one where we had to write the song?"

Parker had been so off-the-charts smart that he was in my history class his freshman year. (By his junior year, he was mainly in the library, racking up college credits in online courses.) We had written a rousing rendition of "The Devil Went Down to Georgia" about Russian history.

I smirked. "Well, of course. I can see how you fell in love with me then. Stalin could make anyone hot."

He shook his head. "It wasn't then. I mean, don't get me wrong, sitting on the floor of your playroom getting to breathe your air for hours was the coolest thing that had ever happened to me. I told everyone I got to second base."

I gasped in mock horror. "Do you have any idea how much that could have hurt my reputation? You were a *freshman*."

He shrugged. "Yeah. But you got the last laugh. When Mason heard about it, he punched me in the face."

I nodded knowingly. "I always wondered how someone as smart as you managed to open a door into your eye."

"It was at that field party right after. Someone had set up that horrible karaoke machine, and when you got up there, you said, 'I can't sing this one without my buddy Parker.' And we sang 'The Devil Went Down to Georgia,' and when you said, 'I done told you once, you son of a bitch, I'm the best there's ever been,' you touched the tip of my nose with the tip of your finger. It was nothing, but I knew then that you would always be the one that got away."

I remembered that night vaguely. The Smirnoff Ice and keg beer, and Parker, who didn't even have his license, was the one to drive my car home, to get us in the house without a word of complaint. How many times had he come to my rescue, really?

God, that story was so sweet. It warmed all those soft spots around my heart and my belly. I smiled at him in the dark and then leaned my head over onto his shoulder. "The one that got away, huh? I didn't get that far."

He pulled me toward him and kissed one cheek and then the other. "I'll give you time, Liabelle. I'll let you think this through and get to a night when the moon isn't so full and I'm not so damn handsome." He paused to flash me a smile. "But these last few months with you, all of that has come flooding back. I've realized that I'll be okay. I'll be able to move on and have a life. With you."

I flopped back dramatically onto the pillows and looked up at the ceiling. I couldn't look him in the eye when I knew I was about to sound so childish. "That's the thing, Park. How can I compete with your perfect, untainted memory of your one true love? How could anyone compete with that?"

Parker lay down next to me and pulled my arm so that I rolled over and was face-to-face with him. "It's really hard," he whispered, "because she's gone. She isn't here to defend herself. And it feels wrong on every level to say something negative about someone who died so tragically." He bit his lip. "I loved her, Lia, don't get me wrong. And I don't fault her for it, but Greer was . . ." He paused as if afraid to say the word. "Well, she was selfish. I knew it about her, and that was fine. I loved her, and I was fine to move to her town and work for her company and live in her house. But she was the kind of woman who just chose where you went out to dinner and where you went on vacation and what you did with your future. She couldn't help herself." He stopped talking, and I could tell how hard this was for him. "'Selfish' isn't even the right word, because she was so dedicated to helping people who needed it . . . but it was like, sometimes, with us, with the people who loved her most, she sort of forgot that we had needs, too." He paused. "Please don't think I'm a bad person."

I kissed him and said, "Parker, I could never ever think that."

"But when you offered to have a baby for me . . ." He trailed off, tears in his eyes. "Amelia, that was the most selfless thing I have ever seen one person do for another. You just wanted me to be happy. And I want the person I'm with to be happy, but it has occurred to me lately that maybe I deserve a partner who thinks about my happiness, too."

I nodded as best I could with my head practically stuck to the pillow.

He squeezed my knee, then got up and headed to the bathroom. He turned back to me. "And I won't tell you I love you again. That was a little much."

I wanted to tell him I loved him, too, but instead, I said, "Do you still want them, Parker? The babies?"

"No," he said quickly, too quickly.

I looked out my window, at the skyscraper across the way. That was the thing about New York. All these windows. All these people. Together, they seemed vast, infinite, maybe even unimportant. But inside each of those windows are families and lovers and friends and maybe even enemies, people falling together and falling apart. And, tonight, Parker and I, we were doing one of those things. I just wasn't sure which one yet.

Parker

AS DANGEROUS AS THE TRUTH

SO, SURE, LYING TO AMELIA after I had sex with her for the first time probably wasn't the best idea. But the part that was true, the part that was important, was that I loved her. But also, I did want the babies. And now I didn't just want them because they were a part of Greer. I wanted to be a father. And Amelia and I both knew that wasn't going to happen with just the two of us.

Now, twenty-two dates later, my lie seemed amplified. Twenty-two was exactly how many times I had seen Amelia in the past six weeks, how many times I had held her in my arms and kissed her lips and felt that we were going to be together forever. It was also how many times I hadn't told her that I wanted children. It was also exactly the number of times we hadn't told our parents we were dating.

This was as real as either of us had ever dreamed. It was

everything. It was the kind of love that made your heart pound but that also made you feel safe and secure. And even though Amelia still swore she didn't want to get married again, I think we both knew that it was time for us to take another step, whatever that was. We were old enough to know what we wanted. And what we wanted was to be together.

That next, unspoken step required me moving out of Greer's house, cleaning out her closets. It required untangling myself from her family and likely even McCann Media.

It was the only thing that was blocking us from moving forward, the one thing we really needed to address before making a lifelong commitment to each other, whatever that looked like. And yet it was the only thing we couldn't talk about.

It was between us every time we made love, every time we held hands in a movie theater, every time we spent a long Sunday on a couch reading the same book and laughing at all the same places . . . Even now, as we held hands on flight 794 from New York, New York, to New Bern, North Carolina, Amelia's head resting on my chest, dozing.

I laid my head on hers, and felt more than ever the fear I had that if I told her the truth it would all be over, the terror that if I didn't, my secret would eat me alive or, at the very least, blow up in my face. I couldn't lose another woman I loved. And so I sat, smelling the organic fragrance of her hair, listening to the beautiful sound of her breathing, holding my breath, praying she couldn't sense what I wasn't saying.

"Can you believe this is happening?" she asked sleepily.

I kissed the top of her head but didn't answer.

"What do you think they'll say?" she asked.

In the dark interior of the plane, passengers sleeping all around us, I said, "I think we both know that they're going to be thrilled." I felt the panic welling up in my throat again. When we told them, it was all going to become incredibly real; our bubble was going to burst. That's what did it: the thought of the way my mother was going to look at me. She wouldn't say anything, but I would know that she knew what I wanted and that I hadn't told the one woman I professed to care about more than anyone else in the entire world. But it was so late tonight. We would sneak into our respective houses and (hopefully) sleep. We would wake up to big break-fasts, mine cooked by Mom, Amelia's cooked by Aunt Tilley if she was having a good day, which I hoped she was because that woman made the best cinnamon rolls in the entire world, and I wanted one or three or four.

When we arrived in Cape Carolina an hour later, I was prepared to kiss Amelia good night in the driveway. She smiled in a way that made me suspicious. "I'm not tired," she said.

I was exhausted. "Oh no?" I asked teasingly, deciding that whatever she wanted from me was more exciting than sleep. She dropped her bag in the driveway and took my hand, pull-ing me in the direction of the dock.

"I will not do it," I whispered.

"Will not do what, sweetheart?" she asked entirely too in-nocently.

As we reached the end of her dock, the moon so bright on the water it looked like daylight, she pulled her shirt off over her head.

"Amelia Saxton," I whispered again. "Don't you even think about it."

"Think about what?" She batted her eyelashes at me.

Her skirt fell to her ankles and she stood on the edge of the dock, bathed in light. "Amelia!" I hissed again as she walked toward the end of the dock and raised her hands up over her head.

She knew how terrified I was of the water at night. There could be sharks or snakes. But she didn't care. She dove right in. Damn her. And bless her. Because that, more than anything, is what made us work. I stood back. I calculated. I planned. I watched. I took notes. And Amelia? Amelia jumped. Maybe I had spent a long time betting on the wrong horses, taking the wrong risks. But, God, looking at her as she came to the surface, laughing, the moon shining on her wet hair and face, I didn't want to think anymore. I just wanted all of her, whatever that entailed.

As I took my shoes off and unbuckled my pants, I made myself a promise. Whatever it took, whatever I had to sacrifice, even if it was my chance at fatherhood, I would do it. Because being with the woman who made everything in my life seem right was worth sacrificing anything.

And so I dove headfirst into the deep, dark, scary waters. I pushed aside the thoughts of what could be waiting for me. I pushed aside the millions of ways it could go wrong (or that I could be eaten by a shark). And I came to the surface, back to my girl, the one whose arrival in my life had, in some ways, shocked me and, in others, seemed like the most natural progression in the world.

I pulled her to me, treading water. And her body went limp. "For a girl who almost drowned, you sure aren't afraid, are you?"

She looked me straight in the eye, and I saw something shift in hers. "I have been terrified my entire life, Parker. But a man who saved me once isn't ever going to let me drown. And there is so much comfort in that."

And, just like that, everything changed. She was mine. I was hers. Sure, a part of me would always belong to Greer. But Greer was gone. And in my arms, in the dark water, was the woman I had dreamed of since I first imagined what love would be like.

Love was here. Love was now. There was no sense pining for what could have been. And there was certainly no use risking the perfection of these simple moments with the woman I loved for something as dangerous as the truth.

Elizabeth

A SENSE OF URGENCY

I COULDN'T BELIEVE MY EYES. At first, I wanted to call the police. Who were the vagrants swimming outside my house? I was about to walk outside to tell them to scram when I realized it: That girl laughing with wet hair streaming down her back? That was my daughter.

I got out my phone. LOOK OUT YOUR WINDOW.

Olivia: I am trying to sleep, which you know is almost impossible these days.

Elizabeth: OLIVIA, GET UP.

Olivia: Is your phone stuck on caps again?

Elizabeth: No. I am trying to convey a SENSE OF URGENCY.

Olivia: All right. I'm getting up.

Olivia: Call 911! There are intruders in the sound.

Olivia: Wait. Is that who I think it is?

Elizabeth: Am I seeing what I think I'm seeing?

Olivia: No way. Absolutely no way. They aren't together. Are they? Wouldn't they have told us?

This was getting ridiculous. I called her.

"Are they *together* together?" Olivia asked breathlessly.

"Yes," I whispered sarcastically, tiptoeing out of the bedroom. "I've known for weeks, and I've just been keeping it from you."

"Ha ha," she said. "Okay, fine. I knew Parker was coming home, but I didn't know he was coming with Amelia."

"What if this is just a fling?" I asked. "Like, they met up at the airport and they are drunk and making out in the sound."

"Don't even tease about that," Olivia snapped.

"I'm not *teasing*, Olivia." I glanced down at my coffee table, my eye catching Greer's last book. *Other People's Problems*. I grinned, because wanting their kids to be happy . . . That was someone else's problem. For now, it seemed that mine both were.

"Whatever you do," I said, "do not ask them about this. If they want us to know, they'll tell us."

"But . . ." she whined.

"But nothing, Olivia. Promise me."

"Well . . ."

"If you don't promise me right now, I'm going to quit sharing these fun secrets with you. When I see something scandalous, I'm just going to keep it to myself." We both knew that was a lie. What was the fun of even knowing a secret in the first place if you didn't have a best friend to tell?

Falling quiet, we both knew what the other was thinking:

this phase of our lives was about to be over. Well, no, not entirely. Charles and I were only moving one hundred yards to the east. But I would no longer be calling Olivia from precisely the same places I had called her from since we were kids.

Ever upbeat, she tried to bolster me. A good portion of Olivia's childhood memories, too, were tied up in Dogwood, maybe just as many as in her own home. Nothing would change. But so would everything. But neither of us said it, so the thought just lingered in the air, each of us picking it up and putting it back down again, letting it float off into the dark night.

"Fine." She sighed. "I won't say anything." She paused. "But do you think it could possibly be true?"

I had cried myself to sleep for several nights after Amelia broke up with Harris. I wanted her to be happy. I wanted her to find a man who could love her the way she deserved to be loved. And I'd thought he was the man who could do that.

I couldn't fathom why she had broken up with him. I couldn't wrap my mind around it, and yes, as much as I hate to admit it, I had been a little ugly to her about it. But I'm her mother, and I know best. At least, I thought I knew best. I had been bugging Amelia for weeks, mercilessly, about why on God's green earth she had let that perfect man go. And now, watching her kiss the boy next door in the dark, in the sound, knowing I should look away, I finally understood.

Greer

JUNE 17, 2016

THINGS WITH AMELIA DIDN'T GO exactly as I had planned. I don't know what I thought would happen. I guess I thought she would jump up and down, throw caution to the wind, be absolutely thrilled. But she wasn't.

She said, "Why don't you just tell them you can't do it?"

I had scoffed at that. I was here because I was pretty sure she understood me better than most people. But if she had really known me at all, she would have known that I would never say I couldn't do something. Even this. Even now. I knew I shouldn't have put it off. I knew I should have dealt with it sooner, but even though I knew logically that I was dying, I don't think I had quite accepted it yet, and now I was running out of time.

"But I wouldn't be able to tell anyone," she repeated again slowly.

"People do it all the time," I reiterated.

"Do they?"

I mean, yeah. Maybe not exactly like this. But I have to think it happens.

That was when I handed her the check.

Her eyes got wide. I had the feeling that she had never held a check that big before. I hadn't, either, so I understood how she felt. She shook her head. "This is yours."

I tried to explain that I would just endorse it over to her. She looked at me blankly. Now I'm worried. What if Amelia was right? Maybe I should have just said no to begin with . . . Maybe I should just say no now. But I have so much left in me, so much to pass on.

Greer's Golden Goodness. That's what the readers nicknamed my column. Because everything I touch turns to gold. I believed it once, I really did. I was the king maker. I wore the crown. I started to think, like they did, that everyone I touched turned to gold, too. Now, as I stood with Amelia, asking a total stranger for the biggest favor I would ask anyone, I reached out to take her hand. To touch her, a last attempt to hope that she, that this project, would turn to gold.

My legacy, my secrets, my future, all placed on this one woman. Could I trust her? Could she trust me? She squeezed my hand. She nodded. And that's when I knew.

Amelia

GREAT LOVE

I WANTED TO STAY IN our bubble. I wanted to carry on flying to Palm Beach, Parker coming to New York, long dinners and walks in the rain and movie marathons and sending books back and forth in the mail with notes in the margins. I wanted the surprise flowers at work and the writing of real love letters. I didn't want any of that to be over. Which is why, as I spritzed my neck with perfume in my childhood bedroom, I said, "Hey Siri, text Parker Thaysden, 'Not tonight.'"

She replied, "Texting Parker Thaysden: 'At twilight.'"

I sighed, picked up the phone, and typed the message myself.

Maybe it was all so perfect because it wasn't real. Our parents didn't know; a lot of our close friends didn't even know. So we didn't have to field the questions about marriage, which I didn't want, and babies, which I couldn't have. We could stay in our little cocoon of love and not face anything real. The real part was when it got sucky. I liked this—the lovely in-between, where I didn't have to worry.

I reached up and touched one of the hot rollers in my hair and, feeling that it had cooled, removed the metal clip, holding the curl in my palm. There was a knock at the bathroom door, and I called, "Come in!" just as my phone vibrated on the counter with You sure? You know we have to get it over with sometime . . .

But I couldn't type back because my hands were full of curlers, and I couldn't voice text because Aunt Tilley had walked in and was wedging herself right beside me on the small window seat, her legs dangling down between the vanity and the toilet, and her full pink polka-dot skirt with the crinoline underneath filling up pretty much every ounce of the bathroom.

"You look beautiful for the ball tonight," she said.

I studied her face, which was hard because focusing on anything but the vivid red blush on her cheeks took some skill. Was she still here? Was she somewhere else? I never could quite decide. I wondered if this was all an act, a willful undertaking so that she didn't have to remember. What it was she didn't want to remember, I couldn't be sure. But something. Either way, I played along, even when it drove my mother mad. I always played along. Why not? If she didn't know, she couldn't help it. And if she did? Well, if she did, it was fun to be lost in her world sometimes. A lot of days it beat the hell out of this one.

"Not as beautiful as you, Aunt Tilley. You will be the belle of the ball."

She smiled contentedly and fanned herself with one of the

vintage hand-painted fans she was never without. I wondered
if she possibly felt warm in here, inside with the air turned
way down.

"It's the things you don't do that you'll regret, darling."

I eyed her. "What do you mean, Aunt Tilley?" This was
the only hard part. Was she here in my world now, or were we
still two genteel ladies discussing a fictitious ball?

She took my hand. "Amelia, I wish more than anything
that I hadn't let Robert run away. I wish I hadn't sent him off to
war without telling the truth. I sent him away with nothing, no
wife or child to come home to." She paused, tears in her eyes
and said, "I sent him away to die, Amelia. I see it now as clear
as the diamond he tried to give me the night before he left."

I shook my head. "You didn't send him off to die, Tilley. It
couldn't be helped." Robert had not been off at war. He had
been killed in a horrible, freak farming accident with a cotton
baler. But I couldn't explain that to Tilley now. She couldn't
hear me, wherever she was.

She shook her head and looked me in the eye. "Amelia,
you're not hearing me." I put the last curler back in the container, looked straight at her, and pursed my lips, so she
would know I was listening. "It is the things we don't do that
keep us up at night, that ruin our lives, that descend us
straight into madness."

"The things we don't do," I repeated.

She was right. So was Parker.

I glanced out the window to see Parker standing at the end
of our dock, hands in his pockets. I felt warm at seeing him,

but also at having a family that had friends like the Thaysdens. For my entire life, their house, their dock, the contents of their pantry . . . It had all been as much mine as theirs. I knew Parker felt the same. Growing up, I took it for granted.

And now, life as I had always known it was going to change. Mom thought it would take at least a few more months to get Tilley settled and the back house spruced for her and Daddy to live in. It was bittersweet. I was losing my home, but my parents were gaining their lives back.

Once word had gotten around that Dogwood was for sale, the realtor had received two offers that very day, both cash, both over the presumed asking price. She'd tried to convince them to sell right then, but Mom just wasn't ready. Dogwood was one of the most valuable properties in Cape Carolina. Mom and Dad said the sale was contingent on the owner keeping the home intact, not tearing it down and developing the land. While, theoretically, that might work, in reality there was really nothing they could do to control the next owner's whims once it sold. So we all just prayed it went to someone we knew and trusted.

I patted what I thought might be Tilley's knee underneath her massive crinoline. "You're right, Tilley." In moments like these, I worried more than ever about what moving to a new environment might do to her.

"Of course I am," she said, looking offended. "You should never doubt that."

I smiled at her. "There is a boy out there on that dock that I need to talk to."

"Little Parker Thaysden," she said. "He is a doll, isn't he?"

I winked at her. "A real, live, true one. You know what? I think I might bring him to the ball." And then I raised my eyebrows and whispered, "As my date."

She winked back at me. "I think that would be marvelous."

Bare feet in the grass, the long hem of my white linen maxi dress swishing along my ankles, I made my way to the dock, where Parker was standing, almost completely still, his hands in his pockets. He appeared to be staring at his boat, which, mysteriously, was at our dock, not his.

"Admiring your great love?"

He turned around, startled. When he saw me, he pulled me close. "Now I am."

I knew it was risky, but I couldn't help it. I kissed his soft, full lips, and I didn't want to stop.

"They're going to see," he said, resting his forehead on mine.

I shrugged. "Let them all see. I think I've changed my mind."

"About getting married?" he joked.

I rolled my eyes. "Nooooo. About telling them tonight."

His eyes sparkled, and he reached his hand out to me. "Then let's get to it."

Maybe we should have planned what we were going to say or how we were going to say it, but it wouldn't have mattered anyway, because before we had even said the blessing, Olivia started. "Anything you two want to tell us?"

I could feel my mom kick her under the table.

I cut my eyes at Mom. "What do you know?"

Olivia shrugged. "Oh, nothing. We don't know a thing. Just wasn't sure if there was any news you wanted to share, in particular?"

Parker and I shared a glance.

He reached over, took my hand, squeezed, and said, "Well, it appears that you already know, but Amelia and I are dating."

Mom let out a scream so high-pitched and long and loud that I thought perhaps my eardrums had burst.

Olivia gave her a look. "So it's true! Is it new?"

I bit my lip guiltily. "Well, six weeks." It wasn't that long, but it was a long time to talk to my mother every single day and not breathe a word to her.

Now Mom gasped. "So all those times you said you weren't seeing anyone special . . ."

I broke out in a grin that I absolutely could not suppress. "I lied. He is the most special."

"Well, *Robby* is the most special," Aunt Tilley interjected.

"But Robby is my brother, so, while he is special, he is not a man I will ever be in love with," I replied.

"Right," she said. "Of course. Your brother. Sometimes I forget."

"So this must be serious, huh?" Mom asked.

She clearly wanted to ask when we were getting married. She simply could not accept it as true when I told her I wasn't getting married again.

"Any important future plans?" Olivia asked, a little more boldly. "Anything I should get a diamond out of the safe for?"

Neither of us said anything.

"What about a baby?" Tilley trilled.

That was when I jumped in. "No, no, Aunt Tilley. I can't have a baby. Remember?"

Evidently, the ball was over, because she said, just as clear and lucid as anyone else around the table, "Oh, but couldn't you try IVF again? Don't you have a couple more embryos?"

Perfect freaking time for her to come back to reality. I'm sure I looked horrified because Parker and I had never really discussed this. To be honest, I didn't think we had to. We'd tried. We'd failed. We'd moved on. But when I looked into his face I could have sworn that I saw something almost hopeful in it.

I did a double take. "Wait. Do you *want* to try to have the other babies?"

The three sets of eyes around the table drilled into us, and I was suddenly thankful that our dads, Robby, and Mason hadn't gotten out of poker night. I did wish, though, that Trina hadn't had horrible morning sickness—for her sake, obviously, but also because she was always waiting with an upbeat smile during these emotional scenes.

He shrugged. "Well, I mean . . ." He sighed. "I don't think this is the time or place for us to have this conversation, but it might be nice to try for a baby."

Breathless, I felt like he had punched me in my very empty gut. "So you mean to tell me that we have been discussing our future ad nauseam, and you never felt the need to tell me that you wanted children?"

He turned to the table and said, "Excuse us."

Then he took my hand and walked us out onto the porch. "Look, Lia, not necessarily. I want you more than I want children."

I shook my head. "Has any of this been real?"

"Amelia, don't do this. Yes, I kept it from you. I just didn't want to hurt you because I love you so much. And I would rather have you than a baby."

"Is that what this was all along? Some attempt to get me to be your surrogate again?" I knew I was spiraling, but I couldn't stop.

He ran his hands down the length of my arms, a gesture I would have recognized as affectionate if I weren't so angry. "Amelia, of course not. You know me better than that. I love you. I want to be with you. Let's just forget the baby thing and go back inside."

I knew before I said what I said next that I shouldn't. I knew I couldn't take it back. But it flew out of my mouth anyway. "Are you still pining away for Greer, too? Am I just a side distraction?"

"Stop," he said firmly. "Don't bring her into this."

"'Don't bring her into this,'" I repeated. "Her. Her. It's always going to be *her*."

"You're being ridiculous," he said, turning on his heels.

As I watched him walk away, I knew that he was right. Even still, I didn't run after him. She would always be there. But, if I was honest with myself, she would always be with us for a reason that not even Parker knew.

Elizabeth

THE PIECES

THAT HAD GONE AWRY VERY quickly. But life is like that sometimes: one moment, you're celebrating, the next, you're debating how—or whether—to pick up the pieces.

"Well, that went well," Tilley said.

"Thanks to *you*," Olivia practically hissed.

I put my hand up, defending my sister. "We all did our
part. We came on entirely too strong."

I couldn't help but think, though, that our questions
hadn't been out of the ordinary for a couple who had been
through what Parker and Amelia already had. So maybe we
had done them a favor. We had revealed cracks that had been
in the foundation that would eventually make the house come
down. Maybe we'd just made it come down sooner.

But what was nagging at me was that this was a problem
that could be fixed, that we needed to fix. That I could fix.

"Well, I'm out," Olivia said. "I did my part. I gave him the letter. He told her he loved her. They spent six weeks together. I have no other tricks up my sleeve."

I studied Tilley's face. She seemed perfectly lucid. Whatever "ball" she had been attending must have been over in her mind.

"I think we have to," she said.

"I'm not worried about me, Tilley. I'm honestly not. I'm worried about you."

She bit her lip. "I can handle it if she knows. I think she can handle it, too."

"But you understand that once it's out there, we can't control it. We can't control what she decides to do with the information."

"I know," she said quietly. "I understand what we're doing." She paused thoughtfully. "I think it might help her, Liz. And if it can, then I think we have to try."

"Do you want to tell her?" I asked.

She shrugged. "I think it should come from her mother."

I'd been afraid of that.

Olivia looked delighted, which kind of annoyed me. "You could act less thrilled that my life is about to come tumbling down," I told her.

"Oh, Elizabeth, you are so dramatic. It's going to be fine."

But I knew, once I told the truth, nothing would ever be fine again.

Amelia

A BRIDGE

I HAD SEEN MR. THAYSDEN'S boat pull out of the dock. I had dealt with the fact that I had said things I couldn't take back, that I had been angry, but, if I was honest, I wasn't surprised. I had tried to take his assertion that he didn't want children at face value, but, deep down, I knew better than that.

I was very clear on one thing in that moment: I didn't want to lose him. That, at least, was something. But was keeping him fair, when he so obviously wanted things that I couldn't give him? Weren't you supposed to sacrifice for love? Or was a child way too big a thing to ask a person to give up? I sighed deeply to no one in particular as I made my way down the dock. I sat down at the end, my feet trailing in the water, the stars so bright it almost seemed like day.

I guess a part of me wanted Parker to come up behind me, to kiss me, to tell me it was okay. But was it true? Could it ever be okay now? I had known true love with him. And now he was gone. Maybe it was stupid to rely on a journal entry from when I was fourteen, but if a man didn't love me the way I was, if he couldn't accept that I couldn't have children, then how could he really love me?

But, then again, when I was fourteen, there hadn't been an obvious way for me to have children. Now there was. Maybe I should quit being so stubborn. Should I give him what he wanted? Maybe that was the answer. But having a child wasn't like switching sides of the bed. It wasn't like drinking Dunkin' when you really wanted Starbucks. It was forever, the single most life-altering thing a person could do. But, then again, we could try. And it might not work . . . No. I snapped myself out of it. *If* I decided to go through with it, I had to be all in. That was the only way.

I turned to see my mom walking down the dock in her starched blouse and fitted leopard pants. She was so cute. And agile, I thought, as she jumped from the regular dock to the floating dock, sat down, crossed her legs, and said, "So, not exactly the celebratory dinner you imagined?"

I smiled sadly, watching my feet skim along the surface of the water. I looked up at her, and she seemed genuinely calm. "Am I being stupid?"

"You could never be stupid."

"She's dead, Mom. It doesn't matter if he still loves her. I don't know why I'm so hung up on it."

"Oh, honey, of course it matters. I understand completely. No one wants to feel like they're second best, and, as much as

I want you and Parker together, he will always have been married to her first." She put her hand on mine. "I think if you're going to figure out where to go from here you might have to find a way to complete the circle."

I looked at her skeptically.

"You know," she continued. "Build a bridge. Find a way to connect a past you can't change with the future you want."

It sounded so easy, the way she said it. Build a bridge. Connect the past and the future. The answer was obvious. The clearest way to build a bridge between Parker and Greer and me was to have their baby. In fact, maybe it was the only way. Creating a new life out of the past while making way for the future, connecting the three of us tangibly, couldn't possibly be more perfect. So what was holding me back?

I couldn't look at her when I said, "Mom, if I tell you something, do you promise you won't judge me?"

She shrugged. "You're my daughter. I couldn't even if I wanted to."

Sometimes I wanted to kill her, and then, sometimes, in moments like these, I didn't know how I would ever, ever live without her.

I looked directly at the moon as I whispered, "I'm afraid I won't love it."

She cocked her head to the side, studying me as she said, "Love what?" and then, a moment later, "Ohhhhh."

Now we were both looking at the moon, and I was pretty sure she was judging me.

"Amelia, I don't know how to say this exactly. But there's

something I've been thinking about telling you for a while now, something pretty risky for me."

I felt my heart begin to race. What else could possibly happen tonight? I turned to her.

"I don't know how to say this, exactly . . ."

From the look on her face, I was pretty sure that I didn't want her to figure out how.

"It's Robby."

"Oh my God! Is he sick?"

She looked at me for a long moment. "He's your cousin." She paused and backtracked. "Well, I mean, he's your brother, of course. He will always be your brother. But he's not technically, biologically, my child—or Daddy's."

She paused, and I sat stock-still, like if I didn't move, I could pretend she'd never said anything. My breath felt short, and my heart like it would burst inside my chest.

She got a second wind, saying, "Aunt Tilley was pregnant when Robert died—I never could understand why the hell she couldn't just marry him and be done with it—and she just lost her mind, Amelia. Completely lost her mind. Mama and Daddy just hid her away. I hid away with her, and once he was born it was really clear that she couldn't take care of him, and it all just sort of . . ."

My little worries suddenly seemed extremely trite. "Mom, my God," I said, sounding as furious as I felt. "How could you do that?"

"Don't come at me," she said, getting defensive. "You have no idea what I have been through," she practically hissed. "At first, I was just helping her out, keeping him until she could get back on her feet. But as the weeks turned to months and the months to years, he became a part of me."

I shook my head. "For God's sake, Mother. He is her *child*."

She gave me the stoniest look I'd ever seen and said, "He is not. Robby is *my* child. And that's what you might never get the chance to understand. I didn't carry him or give birth to him. I didn't know what to do with a baby. But once I was the one taking care of him, rocking him to sleep at night, staying up when he had a fever, when I was the one he called 'mama' . . ." She trailed off, wiping her eyes. "I wasn't trying to take him away from my sister, but that boy deserved a stable home; he deserved a mother who didn't think she was Queen Elizabeth ninety percent of the time. I could give him that, and so I did."

The way she said it, it seemed so simple. So logical. But it was anything but. I had thought it was Tilley all this time, but maybe my mother was the crazy one.

"God, Amelia. You can't imagine it. All the doctors, all the treatments, all the medications, all the false hope, all these years and years that I've tried to bring her back . . ."

Tears gathered in my eyes. For me, Aunt Tilley had just always *been*. I'd never really considered the toll that all of this had taken on my poor mother, as embarrassed as I am to admit it.

She cleared her throat and composed herself. "That's why Tilley has always lived with us. She couldn't take care of

Robby, but I didn't want her to have to be without him. She gave me the most important gift I have ever received—besides you."

"Wait. Robby knows, right?"

She bit her lip but didn't say a word.

"Oh my God, Mom." I got up, pacing up and down the dock. "Are you kidding me? My brother doesn't know that you and Dad aren't his parents? I mean, am I your real kid?" In that moment, I almost wished that she would say no.

"You're being so dramatic, Amelia. Sit down."

I laughed. "Dramatic? I'm being *dramatic*? I just found out my brother isn't even my brother!" I shout-whispered.

"Don't you ever say that again," she said, low and mean. She meant it.

I sighed and sat back down. "Don't you worry about it coming out?"

"Oh, I worry about it every day."

"And?"

"And I just hope I'm dead when they figure it out."

I was so exasperated now. "So that's your grand plan? Hope you're dead? Good Lord, Mother." I was up and pacing again. "Why would you even tell me this? I wish I didn't know. I'm never going to be able to be normal around Robby again."

She took my hand, and I wanted to yank it away, but I knew she hadn't meant to be so horrible. She'd meant to protect her sister, to protect her nephew-turned-son. And, well, she had. No one could argue that Tilley could have raised a child on her own. She certainly could not have. And Robby had turned out smart and handsome and kind and happy. He had made a great life for himself. What shocked me most of all was my dad going along with it.

"Wait. Does Olivia know?" She gave me a skeptical look. Of course Olivia knew.

"Honey, look. I was scared to death when all this happened, and at that point, I never imagined that I would raise Robby as my own. I just figured we'd have him for a few months until Tilley got over whatever was going on with her and then we would move forward. All of us. But what I didn't understand was that, from those first days, I was madly in love with that child."

"Mom . . ."

"No, Amelia. He was *my* son. *Mine.* I didn't understand how a person could feel that way about a child that wasn't technically theirs. But it was as natural as breathing, the way he became mine. Until all this 23andMe mess, I never even really thought about it."

My mouth was hanging open. "So you mean to tell me that people in Cape Carolina just believed that you had hidden away casually and suddenly appeared with a baby no one knew you'd been pregnant with?"

"Oh Lord, no. But then he turned one, and he looked so much like me that the speculation sort of died down. There were new scandals. People forgot. I'm sure every now and then someone talks about it over a game of bridge at the country club. But, by and large, when no new information ever emerged, people just let it go."

"What about Gran and C-Pop?"

"Well, they knew. They had to. But they were all for it. An unwed daughter with a baby was more than they could take. I swear it bothered them almost as much as her illness." She laughed lightly. "I know it doesn't seem like it to you, Amelia, because it isn't the facts, and the facts are what your life is all about. But my truth is that that little baby boy was my son. And there is nothing that anyone can do to take that away from me. It was the best decision I ever made. Well, that and having you, of course."

"So that's why he's named Robby," I whispered. "Not after C-Pop. After his father, Robert."

I knew what she was doing here, and I said so. I gave her credit because it was a super-ballsy move. She had risked the biggest secret she had—at least, I hoped it was her biggest secret—to make me see the truth I hadn't grasped yet. The gesture meant something to me.

"Look, Amelia, I made my peace a long time ago with the fact that you were going to have a life different from mine. You live the life that you want to live. If that doesn't include marriage or babies, so be it. I'll be fine. But don't walk away from something you really want because you're afraid. That isn't the brave girl I raised."

I looked down at my hands. "It's just weird, you know? I spent so many years certain that I didn't want children, that I didn't want that life. So why now?"

Mom looked at me, eyes bright. "Honey, I know that you're a different generation, that you come from a time where women are supposed to know their own minds before they know someone else's, love themselves before they can love a partner. And I respect that. But when you are so close to a person that you are contemplating spending your life together, things change."

"What do you mean?"

"Well, I mean, when you were with Thad, you didn't want children and neither did he. That was fine. Harris didn't want to get married and, when you were with him, you didn't either. But being with someone new means necessarily shifting parts of your life to fit in with parts of theirs. Parker wants children. Changing your mind about wanting them too isn't a crime, honey. It's a part of being in a relationship."

I could tell she was about to get up, leave me alone with thoughts I didn't want to listen to. "Mom?"

"Yeah?"

"Could you just sit with me for a while?"

She pulled me into her side, and I rested my head on her shoulder.

And so we sat, two Southern women who'd grown up in this same house in this same town on this same street—but who, somehow, wanted completely, entirely different things.

Parker

SOUTHERN COAST

I HAD VERY DEFTLY PROVEN that the conversations you never want to have are inevitable. I wanted to say Amelia was over-reacting. In the moment, I believed that she was. And so I huffed out, walked away, mad that she couldn't bend just a lit-tle, as though giving birth to and raising children that weren't biologically hers were a small favor to ask someone.

I realized hours later, about halfway out to the middle of the ocean, in my dad's boat, alone, that I had probably over-reacted. Okay, *definitely* overreacted. I had also played this all wrong. What better way to show the woman you love that you love her no matter what, that you love her more than the life you had envisioned for yourself, than to escape to the sea? Nothing says *I'll do anything for you* quite like getting the heck out of Dodge.

What if she was looking for me? The water was dark and

still, the sky bright with stars and a full moon whose reflection off the water increased the ethereal feeling. It also felt ominous. My stomach churned with the knowledge that I had done the wrong thing and that it might cost me the love of my life.

The *other* love of my life, anyway. It hit me like a punch in the face (probably from Mason) then. The other love of my life. Yeah, it was hard for me to move on. But Amelia was having to live with the fact that, no matter what, there would always be this other person between us. Roles reversed, I wasn't sure I would have been able to do it.

Now I understood that the crux of the situation wasn't even really about babies. I had been too self-centered to realize that Amelia still worried about being in Greer's shadow. I had done everything I could to let her know that she was the one I wanted. But maybe I hadn't done a good enough job. Or maybe there was no use trying to hide something so huge from someone who knows you so well.

I should have been more honest with her. Was I even capable of making the right choice anymore?

That was when I turned the boat around. When I looked down at my phone, I saw I was still too far offshore to get service. But as soon as I did, I texted Amelia immediately. Babe, I don't know why I got on this boat when all I want is you. I'm sorry. I swear.

Nothing. No dots. She could be asleep. But if she was asleep, then she wasn't as worried about all this as I was. I looked down again. No dots.

I pushed the throttle forward, tired and distracted and unable to keep my eyes off the phone screen, searching for a response that wasn't coming.

About the time the house came back into view, the phone rang. It was exactly five a.m. I pulled the throttle to slow the boat and answered frantically, "Hello!"

"Parker, my boy," George said, not frantically at all. George. Not Amelia. "I just sent you a prospectus. *Southern Coast* has gone under. It's being dismantled for parts. We might not want it, but we could pick it up for nothing, head-quarter it wherever."

Southern Coast. Greer and Amelia's favorite magazine. Now my head was pounding. I was too tired to think about this, too drained to deal with it. But my instincts were sharp even when I wasn't. I couldn't let Amelia's favorite magazine fold. I knew she would want it. Whether she forgave me or not, I wanted her to have it. "We can revamp that one, George. It has to be relocated to a Southern town." I paused. "Maybe even a small one. It needs Southerners writing for it . . ." I trailed off. "Let me sit down at my computer, and let's meet about it next week."

"Ten-four. Good man. You'll take the lead on this one."

I nodded and hung up. It was as clear as day to me that Amelia had to be editor in chief. I couldn't imagine anyone in the vast numbers of McCann employees who could reenvision it like she could.

An hour later, as I was pacing around the bedroom in the guesthouse, all thoughts of *Southern Coast* gone, I couldn't stop thinking about my favorite passage in Greer's last book. It rang so true I had committed it to memory.

Everyone always thinks that thing is going to happen to someone else. That cancer or car wreck, infertility battle or bankruptcy declaration. Other people's problems. But we tend to think that the really great things only happen to someone else, too. They never believe they will be the one to become CEO, to start the nonprofit, to get the record deal, to change the world. Other people's successes. But none of these things belong to other people.

The good and the bad could both be yours at a moment's notice. Me? The thirty-two-year-old dying of cancer? I could be you. But also me? The young woman who transformed a media company for a new generation? (She said humbly.) I could be you, too. So what do you want to do? Who do you want to be? Decide now. And then go out and get it. Decide your own future before someone—or something—decides it for you.

I knew what I wanted. I wanted to propose to Amelia. Badly. It was right. We were right. And as much as the pain of losing Greer was still with me every day, I could have this love with Amelia in a new and completely different way; one didn't have to outweigh or obscure the other. It was possible.

How I felt right now had also seemed one hundred percent impossible: I was happy. I was so damn happy. I could hear birds chirp again. The sky looked blue again. I had things to look forward to. Only, this woman who was woven into the net of my happiness had sworn, every time I brought it up, that she would never get married again. But hadn't she broken up with Harris because he had taken marriage off the table? That had to mean something, didn't it?

And so I realized, for the millionth time, that life and relationships are all about compromise. It had taken this moment, this feeling of desperation, of panic, of wondering if she would ever speak to me again, to realize that I wasn't the one that had a right to be mad or worried. Amelia was. She had been completely honest with me from the beginning. I should have believed her.

I thought about that house that had nothing of me in it. Yes, Greer and I had bought it together, but it was all Greer. Every couch cushion and picture frame and tiny trinket was hers. Amelia was right; I couldn't fully have her in my life unless I was willing to let go of the suffocating grip I had on the past—and it had on me.

When I heard a tap at the living room door, I almost jumped out of my skin. I turned and saw Mason, dressed in his old Cape Carolina High baseball uniform, cap on head, cleats on feet, glove on hand. I could feel my eyes get wide as he opened the door.

"You all right, bud?" I asked cautiously.

He was tossing the ball from his hand to his glove, his glove to his hand, like I had seen him do a million times before.

"I thought about what you said."

Now my mind was racing. What had I said to turn my brother into the high school baseball version of Aunt Tilley?

"You're right. I wouldn't still be playing baseball now. So

I started thinking about what I would be doing. What would I have wanted to do after a long and successful career setting records on the field?"

I controlled my eye roll. "And?" I asked, still concerned.

He grinned, and the baseball stilled. "And you're looking at Cape Carolina High's new baseball coach."

As impossible as it had felt only a moment before, I actually felt happy. I hugged my brother and slapped him on the back.

"Good for you, man. Good for you."

He grinned at me, and the sparkle in his eye told me that, for the first time in a long time, my brother was happy, too.

"Okay," he said, looking at me intently. "I did it. I moved on. It's your turn."

"Mace," I said. "I'm sorry."

"I know you are, bro."

"No, but I need you to hear it. I'm sorry that I fought with you that night and I'm sorry that I broke your arm. I'm sorry that I ruined your life." *Ruined your life.* I felt tears pooling in my eyes. I had ruined his life and now, it seemed, I had also ruined my own. "I think I give you such a hard time because if I'm mad at you I don't feel as guilty for what I did. If I blame you for not moving on with your life, it helps me ignore that I haven't moved on with mine."

The way Mason was looking at me, I expected a smart-ass response. But, instead he said, "I know all that, Park. I'm your big brother. Of course I know."

I nodded as he walked back out the door. My phone

beeped. For hours, all I had been able to think about was that text that wasn't coming. And now, as soon as it did, I wished it hadn't.

I won't do this. I'm sorry.

I dropped the phone onto the couch and flopped down beside it. Well, damn, of course she wouldn't. It had taken me until right now to understand that I was asking this woman whom I loved to basically step into my dead wife's position. Live in her house, work for her company, have her babies. It was absurd. It was insulting.

And now I was going to have to do something huge to prove that I understood where she was coming from. I was going to have to prove that I could fix it.

I picked up the phone again, wanting to say something to her. But no words came. Instead, I opened up my email and typed, to my father-in-law: *I need to sell the house. It's time. You have been so kind to me; you are my family, always. But I can't move forward by doing the same things I've been doing. It isn't fair to anyone. Thank you for allowing me to marry your daughter. Thank you for letting me work at your company. Thank you for being my family. I am forever grateful.*

Not ninety seconds later, I got an email back.

Sell the damn house. I don't care. But I can't run my company without you, so suck it up. You have a big raise coming your way.

George

P.S. If you'll stay on, I'll give you my velvet slippers you're so fond of.

I burst out laughing, and then the laughter turned to tears. I was sobbing, loudly, unabashedly, when I heard a small tap on the glass door in the living room.

"Amelia?" I asked as I opened the door.

She smiled and then, when she saw my face, her smile turned to concern. "What's the matter?"

"What's the matter?" I asked. "What's the matter?" I repeated, louder. "Did you think that you could text me that you wouldn't do this and that I would just be fine with it?"

Now she looked really confused. "Parker, what the hell are you talking about?"

"Your text . . ."

I thrust my phone in her face.

She read the text. She paused. Studied it. Read it again. And started laughing. Hysterical, tears running down her face, hands over her mouth, laughing. "Oh God," she said, gasping for breath. "No, no, no. That was a voice text. It was supposed to say, *I want to do this. I'm sorry.*"

"I want to do this," I repeated. Then I started laughing, too, with pure relief. Through my laughter, I said, "Well, you can understand my concern." Then, getting it together, I said, "I want to do this, too. I'm moving out of the house in Palm Beach. I want to make a new life with you."

She kissed me. Then she sat down on the couch and patted beside her. "Park, I've been thinking."

She was suddenly very serious. And I was terrified for the fiftieth time in the last few hours.

"And?"

She nodded, tears coming to her eyes. "I know I've always said I didn't want children . . ." She trailed off, her gaze on the water beyond the door.

"Sweetheart, I know you don't want children, and it was wrong of me to push you into that. I love you no matter what you want to do, and I shouldn't have tried to change you. It wasn't fair."

She nodded. "Okay, yeah, but that's not what I'm saying. Parker, loving you has changed everything. I *want* to have a family with you. And, honestly, at first, I wasn't sure that this was the way. I wasn't sure that I could have Greer's babies, that I could have that reminder all the time of the life you had before me." She paused and cleared her throat, wiping her eyes. "But Greer will always be a part of our story."

My mind was racing. What exactly what she saying?

"Greer will always be one of the most important parts of your story, and if it weren't for her, we never would have gotten together. So I think those babies are the bridge. They're a part of you and a part of Greer, and if I carry them, they'll be a part of me, too."

I was stunned completely silent. "Amelia, are you sure? Are you absolutely sure? You don't have to do this to make me happy." I paused, trying to wipe the grin off my face, resisting the urge to say, *But this would make me very, very happy*.

"I want to," she said. "I'm sure. I want to be a family, Parker. I want to have a future."

I put my hands on her cheeks and kissed her lips. I put my forehead on hers and said, "Liabelle, that is the most beautiful thing I have ever heard. And I agree. Those babies would complete this weird, convoluted circle." I felt invincible. "And, Lia, I'm going to quit McCann."

"Are you crazy?" she practically shouted. "You can't quit McCann. We're going to have a *baby*, for heaven's sake. We need health insurance, benefits, salaries." She paused and took a deep breath. "No one is quitting McCann." Then she added, "Plus, they're George's grandchildren. We're family forever."

I nodded, laughing and pulling her close to me. "Okay, okay. You're right. Health insurance is good." Then I paused. "Wait. Are you only doing this so that I'll be the last source for your frozen embryo story?"

We both laughed and then sat there soaking in the quiet, the view, the perfection of this moment when we decided to become a family.

"I'm scared," she whispered. "What if it doesn't work again? What if they don't take?"

"Whatever happens, we'll get through it together." I leaned back and looked at her face. And I knew then that this woman who I had loved since I was fourteen years old just might marry me. I would ask her, I decided firmly. Now all I had to do was pray that she said yes.

Amelia

WRITTEN IN THE STARS

I STILL CAN'T SAY WHY I did it, why I agreed to Greer's crazy proposal when she came to me a mere three months before her death. Maybe because it was Greer, and I knew this was one of the last favors she would ever ask. Maybe some sort of delusional type of hero worship. My instinct, when she showed up in my Palm Beach apartment, was a hard, fast no. But, for some reason, it just wouldn't come out of my mouth.

"Why me?" I asked. "Why not your sister?"

I could feel the energy in the room starting to shift. It was like the more panicked I became, the calmer she got, like I could almost see the energy leaving her and transferring into me.

"Why not one of your friends?" I asked.

"Because I don't trust them," she snapped.

Now things were starting to come back into focus for me;

I was starting to see things more clearly, more rationally. I mean, I could do this. Every article I'd ever written, every interview I'd done, it had all been leading up to this moment. Because, with every profile piece, every emotional article, wasn't I becoming the person I was writing about?

Every Greer selfie and vacation Instagram post and witty column was merging in my head, forming a vision of her, but also making me wonder if my vision of her was correct. Could I capture her complexity in a meaningful way?

"The only person I trust is Parker," she said. "And Parker trusts you."

Parker Thaysden trusts me.

It seemed foreign at the time. But when she said it, it all— nights chasing lightning bugs, the family cookouts, the neighborhood picnics, his face over mine the day I nearly drowned—came flooding back to me. Parker was my family. It was as simple as that.

"What did he say about this?"

She laughed. "Oh no, no, Amelia," she said. "You've misunderstood. Parker can never know about this."

"I could never pull this off," I said firmly, realizing that was my insecurity talking. Of course I could pull it off.

This was not a typical business deal, a ghostwriting job set up and carried out by a publisher. I would be impersonating a person who the world loved, who women everywhere relied on. She already had one book out. Could I write a second so seamlessly that no one would be able to tell? I was messed up, I was fragile, I was terribly imperfect. There was no way I could even attempt to sound like Greer, the embodiment of perfection itself.

In retrospect, that's when Greer started to win this argument. As soon as I started making empty excuses, that was proof positive I was pretty much on board with this crazy plan.

"I'm too weak, Amelia. I'm too sick. I sit down to start writing this book, to leave the world with what I want to say, and there's just . . . there's nothing." Tears started to form in her eyes.

"So how does this work? Do I interview you?"

She nodded. "And I have some notes," she said, as though she were too tired to even discuss this. "But, to be honest, not many of them."

That was when I knew I was going to say yes.

"I can't even write things for you to polish," she continued. "It doesn't come for me anymore. I just can't do it."

A cold chill ran through me, because that was one of the worst things I could imagine. We were writers, Greer and I. Being able to see something and tell a story about it, interpret emotions and feelings and facts in a way that moved someone to action, was what we did. For that to be taken away was unthinkable. I would do what she couldn't.

"What I was hoping is that you could write chapters and then call and read them to me. I can help you edit them over the phone. But we have to pick times when Parker won't be around."

Or Thad, I thought.

It was crazy. But I was going to do this. I sighed. "Want to get started?"

Two. That's how many chapters of Greer's book I actually ever read to her. After that, she was too sick, too tired, her attention span too short. The cancer was in her brain by the time I got to chapter five. Then it was over. I was on my own. But, by then, my doubts were over, too.

The more I wrote, the more I became Greer, the stronger I felt, the more I realized that this was the most important writing project I had ever had, the piece that I'd waited my entire life to write. It didn't matter that my name wasn't on the book. That was irrelevant.

Her publisher and her editor knew, obviously. But we had all agreed that this was our secret. They even issued a press release on her death about how she had managed, against all odds, in true Greer fashion, to complete her final memoir.

It debuted at number six on the *New York Times* Best Sellers list when it released, a shockingly fast five months after her death. A book I'd written hit number six. It would never be on my résumé, would never be a tale to spin to my friends. It bugged me the tiniest bit, but really, it also made me proud. I had done it. I had pulled it off. I had talked and researched and become Greer so thoroughly that no one ever knew the difference. Not even her husband.

I took the absurdly large advance check she had signed over to me and donated it to her foundation. I weighed that decision for a long time. It was money that I could have saved for a rainy day, money that would have elevated the paycheck-to-paycheck life I had lived since graduation. It was money that my parents could really use. But, ultimately, it was Greer's story, Greer's voice. Her money should return to her, even indirectly. I'll admit that I wasn't as generous with the royalty checks that came every six months afterward. They weren't huge, but on more than one occasion, they saved me. I was being reimbursed for my work in a reasonable way, in a way that helped me move forward, especially after I left Thad.

And so no, I would never be able to take credit for Greer's book, the book I wrote. But she would never be able to take credit for my babies, the babies she made, which I was carrying right now, inside of me.

"Are we doing this?" I asked Parker for roughly the five hundredth time.

"Oh, we're doing it, all right," he said, taking his hand off the steering wheel, reaching over and patting my belly.

"You know I've never been an editor in chief," I said stupidly, like that should have been my largest concern. I had actually argued with Parker when he told me his plan about *Southern Coast*. I told him I wasn't ready. But he (rightly) argued back, "Amelia, you have worked in magazines since you were eighteen years old. You were the managing editor for one of the country's premier publications, and you know this market and its needs better than anyone. A better candidate for this position literally does not exist. If I had never met you, I would have hired you on your résumé alone."

We had tabled the discussion, but once I had hired the

staff, set up the office, approved new layouts with the head designer, and brainstormed the content for the first issue with the skeleton crew that would be reporting, writing, copyediting, and fact-checking, Parker had insisted. He was right. I was ready. This was my dream job. With Parker as publisher and me as editor, we were creating a real-life family business. I had always thought that I would have to move far away to do the job I wanted. I had been wrong. I would miss Martin. I already missed Philip and Sheree. But they would all visit often. Sometimes, especially when one was on the verge of becoming a mother of twins, there was no place like home.

Parker laid on his horn for no reason I could discern, and I was grateful for the thousandth time that I wasn't the one navigating Manhattan traffic in a U-Haul truck that smelled vaguely of old sub sandwiches.

"I've never been a father." He grinned at me. "Wouldn't it be boring if we just stuck with what we knew?"

When Parker and I had gone, together, to tell George that we were pregnant, that his grandchildren were going to come into the world after all, when we had pitched him the idea of us relocating *Southern Coast*—and ourselves—to Cape Carolina, he had fallen as to pieces as I've ever seen a man. He had to leave the room to compose himself.

But once he returned, it didn't take him long to spring into action. He had planned to give Parker a big bonus. He would relocate us, buy us a home. But he wanted a huge house, one big enough for him to have his own wing, somewhere that he could come visit his grandchildren for weeks at a time without disturbing us. And, well, we knew just the place.

"Well, at least the house is familiar," I said now. I had pushed Parker on Dogwood, made him express his opinions, voice his concerns. I had insisted that he take the small third floor with the peerless view and make it into a space for himself. His house in Palm Beach had been all Greer. Dogwood was, by default, all me. But I wanted him to stake his claim there, to make it his own. Some days I knew the details drove him nuts, but I thought he would be glad when he walked into the kitchen and saw the dishwasher that he had researched in *Consumer Reports*, when he sat at the dining room table and remembered that he had helped choose the art hanging over it, when his bedroom was a mix of soft blues and creams that he had chosen.

"I can't wait to see the new master bath," Parker said. Parker had dreamed of having a master bathroom with a steam room and sauna right inside—especially since there wasn't a gym in Cape Carolina that had them.

I nodded, happy and proud that we had created this home together for our life together. "I think I'm most excited about the kitchen. No, no! I'm most excited about the nursery."

After Parker and I had told George the news that day, I had to visit one more place in Palm Beach. Walking up the three flights of stairs to that apartment I used to share with Thad didn't hurt like I'd thought it would. I hadn't told him I was coming. And if he hadn't been there, that might have been that. I would have just left that day. I'm so glad he was home. So was Nita, a sprightly, bright-eyed eight-year-old who Thad and Chase were fostering and hoping to adopt.

"She's so special," Thad said. "But she has so much to overcome, so many scars."

Sitting in this living room where I'd had some of the best and worst moments of my entire life, I felt at peace, and I knew for certain that everything had worked out for the best. When Nita went to the kitchen to get a snack, I said, "Thad, I'm pregnant. The second pair of embryos took."

He smiled. "That's such a nice thing for you to do for Parker. You have always been so selfless."

I shook my head. "We're having them together."

It took a moment for the news to register, but when tears gathered in his eyes, I knew he understood. He took my hand. Neither of us said a word, and that made the moment so perfect. We had already said everything there was to say. We had moved on. We had healed.

As we said goodbye, I was struck by the most overwhelming need to know that I would see Thad again. "When we get settled in Dogwood, when the babies come, will you, Chase, and Nita please come visit us? Maybe spend Thanksgiving or Christmas?"

Thad wiped his eyes and nodded. "I'll be counting down the days."

Parker and I had flown home that night to tell our parents the news about the babies. We had originally thought we were flying home for our last family Thanksgiving at Dogwood. I had been devastated, of course, but my joy at this pregnancy had blocked my sadness. I had Parker. I had the babies. I had a new life and a new lease on it, too. After our conversation with George, I realized I didn't have to be sad anymore. Dogwood was going to be a part of our family for another generation.

I'll never forget walking into Dogwood last November, the smell of pine absolutely everywhere, giant Frasier firs flanking the staircase in the entrance hall. Mom always decorated for Christmas the day before Thanksgiving, to make the season last. I could imagine that she wanted this one to last even longer. *Christmas Songs by Sinatra* was playing soft and low, and this old house shone. Its presumed last Thanksgiving in our family might very well have been its most glorious. I paused for a moment to try to picture being the one in charge, the one who had the final say on the Christmas decorations.

I had snuck up on Aunt Tilley in the kitchen, kissing her cheek from behind. She turned and laughed and hugged me full-on. "My girl is home," she said, wiping her hands on her black slacks. I wondered how it felt on days like today, when she was okay, to sit across the table and know that Robby was hers, that she had spent a lifetime playing his aunt when really she was his mother. In my current twins-induced hormonal firestorm, I couldn't control my sobs. Aunt Tilley smiled at me knowingly and squeezed my hand. Mom and Olivia's voices drifted toward us as Olivia said, "I just think the Lismore crystal is more classic for the last Christmas."

Parker was getting my luggage out of the car. So as not to be caught unaware like we had been the last time we had made a large family announcement at the dinner table, we had care-fully scripted how we would break our latest—and best—news.

But then I saw them. Those meddling little women in bal-let flats with matching bobs. And as they hugged me and asked in soothing tones what was wrong, I couldn't help but blurt out, "I'm pregnant." I sobbed, and added, "With twins."

The shrieks could have been heard 'round the world. As I began to recover from the deafening noise, I realized Parker was standing in the kitchen doorway. "Babe, you're not great at sticking to a plan, are you?"

But he couldn't say anything more because three women were covering him with kisses.

That night at dinner we told them all about the plan, about moving to Cape Carolina, about buying Dogwood, about taking over the magazine. I am quite certain there have never been that many cheers, tears, or toasts at a Dogwood dinner table. When everyone was somewhat settled down, Daddy said, "Amelia, Dogwood is yours for the taking. That was always the plan. We don't want to sell it to you. We sim-ply want to pass along the nightmare of its upkeep." He laughed heartily.

"I insist," Parker said. "We can't take the house . . ."

But Mom put her hand up. When Mom puts her hand up, no one argues. "It is a family home, meant to be passed down through the generations. As of this moment, the house is yours," she said.

"Thank you," I said. It was all there was to say.

"Then we insist on renovating the back house for you when we renovate this one. It's the least we can do," Parker added.

No one argued.

"As homeowners, you are now in charge of washing all these dishes," Aunt Tilley added.

Robby put his arm around her and squeezed her shoulder.

"I am so excited that I will help you!" Trina squealed. "Oh, to have babies in the family again!"

She was currently nursing her four-month-old—a fourth boy—at the table, so I wouldn't exactly say there weren't babies in the family, but if she was happy, I was happy.

But Parker looked perturbed. "It isn't right," he said. I gave him my best *What do you want me to do*? look. "It isn't right," he continued, "for us to be living here at Dogwood, in Cape Carolina, with these babies, without making it official."

I was ninety percent sure I knew what was coming next, but I didn't quite have time to protest. Parker was on his knee and reaching his hand out to his mother, who slipped a ring out of her pocket so fast I barely saw it happen. "I never dreamed that I would get lucky enough to fall in love with the girl next door. I really never dreamed that I would get lucky enough to have the girl next door be the mother of my children. But I think what would really make me the luckiest of all would be to marry the girl next door." He took a deep breath, and I could tell he was nervous. "So, Amelia Saxton, will you marry me?"

I had been a wife before, and it hadn't ended well for me.

But, this time, I was determined to do it differently, to do it better. This time was different anyway because, without any thought, without any action, without so much as a good therapy session, I had fallen into Parker. I trusted him so fully that my old worry of never being able to commit to another person had vanished. It never even crossed my mind. And maybe it was because I had committed to four people—to Parker, to these two babies of ours, and to Greer, the woman that, though I once feared she would always be between us, had somehow become the glue that held us together.

I wondered what he had said to Greer in this very same moment. I wondered how she had felt. All those years ago, Parker had walked into marriage wide-eyed, naïve, and fresh. Tonight, he knew what could happen, knew the risks. He was a soldier choosing to go back to war.

To walk back into the line of fire was a big love, a love so big maybe I couldn't even comprehend it.

"Everyone is looking," I whispered.

"Sorry," he whispered back. "I was going to do this later on the dock, but I couldn't wait any longer."

I smiled at him and took the ring out of his hand. "I love you, Parker." I took his hands in mine and said, "Let's do this." I kissed him to applause around the table and then turned back to the moms. "But not until after the babies. They don't need the stress of wedding planning with Elizabeth Saxton and Olivia Thaysden while they're forming neurons."

Mom looked at me with mock seriousness and said, "Whatever the new mistress of Dogwood wishes."

• • •

Now, bouncing down the highway in the U-Haul, thirty-five weeks pregnant, that night felt like a faraway dream, like something so wonderful it couldn't have been true. Tying up the loose ends and coming home felt right.

Maybe it hadn't all happened in the usual way, but it had happened. I had grown two human beings that, even if they were born right now on the sidewalk, would be healthy, viable little people. It is the most ordinary thing in the world until it happens to you. And then it is extraordinary beyond belief.

Twenty-seven bathroom breaks and an overnight stay in DC later, my little map dot, our beautiful home, came into view. And, roughly every ten feet, another red and white SAXTON FOR MAYOR sign appeared.

Parker groaned. "He's going to make us work polls, isn't he?"

I patted his arm. "Well, before that, he's going to make us put out signs. I told him you would do it, because I couldn't, with my swollen ankles and everything."

"And he let you off the hook that easily?"

I smirked. "Nope. He sent me compression socks."

Parker burst out laughing as we pulled into the driveway of Dogwood. "When are you going to run for mayor?" he asked. The babies kicked sharply, voicing their disapproval. Or maybe they just knew that they were home.

I never thought I'd be a mother. I never thought I'd be a fiancée again. I certainly never thought I'd move to Cape Carolina or give up investigative journalism for lifestyle editing.

While I had always believed that I was the master of my own destiny, perhaps this was written in the stars after all. And while driving away from a city I had come to love had been a little sad, I had to admit that, in Cape Carolina, the stars shone a whole lot brighter.

Parker

MEMORIES

WHEN AMELIA WOKE ME IN the middle of the night, I was sure she was in labor. It was our first night in Dogwood, in our new house, in our new bed. It felt different. And the same. It's hard to explain. We had renovated the entire house. New plumbing, new electrical, new wood, new paint, refinished floors, and new furniture with the old heirlooms still mixed in. You don't donate a dining room table with George Washington's initials carved in it.

I jumped up and started putting on my shoes, which was nonsensical since I wasn't wearing any pants.

"Park, what are you doing?" I turned back. Amelia was lying on her left side, her head propped on her hand, staring at me.

"Get up! What are you doing? Unless you want to have

our babies in the same place your great-grandmother had your grandmother, I suggest you hurry."

"Sweetie, I'm not in labor," she said soothingly.

I exhaled, unlaced my shoes, and flopped back into bed. "Do you need ice cream? Pie? Jalapeño pizza?" These were the three most common requests of Amelia's pregnancy. I did my best to accommodate her because she looked so uncomfortable all the time.

"Parker, I want to get married."

I looked over at the bedside table. It was four thirty. I switched on the lamp so I could see her face. "Amelia, are you having a dream? We are getting married. In November. Remember? You wanted to get married Thanksgiving weekend so the leaves would be falling?"

She nodded. "Yeah. But I'm just lying here thinking about how we won't all have the same name when the babies are born, and I'd like to be married when they come."

I would have done anything in the world for Amelia at that moment—except tell our mothers that we wanted to get married now. They were trying to hide their incessant planning from Amelia so as not to stress her out, but they didn't mind stressing me out. I knew more than I had ever planned to know about flowers. And we were only inviting, like, forty people. I couldn't imagine if this were a first wedding.

"Babe, I don't know if we can pull that off," I said soothingly.

"We won't tell anyone!" she snapped. "I just want to go to the courthouse and get married."

"We do have the license already," I mused, more to myself than to her.

"Right," she said. "So, tomorrow, let's please go get married."

She seemed almost frantic about it, and I have to admit that it made me worry. Was there something she wasn't telling me? But then I looked at her, lying there, so uncomfortably pregnant with my babies.

"I can't wait to marry you." I kissed her passionately.

"Don't get any ideas," she snapped.

I tried to stifle my laugh as I rolled back over.

But as I lay there, I couldn't sleep. I was back in Cape Carolina. With Amelia. With our soon-to-be children. I had sold the Palm Beach house I had shared with Greer. I had done it in baby steps. One day, I donated files of her work to libraries. The next, her friends came and sat on the floor of her huge closet, helping me choose what to donate and what was too precious to let go of. They each walked away with dozens of mementos of the friend they had loved until her last day.

Greer's sister, much to my surprise, had flown down to help me pack boxes and instruct the movers. I didn't know which pieces were family heirlooms. We donated a few things; some went back to various family members. But, yes, I still have a storage rental in Palm Beach filled with remnants of our life that I couldn't say goodbye to. It was too hard, too permanent. I may never go back there, but it soothed me to know that I could.

Greer's jewelry was the one thing I wasn't sure what to do

with. She was buried in her diamond wedding band, and her engagement ring was in the lockbox. I hoped that I would have a daughter to give it to one day or maybe a son who could pass it on to his wife. The emerald ring she had loved so much that belonged to her grandmother, I gave to her sister. It was right that she have it. Everything else I saved so that our future children could have a piece of their biological mother.

The most curious part of my unearthing process was an envelope inside the felt-lined drawer where Greer kept all her jewelry. On the front, it said, in Greer's handwriting: *Please give to Amelia Saxton.* I was extremely confused. There was no note, no indication of why on earth my wife, who hadn't dictated who a single other item should go to, would have wanted to give a piece of her jewelry to a woman she barely knew. I pulled out a bracelet. It was a thick but plain gold chain and from it hung a gold typewriter with ruby keys and pearl turning knobs. I took it with me, but I never gave it to Amelia. I wasn't sure if she would want it or if it would be a setback.

The house sold, over asking price, in ninety minutes. I sat on the floor in the empty place for hours, looking out at the water. I thought about how Greer's face lit up when we first toured it, how exhausted we had been after move-in day. I remembered carrying her over the threshold. And, yes, I remembered her dying in my arms. I felt numb but proud. Letting go of this house had felt impossible, but I had done it.

The one thing I hadn't let go of was Greer's journals.

I got out of bed and walked to the end of the hall, to the

library, where the journals were all in a row on the bookcase. I had told Amelia about how I read them. It couldn't have sat well with her, but she must have understood, because when we moved, she pointed to a shelf and said, "I thought Greer's journals could go here."

I pulled them out, flipping through them, reading a passage here and there and then, one by one, putting them in a box. I didn't know what I was looking for. I couldn't imagine what the "right" entry would be. Maybe a reminder of her true and eternal love for me?

That was what I expected. But, in true Greer fashion, she gave me a goodbye better than my wildest dreams.

Greer

JULY 13, 2016

HOW CAN SOMEONE SOUND MORE like you than you do? If it's possible, Amelia has done it. She's only two chapters into my book, but I barely have edits for her. She nailed it.

I feel guilty, of course. I feel badly that when this book comes out, everyone will give me the praise. Dead me, probably. Unaware me, at the very least. I don't like thinking of that. Not at all. I said to Amelia today that maybe we should do this differently. Maybe the cover should at least say "Greer Mc-Cann Thaysden with Amelia Saxton." Then she could have the glory that I won't be here to have.

But she said, "This is your life advice, Greer. It's your memories. The men and women who buy this book are buying it because they want to hear from you. Who technically wrote it isn't important."

Maybe it isn't. And I know it's selfish, but it soothes me

that my legacy won't be that I was too sick, too depleted, to even finish my own book. I'm sure there's someone out there who would argue that my truth would help people. But this will help people, too. It comforts me that I will leave people believing that I was fighting with all I had until the very end. That's a lesson the world needs, too.

I used to think of Amelia as a threat. But now I realize that wasn't true at all. Amelia Saxton isn't just Parker's family; she is mine, too. We are bonded together, connected forever. I trust her in a way I have never trusted anyone. I trust her with my deepest secrets, with the most important parts of myself. I trust her with the future I won't be here to live. I hope she knows how indebted I am to her. I hope she feels my gratitude. I will be gone. But thanks to her, I will live on. Because of Amelia, the best parts of me, the truest, are yet to be.

Parker

OFFICIAL

I ACTUALLY LAUGHED OUT LOUD as I read it. Well, damn. Amelia had written Greer's last book. I wondered how she had pulled it off. No doubt about it, Greer had had her secrets. But we all do.

As I read, contentment washed over me. It was like she knew. Yes, she was talking about Amelia writing her book. But Amelia was letting Greer live on. And she had been grateful for that. She couldn't have known . . . but, somehow, it was like she did.

Greer had been my world. She had been life and all the light inside of it. But I had a new light now—three of them, in fact.

It was time.

As I closed the journal for what I knew would be the final time, I put my hand on the soft, smooth cover. "Goodbye,

Greer," I whispered. "I love you forever. Thank you for giving me permission to move forward." I took a deep breath, swallowed the lump in my throat, and put the journal in the box for the very last time.

I was closing the box when Amelia walked into the library. I glanced down at my watch and was shocked to see that it was almost nine a.m.

"What are those?" she asked. Then she looked at the shelf. "They don't bother me, Park. I swear they don't. I understand needing to hold on to a memory. Hell, I'm living in mine."

I smiled and pulled her to me. "I know. But, Amelia, I'm marrying the love of my life today. I just don't need the journals anymore." I kissed her gently.

Her eyes filled with tears, and I turned and placed the heavy box on the top shelf of the closet. She put her hands on her belly. "For the babies?"

I nodded.

"No," she said, gesturing for me to take them down. She walked down the hall into the baby blue room overlooking the sound with the matching cribs in the window, the chaise in the corner, the antique chest with the changing table pad on the side, and a huge bookshelf that was already filled with books—some from our childhoods—for our babies to read.

Amelia pointed to the top empty bamboo shelf. She opened the box I was holding and pulled out a stack of journals. "They should go here," she said. "I never want to hide Greer away. I never want you or the babies to feel like we can't talk about her."

When we were finished unpacking the box, I set it on the floor. I put my hand on a volume on the bookshelf, Greer's second book, the hardback with her glossy picture—and her name in massive type—on the cover. I pulled it off the shelf and handed it to Amelia. "I don't know how you did it," I said.

She froze and said nothing.

It was then that I realized the irony: Amelia's words had actually convinced me to ask her—a woman who insisted she didn't want to get married—to marry me. But that seemed like a conversation for another day.

"Why didn't she tell me?" I whispered.

She didn't skip a beat. "She was trying to protect you."

"Protect me from what?"

Amelia turned and looked out the window. I don't know if she was deciding whether to tell me. But when she turned back she said, "She didn't want you to know how far she had deteriorated. She didn't want to admit to you that she couldn't do something that used to be second nature."

That did sound like that girl I loved. "Well, then why didn't you tell me?"

She looked down toward her feet, obscured by her belly, and then back up at me, her eyes shining. "I was trying to protect you, too."

I hadn't been the only one preserving a perfect image of Greer; Amelia had been, too, in a way that was even bigger and must have been more difficult.

I pulled Amelia to me and kissed her. She was strong, that woman. Stronger than I was.

And that was when it all began to make sense. "I have a gift for you," I said.

"For me?" she said coquettishly.

"It's from Greer."

Now she looked confused.

I motioned for her to follow me back to our bedroom, where I pulled the envelope out of the top drawer of my dresser and handed it to her.

As she opened it, her eyes filled with tears, and she put her hand to her mouth. "I loved this bracelet," she whispered.

She studied it and then laughed. "She had it engraved."

She handed me the bracelet and I read, "'To *New York Times* bestselling author Amelia Saxton. All my love, GMT.'"

I undid the clasp and put it on her arm.

"It feels right that I should be wearing this when we make it official."

"You sure?" I asked.

She nodded.

I winked at her and held my hand out. "Shall we get married, then?" She took it, and I stopped. "Wait. What about a witness?"

"Someone at the courthouse will do it."

But as we walked down the stairs and I could hear morning sounds in the kitchen that meant Tilley was having a good day, I decided a courthouse witness wasn't enough. Amelia and her family had protested when I insisted that Aunt Tilley remain in the east wing. But it wasn't a selfless act. Tilley wasn't just Amelia's nutty aunt; she was the entire town's nutty aunt. Plus, as I said to Amelia, it really added to the allure of our story. Unwed couple—surrogate to the dead wife's babies and the boy next door—take up residence in the family home. What kind of story was that without an aunt Tilley? Not one at all, if you asked me.

Amelia and I smiled at each other. "Aunt Tilley," she asked, "how are you at keeping secrets?"

Something I didn't understand passed between them when she said, "Well, my dear, I think you know that, when it comes to keeping secrets, I am quite possibly the best."

As we drove to the courthouse, where Amelia and I would become husband and wife, so we'd share a name with our babies on the day they were born, I wondered why things happened the way they did. Wouldn't it have been easier if Amelia and I had fallen in love the summer after college and never looked back? But when I thought about erasing that entire chapter of my life, the one where Greer was the center of my world, when I thought about not having these babies that were half-her and half-me, I changed my mind.

I thought about a few minutes earlier when I'd put all her words, all her feelings, all her secrets, on a shelf in her babies' room. And then I put my hand on Amelia's belly.

The best part of Greer and of me was right beside me, living inside the woman I loved. They were real and would be here any day. I didn't need my old memories, because now, finally, I was ready to make some new ones. I had spent years worrying about preserving Greer's legacy. Now I was ready to create my own.

Amelia

UNDER THE SOUTHERN SKY

THE DAY MY BROTHER RAN into the makeshift *Southern Coast* office in what had once been the ballroom of Dogwood but that now held our staff of twelve—who had, in my humble opinion, made magic of a dying magazine—and handed me two newspapers, something extraordinary happened. My past and my future merged, became a seamless, undeniably right present.

The front page of the *Cape Carolina Chronicle* boasted, "Saxton Wins Mayor in Landslide Victory."

The Life Styles section of the *New York Times* proclaimed, "Modern Motherhood with Amelia Saxton Thaysden."

I smiled up at my brother. "Banner day for the Saxtons, huh?"

It wasn't lost on me that giving birth to two beautiful babies had made the gap I had worried would form between my brother and me—after my mother told me the truth about Tilley being his biological mother—nonexistent. I understood now that it wasn't my truth to tell. It was my mother's and Tilley's.

"I think it was you standing out there with one baby on your front and one on your back all day and handing out rulers to voters that put me over the edge." He winked at me.

Yeah. My brother had received 1,274 of the total 1,709 votes because of me in an overstressed BabyBjörn with two cranky infants. But whatever. It wasn't November if I wasn't standing in front of Cape Carolina High's gymnasium, our town's polling place.

I hadn't let Parker read the column before it had gone to print. I said I wanted it to be a surprise, but really, I didn't want his input. I loved and cherished him, but this was my side of the story. I couldn't think about it through his eyes. I needed part of this journey to be mine and mine alone. Almost two years after I walked into that fertility clinic for the very first time, I had finally managed to write the story I had started that day. Only, when it came time to put it on paper, it felt like a different story. Yes, I'll use those facts one day. The interviews, too. But, for now, a column seemed like the way to go. A Modern Love column, in fact.

This time, I didn't have to run home from work to show my husband the story I had written about him. He eagerly grabbed it from me the minute he saw it. I looked over his shoulder as he read.

When I was fourteen years old, I cheated on a test. It was wrong. I knew it then, and I know it now. I'm sure if I had gotten caught the teacher would have said I was only cheating myself, but I think we all know that isn't true. I was cheating off Parker Thaysden, who, even though he was three years younger, was the smartest guy in my math class. I told myself I hadn't meant to look over and see his answer, that it was simply a coincidence that the problem I was stuck on was one that happened to be right in my view. But, deep down, I knew the truth.

Eight days later, I found out I could never have children, that I had primary ovarian insufficiency syndrome.

I thought it was because I'd cheated on my math test.

Twenty-ish years later, I still can't explain the exact laws of karma (or, as might be obvious, the laws of exponents), but what I do know is that fate very rarely delivers upon that straight of a line. Maybe I did something—or a whole string of things—right, because, despite the odds, despite the truth I had long known, I did end up with babies. A perfect, matching set of them, in fact. They came from the journalist and philanthropist Greer McCann Thaysden's gorgeous eggs.

I was always better in science than I was in math, thank goodness. Maybe that's what drew me to investigate what people do with their extra frozen embryos. Maybe that's what led me uncover that Greer's embryos had been deemed abandoned.

The day in eighth grade I told Parker Thaysden I'd

copied off his paper, I didn't know what was going to happen. In fact, I had stayed up half the night worried and wondering. Would he tell the teacher? The principal? Would I get expelled? None of that happened. He said, "Who cares, Amelia? I had the answer, and you didn't."

That rings true now, as I hold this beautiful pair of babies in my arms. My ladybug and four-leaf clover. That's what Greer had nicknamed them; that was what they looked like under a microscope. Who knew they would turn out to be my lucky charms? Who knew that what I didn't have, Greer would end up giving me?

I would eventually pay Parker Thaysden back by writing a biology essay for him. On mitosis, in fact. The cell division that results in two child cells having the same number and kind of chromosome as the parent.

No, these babies don't have the exact number and kind of chromosome as Parker. Only half. Half-Parker, half-Greer. But when they kicked inside of me, when the doctor laid their warm, tiny bodies on my chest, they became mine, too.

I never expected to fall in love with the boy next door, with the one whose paper I'd cheated off of. I never expected to get pregnant with his babies. And I never, ever imagined that doing each of those things would heal what was broken inside of me, what had been broken, in fact, since that day I sat on a cold doctor's office table in a thin gown, receiving the hardest news of my life. I never expected that thirteen pounds, eight ounces of babies could connect Parker and me to his late wife in such an inextricable way, while also giving us both permission to truly release her.

But maybe Parker did. In fact, his childhood voice rings in my ears now, as I place my babies side by side in their crib overlooking a mesmerizing stretch of sound that is always the same and yet never the same. *I had the answer, and you didn't.*

It isn't math; it most certainly *is* science. And, at first, I thought that, surely, it was modern love.

Generations of Saxtons and Thaysdens have welcomed their children home to this tiny peninsula, this singular spot in one of the world's most beautiful forgotten corners. I watched the way my babies turned toward each other, by instinct, the way they fussed and then, their eyes fixing on me, their mother, settled. And I finally realized that, this love? It wasn't as modern as I once believed. Quite the opposite, in fact.

This was a love as old as time.

In a lot of ways, the day this column published was the same as the day the last one did. Tears were shed. Indelible memories were made. But, this time, the life I had carefully cultivated didn't fall apart. In fact, I'm proud to say, my life isn't cultivated in the least. It's messy. It's busy. It's happy. It's exhausting. And, most of all, it's real.

I went upstairs, saying I had to check on the babies. But instead of turning right toward the nursery, I turned left toward my childhood bedroom. I pulled that tiny pink-and-purple notebook out from underneath my mattress and sat down on the bed, looking out the window. I flipped through until I found the entry from that fateful day. Pen in hand, I put a big check mark next to *Become editor in chief of a magazine.*

Then I read *Find a man that loves me and doesn't care that I can't have children.* I crossed it out and rewrote, *Find a man that loves me for exactly who I am.* Because that had been what I was asking for, really, hadn't it? Now, with time and a grown-up dose of rationality, I realized it wasn't having those gorgeous, perfect babies that healed me. It was realizing that no matter how my life played out, I was who I was born to be. I was enough.

I thought of Parker, downstairs, and I smiled. I picked up the pen again. *Find a man who loves me for exactly who I am.* Check.

Life, I have realized, ebbs and flows like the tide outside my old bedroom window. Some days the wind is too strong, and sometimes you are carried along on a gentle breeze. The hurricanes come; the landscapes change. Any expert seaman will tell you that, in the roughest seas, it's best not to fight the tide. It's better to let it lead you where it wants to, to let it lead you where, maybe, you were supposed to be all along.

All those years I was planning and plotting my course, controlling my every move, I wasn't controlling anything at all. Now I've given in to the pull of the moon, to the song of the sea, to the magical divinity that exists under the Southern sky. It will fill up your heart and never let you go, I realized as

I walked down the hall to the nursery, to gaze over my sleeping babies. It will never stop its quest to bring you back where you belong.

And somehow, if you're really lucky, you'll do what I did: you'll find your way back home.

Acknowledgments

IT IS FITTING IN SOME ways that *Under the Southern Sky* is a story of feeling untethered, of life getting in the way and having plans vastly different from our own. It was written in rental houses, condos, and apartments during the fifteen months our family was displaced after Hurricane Florence ripped through our beloved town and home, and edited during a pandemic that has felt straight out of a dystopian novel. But in *Under the Southern Sky*—as in life—miracles are born from adversity. Relationships are created in the void of lost love and dashed hopes. New life springs from the ashes.

For me, one of the greatest gifts—besides this book—to come from a challenging time was a weekly Facebook Live show, *Friends & Fiction*, with my dear writer pals, Mary Kay Andrews, Kristin Harmel, Patti Callahan Henry, and Mary Alice Monroe. Thank you, lovely friends, for creating a spectacular way for us to connect with our readers even when we couldn't be on the road. And thank you to the tens of thousands of readers who have joined us on a literary journey of hope and connection. (Shameless plug: If you aren't watching *Friends & Fiction*, join us on Facebook Wednesday nights at 7 p.m.!) Big love also to Meg Walker and Shaun Hettinger for being such an invaluable part of this journey. Michelle Marcus and Brenda Gardner, all the thank-yous for taking on the task of organizing our Friends & Fiction book club. We are all so grateful!

On that note, Friends & Fiction began with the mission of supporting independent bookstores—and I would not be here without the indies who have hand sold my books, hosted events and cheered me on since the beginning. This past year more than ever when in-person events were canceled and pivoting on a dime was necessary, you all stood by my side and sent *Feels Like Falling* into the world with aplomb despite the challenges. Thank you, thank you, thank you for all your support.

To my incredible, amazing, brilliant team, I can't possibly thank you enough for all you do to bring my stories to life. Kate Dresser, you "got" this book right away and traveled this path with me until it was the best story it could be. Molly Gregory, I am always grateful for your positivity and willingness to go above and beyond. Elisabeth Weed and Olivia Blaustein, agents extraordinaire, I wouldn't be here without either of you. Kathie Bennett, thank you for rolling with the punches, for rising to every challenge imaginable, and, most important, for being almost as invested in these books as I am. Michelle Podberezniak, you amaze me every single day with your fresh ideas—and organization. Jen Bergstrom and Jen Long, I am so grateful for all your expertise and insight and for being on this road with me year after year. Bianca Salvant, thanks for your marketing prowess. Gabrielle Audet and Sarah Lieberman from Simon & Schuster Audio, y'all are total rock stars. I'm in awe of your creativity and so thankful for all your help getting my audiobooks into the world. Tamara Welch, as you well know, I couldn't do what I do without you. You have been such an important part of this journey, and I am most grateful for you!

My Tall Poppy Writer tribe has been there for me through thick and thin before my first novel was published. This group—and its members—continue to evolve and change, but the constant is a group I can always turn to for advice. Most of all, I'm grateful for the friendship of each and every one of you! And to the members of our Bloom group: Y'all are so amazing, so supportive, and we love you! (Shameless plug number 2: Are you in Bloom? If not, join us on Facebook via Bloom with Tall Poppy Writers!)

To all the Bookstagrammers, bloggers, reporters, and influencers who have helped bring this book into the world, a huge and hearty thank you. Friend and phone buddy Kristy Barrett, thanks for all the book honey! Andrea Katz, your support and advice is always so welcome and appreciated. Stephanie Gray, I am so happy for the success of Porter Co. Book Shoppe and so grateful for all the book love through it and, of course, the Book Lover Book Club and Porter Co. Marketing. Special thanks to Jamie Rosenblit, Anne Mendez, Addie Wemyss, Judy Collins, Kristin Thorvaldsen, Courtney Marzilli, Bethany Clark, Kate Rock, Jennifer Clayton, and Nicole McManus for always going so above and beyond! And fabulous podcasters Zibby Owens, Grace Atwood, and Becca Freeman, thanks for being so supportive.

Susan Roberts, Susan Peterson, Sheree Kun, Michele Collard, Rose Goforth, Denise Holcomb, Annissa Holmes, and Susan Persons, I adore you and am so thankful you're in my life. Everyone who follows my design blog, *Design Chic*, and all the friends I have met along the way, thank you for also reading my books so enthusiastically, showing up at my events and sharing them with your followers. It means more than I can say!

If you've read my books, you know that I love writing about families. How they come together, why they fall apart, what matters in the end, how they are created. I am so blessed to have the most wonderful family. Will and Will, I couldn't have dreamed up a better husband and son, and I'm grateful for every day with you and, quite honestly, absolutely treasured every minute of being at home together for weeks on end. (Another unexpected gift!) Mom and Dad, you are and always have been the most amazing parents. Thanks for being the best examples. Ola Rutledge, Cathy Singer, Catherine, John, John Ross and Peyton Adcox, Anne and Tommy O'Berry, Raymond and Manika Smith, Rutledge Smith, Nancy and Tommy Sanders, Thomas and Halley Sanders, Sidney, Michael and Emilia Patton, and Jim Woodson, y'all are the best family anyone could ever have and, without even meaning to, you taught me what it means to be family first. You are always a part of my stories.

Perhaps most important, thank you to my readers who come back year after year for another story, another adventure. Can you believe this is number seven? *Under the Southern Sky* has such a special place in my heart. I hope it finds one in yours, too.